Taking a deep breath, I p⌐ "Now I'll levitate throu⌐ With the powers at my command, I will force the Typewriter to his knees!"

"Not to trouble you, but have you considered taking the elevator?"

I took a look at the elevator about three feet away from me. "I see. Are you sure I can't levitate the last thirty or so floors?"

"You're mocking me."

"Yes. Yes, I am," Walking up to the elevator doors, I muttered, "I swear, you take all the fun out of superpowers. I'd also like to register a complaint about the general crappiness of my abilities, too. This whole 'no flying' and 'intangibility for thirty seconds' isn't doing anything for me. You said I could take more damage than a normal person. Am I at least bulletproof?"

"Mostly."

"Do I want to know what you mean by that?"

"No. Try not to get shot."

Well, no one said supervillainy was going to be easy. "I'll try to remember that."

THE RULES OF SUPERVILLAINY

By C. T. Phipps

THE
RULES
OF
SUPERLATIVITY

Dedication and Acknowledgements

This novel is dedicated to my lovely wife, Kat, and the many other wonderful people who made this book possible. Special thanks to David Niall Wilson, David Dodd, Jim Bernheimer, Raffaele Marenetti, and my fans.

C.T. Phipps

Preface

Who would ever want to be a supervillain?
   I pondered this question while sitting down to write my first superhero novel. I've always felt there was a dearth of superheroic literature and have even written a couple of essays on it.

Being a supervillain seems like a raw deal. You get beat up all the time and while you don't stay in prison very long, you bust out just to get beaten up again. There're some perks, especially if you have a gorgeous underling or a kickass secret lair, but these are outweighed by the drawbacks.

You'd have to be crazy to want to be a supervillain.

Then again, superheroes and supervillains live in a crazy world.

Superpowers violate every law of physics, the world is endangered every other week, superheroes wield the power to level planets, and supervillains can resist law enforcement like rooftops resist raindrops.

Regular humans are trapped in a world where they don't matter, and only the opinions of dueling demigods are important. That's when my hook hit me. In a world where everything is exaggerated and surreal, why not be the bad guy?

I've never wanted to be "normal" and could imagine someone who doesn't have the fortitude to be a hero wanting to be the reverse because it's an escape from mundane.

People want to stand out and be something and *The Rules of Supervillainy's* protagonist, Merciless, a.k.a. Gary Karkofsky, dares the world see him.

The Rules of Supervillainy makes no attempt to be realistic.

There're plenty of people who have created more grounded or "realistic" superheroes. I have no interest in this, though. No, my world is unabashedly unrealistic and proudly so.

It is the result of me sticking every comic book I've ever read in a blender and hitting frappe. I wear my inspirations on my sleeve from reading *Marvel*, *DC*, *Image*, and playing a decade of superhero-themed tabletop RPGs. Something akin to every comic book story ever written has taken place in this world and the planet still stands.

Barely.

I invite you to join Merciless on his first day on the "job" after gaining superpowers. He's a lunatic, a cartoon, and someone I'd probably run the other way from if I met him in real-life, but I still love him.

If I've done my job right, at the end of this book you'll be rooting for the bad guy.

Chapter One

My First Outing as a Supervillain

"Cloak, do you think I should cultivate a villain voice?" I asked, staring out at the city horizon from a rooftop.

"*Pardon?*" The hooded cloak of my all-black costume telepathically said. Its 'voice' was dry and otherworldly, as if Christopher Lee had Darth Vader's reverb. In fact, it was Cloak's way of speaking that had inspired me to consider changing mine.

"Something deep and gravelly to strike fear into the masses. You see all these amateurs today and none of them have the *panache* of the bad guys I grew up with. Don't you agree?"

"*I think your plan to become a supervillain is stupid enough as is,*" Cloak said in my mind.

"Spoilsport."

We were standing on top of the twenty-story Falconcrest City National Bank, a place where I'd worked until a month ago, practicing my newly-acquired powers. I'd been *Merciless: The Supervillain Without Mercy*™ for less than twenty-four hours. In a city filled with countless costumed criminals, I was fresh off the boat. Hell, I didn't even have a record. The one thing I *did* have was powers.

*Super*powers.

The weird thing was, they'd been acquired by chance. Yesterday, someone had dropped off an unmarked set of cardboard boxes filled with files, equipment, and the Nightwalker's magic cloak.

The Nightwalker had been the patron superhero of Falconcrest City since the Thirties but had been announced as dead by the Society of Superheroes less than a week ago. Coincidentally, the city's two biggest philanthropists in the Warren Brothers had died too. I had no idea how the Nightwalker's stuff had ended up on my doorstep and, more to the point, I didn't care.

A better man might have wanted to follow in the Nightwalker's footsteps, but I was a poorer one. As in financially. I was *eager* to begin my reign of terror over the city. As long as I didn't have to kill anyone.

"Most people would consider killing to be a necessary component for a reign of terror," Cloak said, reading my thoughts. That was one of the downsides to my new powers; they came with a built-in conscience.

"I heard that," I thought back.

"I don't care. I'm not most people. I can shoot fire from my hands, conjure ice, levitate, turn insubstantial, and take being hit by a car. I don't need to kill. I mean, if they're bad, sure, I'll take them out but not just because. I'm not *crazy.*"

"Ugh." Cloak sighed, despite having no lungs. *"I suppose I should get used to your peculiar logic. We're going to be bonded for a long time and you alone can determine how to use your newfound gifts."*

"I intend to use them to make a lot of money by taking it from other people. It's the family tradition!"

"You refer to your brother, Stingray?"

"Yeah." Keith was my reason for becoming a supervillain He'd died when I was fourteen, in a particularly nasty way.

What followed had been worse.

Cloak was silent for a moment, respectful of my pain. *"Now, can we talk about the downsides to our bond?"*

"Sure. Lay them on me." I lifted my right hand and generated a ball of flame that hovered in the air for several seconds. "What, am I vulnerable to purple or lose my powers on holy ground?"

"Unless your abilities are used on a regular basis, the cosmic balance will go out of sync within the confines of Falconcrest City. This will result in the re-animation of the departed."

I blinked, not sure I'd heard that right. "Could you repeat that?"

"*Ravenous undead will rise en masse if you do not use your powers every day.*"

"Zombies?" I couldn't believe what I was hearing. "Frigging *zombies* are going to rise if I don't use my powers?"

"*Flesh-eating undead are ghouls not zombies but, yes, more or less.*"

"That's a pretty big drawback."

"*Yes.*"

"And the Nightwalker knew about this?"

"*He was aware of the downside, yes. It's why he was always using his powers.*"

"I just thought he was obsessive about fighting crime." I rubbed my temples. This was starting to seem like responsibility. "Anything else I should know about?"

"*You will be harassed by the ghosts of the dead. Those who have been murdered and their killers uncaught will be your most frequent visitors.*"

"So, unless I pursue my new career twenty-four-seven the city will go all George Romero. Likewise, I'm going to be the kid from *The Sixth Sense* from now on."

"*You've lost me with your colloquialisms but yes.*"

I thought through all the implications. "I'm okay with it."

"*Really?*" Cloak sounded skeptical.

"Yep!"

"*You're taking this well.*"

"Well, I figure it's a case of no pain, no gain. If I complained now after getting superpowers, I'd just come off as a tremendous dink." I looked down onto the city, taking in its vast wealth—all of which I intended to plunder. "There's nothing *too* bad about these drawbacks, anyway. I have no intention of quitting my new career. That should keep the zombie population down. As for the ghosts, well I'll avoid cemeteries and morgues."

"*Your cavalier attitude frightens me.*"

"Some things you do for love." I winced. The word love made me realize I had a big problem on my hands. "Now I just need to figure out how I'm going to break this to Mandy."

"Your wife?"

"Yeah, who else?"

I wasn't going to be one of those supers who kept their secret identities secret even from their spouses. Supervillainy seemed like the sort of thing you needed to be upfront with your spouse about.

Unfortunately, there was the slight fact that Mandy hadn't been raised in the lifestyle. She had almost no experience other than some college experimentation. The trick was figuring out how to broach the subject without her going ballistic.

"Perhaps she will be understanding about the fact you're going to put her in constant danger as well as make the world an objectively worse place by your presence."

"Let's hope!"

I was saved from having to think on the subject further by the sound of an alarm going off. I was surprised I could hear it until I realized it was coming from the bank itself. Pulling out the pair of binoculars I brought, I saw a group of thieves moving in and out of the building's front doors.

The bandits were dressed in Eskimo parkas and traveling in an ice cream truck with a rotating polar bear head. They were loading it up with bags of money as they shooed away pedestrians... with Uzis. Yikes.

I had to salute their choice of getaway car. An ice cream truck was the perfect vehicle for a nefarious gang of ne'er-do-wells. Let other thieves use inconspicuous white vans, Falconcrest City criminals traveled *in theme.*

"Oh those jackasses!" I shouted.

"What?"

"*I* was going to rob this bank!" I shouted. I hadn't put much thought in my supervillainous debut, but I wasn't about to be shown up on my first day. "Okay, Cloak, how do I do the intangible thing?"

"Just think... intangible. It's like ordering your arm to flex."

"Okay!" I gave a shout, thinking of passing down through the floors beneath me. I was surprised when it worked. I heard a number of screams as I descended past hundreds of employees. Apparently, they'd never seen a caped man moving through things like a ghost.

When I landed on the ground floor, I got a good look at the bank and the people robbing it. The Falconcrest City First National Bank was pretty typical as corrupt metropolitan banks went. There were teller windows, fancy carpets, and a huge vault door just waiting to be robbed.

Of course, the huge icicles hanging from the ceiling and skating-rink-like ice spread around the floor were new. So were all the customers and personnel on the ground with their hands behind their head.

Five or six cold-weather-costume-wearing hoodlums armed with assault rifles were already emptying out the vault. Their leader, the Ice Cream Man, was leaning up against the frozen form of what I suspected was the bank president. Thankfully, none of them were looking in my direction.

The Ice Cream Man was the Malt Shop Gang's leader, and the third-most famous supervillain in the city. He was dressed in a pink button-down shirt, white pants, suspenders, and a little paper hat. The Ice Cream Man also had cut off his lips and sharpened his teeth to shark-like levels. It was damned scary and reminded me not everyone took supervillainy in quite the same easygoing manner as myself.

Also noteworthy was a girl standing on the other side of the deceased bank president, holding a two-handed gun that looked like it came from the 40th century. She was an attractive girl with long red hair, shades, and a furry hood. There was something *familiar* about her, but I couldn't place it.

"The Ice Cream Man, shit just got real," I muttered. I hadn't expected one of America's worst domestic terrorists to be making an appearance here. It was too late to back out now, though.

"Are you sure you know what you're doing?"

"Not at all. But I've got an entrance to make."

"Fine." Cloak sounded irritated. *"Get yourself killed. We're only bonded for life after all."*

"Ice Cream Man!" I hissed in the throatiest grave-like voice I could muster, drawing the gang's attention. "You've made a big mistake coming to my city."

"Wait; are you a supervillain or a superhero? I'm confused."

I didn't get to respond because the Ice Cream Man's reaction to my threat was to say, "Kill this idiot!"

The other members of the Malt Shop Gang pulled out their guns and started shooting at me. You had to admire their discipline since they dropped at least a dozen bags of money to murder me.

I was still intangible, however. Thus, all the bullets flew through me. Raising my hands, I started causing the crook's guns to catch fire one by one. It worked well, causing most of them to drop their weapons and stare at me in horrified shock. The one exception was one of the robbers who caught fire instead of his gun and ran out of the bank screaming.

I needed to work on my aim, it seemed. Well, practice makes perfect.

"Holy shit!" One of the gang members shouted, staring at me in horror. "It's the Nightwalker! He's back from the dead!"

"No." I raised a finger to correct him. "I'm not the Nightwalker. I'm—"

That was when a glop of green ice cream passed through my intangible head. The stuff hit a desk behind me and melted it into a pile of sizzling goop within seconds. With that, the goons panicked and made a break for it, tossing their guns to the ground and screaming as they ran.

I turned around, looking at the Ice Cream Man. "Did you fire acid ice cream at my head?"

"I agree, that is tacky. Of course, it's not the first time I've had acid ice cream shot at me. I remember when Master Warren and I—"

"Shut up!" I snapped at my cape, looking very strange to the dozen or so terrified bank employees watching my altercation with the Ice Cream Man. "Ahem, I mean tell me the story later. I'm working on my ambiance."

The Ice Cream Man was holding a brown cone-shaped weapon, looking quite irritated with me. "Listen pal, I don't know how you got the Nightwalker's outfit, but I knew the Nightwalker. I tried to kill the Nightwalker and you sir, are not the Nightwalker."

The henchgirl jumped up and down, pointing her futuristic gun in my direction. "Yeah, you're just a cheap knock-off superhero!"

I raised a finger to correct her. "I'd like to point out I'm not a superhero either."

That was when the Ice Cream Man swung his weapon around, slamming me across the face with it and sending me spiraling backward into a loan officer's desk.

"What the hell?! I thought I was intangible!" I coughed.

"You can only maintain intangibility for a limited time. Additionally, using your other abilities shortens that time by a considerable amount."

"Now you tell me!" I struggled to get up.

"Maybe next time you should familiarize yourself with your powers **before** *trying to thwart a bank robbery?"*

I didn't have time to argue further with the garment because the Ice Cream Man was already lifting a triple chocolate fudge covered stick of dynamite to stuff down my pants. I'd seen him do it on CrimeTube. The results...weren't pretty. Funny, but not pretty.

Pulling my fist back, I spun around and clocked the insane confectioner across the chin. It spun his head around, giving me hope he was stunned.

The Ice Cream Man turned back to me, a terrifying grin on his face. "Was that supposed to hurt?"

I remembered super-strength wasn't amongst my powers. "No, but this is."

I grabbed the loan officer's chair behind me and struck the Ice Cream Man across the face. I had to hand it to myself—that was a pretty good comeback.

I wasn't the sort of guy to miss an opportunity and beat the Ice Cream Man with the chair until he was on the ground unconscious... or dead. I wasn't sure and didn't care. I then hit him again across the head for good measure.

"Was that necessary?"

"Necessary? No. Fun? Yes." I smiled before something started bugging me. "There's something I'm forgetting. What is it?"

"The girl," Cloak reminded me. *"You still haven't subdued her."*

"Oh, right."

Looking up, I saw the terrified-looking figure of the henchgirl with the futuristic gun. I had the suspicion she was the one responsible for all the ice filling the bank, plus the dead bank President. She could have just blasted me and taken off running. I got the impression she wasn't the mad dog killer type, though. Either that or she wasn't sure whether her gun could harm me since I could turn intangible at will.

Smart woman.

Really, she was *very* familiar. Her Eskimo parka was wrapped around her head so I couldn't make out her features but there was something about her that made me feel like I was next to someone I knew *very* well. It helped that her hands and neck were as pale as a vampire's, which just a few people I knew had. I was ready to walk up to her and pull down her hood so I could get a good look.

In an accent I recognized as coming from the South Side, the woman hesitated then asked, "Um, am I next?"

I finally realized why she was so familiar. "Cindy? Cindy Wakowski?"

"Gary?"

"Shhh!" I made a shushing gesture. "Don't advertise it to the world!"

Cindy and I had gone to school together, South Falconcrest High. We'd shared glee club, a love of supervillainy, and the joys of sex in the backseat of my father's car. Hell, we'd even gone to prom together. Last I'd heard she'd been studying to be a doctor.

"You know this woman?"

"Don't act so surprised. I grew up in South Falconcrest. Half of my class went on to become henchmen or supervillains."

To understand Southies, you had to take the bad part of town then put it next to a part of town its residents didn't want to go into late at night.

That was South Falconcrest.

"You're a *superhero*?" Cindy asked, disbelieving. "Your parents would be so ashamed!"

"Not quite," I said. "How did you end up a henchwench?"

Cindy huffed, lifting her gun. "That's an offensive slur. The proper term is hench*person*. In any case, it started small. I needed to pay off my student loans and there was an ad on Crimeslist. It spiraled from there. I've worked for six different supervillains in the past month. There's not much demand for a permanent sexy underling."

"I understand, I do." I nodded, giving her a once over. "By the way, that's not a flattering look for you."

Cindy pulled down her parka and revealed her long bright red hair and cute round ears. "Well, excuse me all to hell. It's not like I'm going to start taking fashion tips from a guy dressed up like the Nightwalker."

"I prefer to think I look like an evil sorcerer or necromancer. In any case, you're free to go. Try not to hook up with guys like the Malt Shop Gang again, though. Those guys are *crazy*."

"Tell me about it," Cindy said, lifting her futuristic gun. "You want the freeze ray?" She got a dreamy look in her eye. "I miss working for the Mad Baker. He made the most delicious cookies. They're made with ingredients from the future."

"What IS it about this town? I never thought I'd long for the good old days of Nazi robots and dragons."

"I'd love the freeze ray!" I said, ignoring Cloak's mutterings before taking the bulky weapon in hand. "Oomph. Heavy. I can make it my first trophy, though."

"You're letting her go?" One of the bank employees, a middle-aged black woman, interrupted us. She was still kneeling on the ground with her hands on her neck like half the bank personnel.

"You're welcome!" I snapped back at her.

"You realize she killed the bank president, right?"

I gave a dismissive shrug. "Last time I came here for a loan, the Bank President had a pregnant mother of two thrown out by security. Somehow, I think God will forgive her. If not, eh, Hell has better parties anyway."

Taking a look back at the frozen form of the bank president, I saw he was still standing there, hands in the air. It looked like he was trying to wave off whatever blast had covered him in a thick layer of frost. Standing next to the block of ice was a figure identical to the frozen man, only lacking in the thin white covering. The identical figure looked lost and disorientated, which made sense since he was standing next to his own dead body.

"Is *that* one of the restless dead?" I asked my cape.

"*I'm afraid so.*"

Walking over to the man, I hefted up the freeze ray in my arms. "Uh, sorry. I wish I could have saved you. Well, sort of. In fact, I'm glad you're dead. Still, it sucks for you and I suppose that's all that matters."

"*That was horrible.*"

"I'm a beginner at this!" I said, throwing my hands out.

The bank president, a balding middle-aged Caucasian man with glasses, looked up. "I don't understand. What's going on?"

"You're dead. *Finito.* Kaput. You've kicked the bucket. You're now a ghost," I shook the freeze ray in my arms for emphasis. "Take a look beside you at your corpse."

The man shook his head and turned around, jumping with a start at his dead, frozen, body. "Oh, my God! No! I was just fifty-two!"

"Yeah." I gestured to the sky with the gun. "Well, you should let go of your earthly confines or whatever. Go into the light, or given the way you've behaved, the big burning pit."

"*Master Warren handled these little heart-to-hearts with the recently deceased better than you.*"

"Well, we all can't be billionaire philanthropists."

"*Hmm? No, Arthur Warren merely* **funded** *the Nightwalker's crusade against crime. I was referring to Lancel Warren, the ex-police officer and Arthur's brother. He was the Nightwalker.*"

"Oh." I was a little disappointed. "I just figured Arthur Warren would be the Nightwalker because he was independently wealthy and would have a lot of free time on his hands."

"*That was cliché when the Scarlet Pimpernel was published.*"

"Uh?" the bank president started to ask. "Which light? There's—"

"Shoo! Shoo!" I gestured with the freeze ray, causing the ghost to back away and disappear. Hopefully, he went on to whatever afterlife awaited him. It occurred to me to ask Cloak what cosmological and religious system was true, but I wasn't sure I wanted to know. I'd hate to find out the Ultraologists were right.

Cindy grabbed a sack of money on the way out, and I helped myself to the other sacks. None of the bank employees made any attempt to stop me. Either they were too grateful at being rescued to care, or they were too terrified of the crazy set of superpowers I'd displayed.

Maybe both.

The woman from earlier, the one who objected to my letting Cindy go, shouted, "Wait a second! Who are you?"

I was tempted to say I was the Nightwalker. He was the coolest superhero ever. It's a pity the world would never again see his equal.

Or so I thought.

Walking out the door and levitating away, I, instead, shouted back, "I'm Merciless! The Supervillain without Mercy!"

"You realize, of course, that's redundant."

"Eh, it's a work in progress. Like me."

"God help us all."

Chapter Two

Where I Tell the Wife

Informing the wife about my new career went about as well as could be expected.

Better, even.

"Are you out of your mind?"

Mandy was wearing tight blue jeans and a GladiatorFest XXX t-shirt, her gorgeous brown hair hung over her shoulders. Her skin was pale, albeit less so than Cindy's. Mandy was a bit on the short side, five-foot-four to my five-foot-eight, but I liked petite girls. Mandy was Eurasian with a Korean mother and Caucasian father, favoring neither completely.

Mandy and I had met when I was studying Unusual Criminology at Falconcrest City University. She was the lead in the all-girl band known as the Black Furies, captain of the track team, a martial arts master, and capable of out-drinking a demigod. We'd dated some of the same people and decided to hook up after a concert. We hadn't looked back since. My conservative Jewish parents had, of course, had a hissy fit but they'd overlooked their first son being a supervillain and I eventually won them over.

"I..." I tried to think of a way to respond to her accusation. "Kind of?"

"You're out of your mind and you're an idiot to boot."

"I thought you'd be happy." That was a lie, of course. I'd been pretty sure she'd be pissed off.

"You robbed a bank!" Mandy gestured to the television set in the living room, which was tuned to the local news. They were covering my earlier escapade with the Malt Shop Gang. Well, that and a dog that had learned how to dance. The reporters in Falconcrest City were just slightly more competent than the police.

"Eyewitnesses report a terrifying masked man interrupted a robbery by the Malt Shop Gang," Sally Sutler said. She was a pretty Chinese American in her thirties and on-site at the bank. Rumors were she was dating the Prismatic Commando. Reporters *loved* raising their profile that way. "It has been suggested he may have been using some form of magic."

"Which is true." A block of ice appeared in one hand while a bit of flame shot out from the other. "I'm all sorts of magical now."

"Don't do that in the house," Mandy snapped before turning back to the TV. "You're scaring the dogs."

Our snow-white bull terriers, Arwen and Galadriel, were hiding underneath the kitchen table. They hated when we fought.

"Fine, fine." I used my flame powers to evaporate the ice in my hand.

"I thought we'd agreed you wouldn't be a criminal. That was one of the conditions of my marrying you." Mandy was right, of course. I'd given up my college career of hacktivism and petty sabotage upon graduation.

It was the worst mistake of my life.

"Being an unemployed bank teller isn't working out for me. Opportunity knocked, and I couldn't help but let her in."

Mandy tried to calm down, but it was difficult for her. We didn't fight often, but she was a very passionate woman. "We don't know where this costume came from."

"Obviously, it came from the Nightwalker."

"He had nothing to do with it."

Sally's report on the television was less than flattering. "Alternately described as the 'most terrifying man they'd ever seen' and 'somewhat goofy', the supervillain calling himself Merciless beat escaped serial killer Charles Creamley, a.k.a. the Ice Cream Man, to death before helping himself to fifty-five thousand dollars in cash. Spokesmen for the Malt Shop Gang have called for vengeance against this newly-debuted figure in the city's underworld."

"He died? Huh. I guess it *is* a reign of terror."

It was strange how little the revelation of my killing the Ice Cream Man affected me. He wasn't the first person I'd killed, there had been one other. That time, I'd been an emotional wreck for almost two years. The Ice Cream Man, by contrast, felt like I'd done the world a public service. Maybe that first murder had drained anything objectionable about the act from me, at least with fellow killers.

Mandy put her hands over her face. "Goddess, Gary! You're guilty of murder now!"

My wife is a Wiccan, by the way. Sadly, that didn't come with supernatural powers, unlike some witches I knew.

"Hey, killing people doesn't count if they're bad! Hollywood taught us that."

Mandy glared at me.

I grimaced. "Okay, that sounded psychotic even to me."

"I was thinking stupid." Mandy sighed, gesturing to the bags of money sitting in a corner. "You can't keep this money, we have to return it."

"I can't return it!" I choked out, horrified. "That would ruin my rep!"

"You're not a supervillain!" Mandy shook her hands in frustration. "You're Gary Karkofsky."

"Why can't I be both Gary *and* Merciless?" I asked, spreading out my arms. "Didn't you once date a supervillain?"

I shouldn't have done that, as that was a game I couldn't win. While Mandy had dated the Black Witch, I'd been involved with Cindy and one other woman my wife often wondered if I'd rather have been with. Mandy and I had fallen in love after we'd broken up with our former fiancés and there was always the unspoken agreement we shouldn't talk too much about our romantic pasts.

"The Black Witch just spoke to me with her words about the bleak poetry of the human condition." Mandy frowned before looking away. "Selena hadn't started her whole, 'world domination through dark magic' thing."

I tried not to think of my wife dating one of the world's sexiest supervillains. The last thing this conversation needed was me getting turned on. We could save that for later.

"I could have gone all day not hearing that particular thought."

"Cloak, back me up here."

"Leave me out of this. I had enough problems with Master Warren's love interests," Cloak replied. "Besides, no one other than you can hear me, as long as we're joined."

Mandy looked at me. "What are you doing?"

"The cloak talks," I explained.

"Only to you?" Mandy asked, raising an eyebrow.

"Yes."

"Okay, Gary. That explains it. You've had a psychotic break. We're taking you to see a doctor tomorrow."

Instead of rising to her bait, I replied, "Good idea. If you can prove you're insane to a court of law, they'll pretty much let you get away with anything in this town."

"Argh!" Mandy looked ready to strangle me.

I took a deep breath, trying to articulate how I felt. "This is important to me. It's something that has meaning."

"Meaning? Do you *want* to be remembered for robbing banks and fighting superheroes?"

"Yes?"

I was spared her rebuttal by the sound of a telephone ringing. Not the ring of a modern phone, but the kind belonging to one from the 1960s or 70s. The last time I'd heard one was when I was at my grandmother's house as a child. It was coming from one of the cardboard boxes still in our living room. Not the one the Nightwalker's cloak was from but another that came with it.

"Excuse me." I seized the opportunity to take a break from the conversation. Picking up the kitchen knife from earlier, I sliced open the box the sound was coming from. Inside, I found a glowing midnight black phone resting on a pile of journals. It had no chords or dial, despite looking like an antique. I'd seen similar devices, though, at the Nightwalker Museum.

Picking up the receiver, I held it to my ear. "Hello?"

"Is this one of Nightwalker's associates?" A voice spoke

on the other end of the line. "It's Chief Watkins. We need your help."

"Wow," I said. "I thought the Nightwalker's hotline to the police chief's office was an urban legend."

"Who is this?" Chief Watkins asked, offended.

"Uh, that's not important." I considered hanging up. I didn't want anyone tracing the phone call back to my home. Still, I was curious. "Is something wrong?"

Chief Watkins cleared his throat. "I was hoping someone was going to be sent by the Nightwalker's associates in the Society of Superheroes to replace him. We've had a kidnapping and we need someone with his expertise to solve it."

God, the police in this town were lazy. Eighty years of a vigilante protecting them and their detective skills had gone to shit.

"What happened?" I was more curious than anything else.

"Are you talking to the Chief of Police?" Mandy asked, beside me.

"Yeah. He wants my help. Our tax dollars at work."

"Wow," Mandy said, her earlier anger dissipating. "Tell him he's doing a good job, and we're glad for all the sacrifices the police department has made."

I put my hand over the phone's mouthpiece. "Except, he's *not* doing a good job. Have you been downtown lately? That place is full of freaks and weirdoes."

Mandy crossed her arms. "That's unfair and you know it. The police are doing the best they can."

"They keep a freaking hotline to call a vigilante for help!" I said, appalled. "If that doesn't shake your confidence in the city's patrolman, I don't know what will!"

Mandy narrowed her eyes. "Don't take that tone with me."

"Sorry. It's a sore subject with me."

"Nightwalker, are you talking to someone?" Chief Watkins asked, either assuming I was the Nightwalker's replacement or just used to calling whoever was on the hotline that.

Or he was a moron, which I couldn't discount.

"Ahem!" I cleared my throat and lowered my voice. "No, Chief. Go on."

"Billionaire heiress Amanda Douglas was taken by the Typewriter," Chief Watkins said.

"Isn't she married to a rap star?"

"Wrong celebrity."

"Sorry."

I remembered Amanda Douglas now. She was a local the tabloids loved to portray as a massive party-girl with self-entitlement issues. The sex tape hadn't helped. Mandy was a fan of hers and indicated there was much more going on there than most people thought. One thing I did know was that her father was loaded and probably willing to pay out the nose for her return.

"Her father has offered a half-million dollar reward for her retrieval," Chief Watkins said. "I know it doesn't affect heroes like yourself—"

"Ca-ching! Hell yes!"

"What was that?" Mandy asked, leaning in.

I put my hand over the mouthpiece, again. "Dudley Douglas is offering five hundred grand for the safe return of his daughter."

Mandy blinked, all trace of her earlier disapproval gone. "Amanda Douglas has been kidnapped? That's terrible!"

"Yeah. It's too bad I'm not a superhero." I gave a little whistle before looking away. "Oh wait, superheroes can't take money for their good deeds."

Mandy stared at me. "Okay, fine. If it saves that poor girl's life you can run around in tights."

"I am not a set of tights."

"Thank you." Pulling my hand off the mouthpiece, I asked the Chief, "Could you put the father on the phone?"

Seconds later, I was on the phone with Dudley Douglas. Like a certain other business tycoon, he was richer than God and had no objections to showing it. Still, he seemed to love his daughter and sounded incoherent with grief.

"My daughter," Dudley Douglas spoke with a thick Texas accent. "You've got to save her, Nightwalker!"

I almost shouted, "I'm *not* the Nightwalker!" but held back. Instead, I said, "I'm willing to do what I can, sir. Tell me what happened."

"It all started like this..." Dudley trailed off, violently coughing in my ear. "Sorry, that was my cigar. They cost a thousand dollars each, you know."

"Really?" I asked, losing all sympathy for the man. "How do you know she was taken by the Typewriter?"

"Because he sent us a typewritten note telling us where he could be found and that he was responsible for the kidnapping," Dudley replied. "He's at the top of the Douglas Grand Hotel."

"I see we're dealing with a real criminal mastermind here." I was unable to process how any villain could be that stupid. Maybe there was something to the old saying all supervillains secretly wanted to be caught.

Nah.

"He wants ten million dollars for my little girl, but the police say he might end up killing her anyway," Dudley sobbed out through cigar puffs. "I haven't been so distressed since mah poor wife disappeared. Tell me, Nightwa—ahem, stranger, will he kill her even if I pay?"

I decided the truth was better than candy-coating it. "It's possible. Supervillains aren't as nice as they used to be. If this were Diabloman or Doctor Sin, yeah, I'd say they'd return her, but this sounds like amateur hour stuff. A lot of potential to go bad." I paused, deciding to cut the guy a break. This wasn't the kind of business I wanted to get into, but I figured I could make an exception. "Okay, I'll get your daughter back for half a million dollars."

"*What?*" You could hear Dudley Douglas choking on his cigar as he spoke. "Aren't you a superhero?"

"Hey, man, you posted the reward." I snorted at the man's cheapness. "Don't blame me for taking advantage of it."

"Yes, but I did it for the publicity!" Dudley choked. After a second, though, he calmed down.

"Gary!" Mandy said, listening in.

I raised a hand for her to wait, covering the receiver with my other hand. "I'm negotiating, honey. It'll be fine."

Finally, I heard Dudley crack. "Oh, all right, fine. If you can deliver her back to me safe and sound, I'll write you out a check."

"Make it cash. Remember, I know where you live." I hung up the phone before he could respond. "Well, that went well."

"You know, for a supervillain, you seem to be foiling a lot of crimes."

"Only for selfish reasons!" I placed my hand over my heart.

"Is your cloak talking again?" Mandy asked, looking concerned.

"Yes. He's trying to talk me out of my chosen career path. He thinks supervillainy is a poor career choice."

"I can't imagine why." Mandy looked worn out despite having just found out about my new career a half hour ago. "We need to talk more about this."

I took a second to ponder how much my new career meant to me versus the approval of my wife. It was easy to see that meant more.

"Listen, Mandy, I can't do this without you. I've wanted to be a supervillain since I was eight but that doesn't mean anything compared to my love for you. If you want me to, I will give up my cloak after tonight."

I meant it, too. Say what you will about supervillains all being psychopaths, I loved my wife and she meant more to me than my dream. If she wanted me to quit, I would. I'd take up a similar but unrelated career like politics or law.

Mandy seemed torn, perhaps realizing how much this meant to me. "Are you going to save this girl's life?"

"Yes," I answered her.

"*And* get paid for it?"

"Yes," I repeated, this time more forcefully, sounding almost like Cloak.

"You're not going to kill *anyone* else?"

I bit on my back teeth. "How about I promise to only kill people who have it coming? Like clowns, communists, serial killers, Nazis, or Islamic terrorists?" I neglected to mention people who annoyed me. That wouldn't have gone over well.

"You do realize you could end up in jail because of this. I don't want to spend the rest of my life married to a man behind bars."

"Please, supervillains *never* stay behind bars. There are whole fields of law devoted to beating the system for super-humans." I put the phone receiver in its box. "It's one of the reasons I voted for the current President. The whole 'three strikes and you get sent to the moon' policy is the kind of hardcore stance we need on super crime."

"You're a supervillain who supports 'tough on crime' policies?"

"Less competition that way."

"Okay then." Mandy took a deep breath. "I'm willing to try this out with a couple of caveats."

"I love it when you talk dirty." I tried kissing her on the lips only for her to push me back with one hand.

"Caveat isn't a dirty word." Mandy raised an eyebrow. "Are you ready to listen? I mean, *really*, listen?"

"Shoot."

"Number One: Don't steal from anyone who doesn't deserve it." Mandy poked me in the chest.

"That should be easy; people who don't deserve having it taken away don't have any money to begin with," I said, smiling. "Next."

"Number Two: I don't want you staying out all day and night doing this. I need you around the house."

I winced. That would cut into my efforts to make a name for myself. "Okay, I'll be a part-time supervillain."

"Number Three: Don't use your powers in the house." Mandy narrowed her eyes. "The last thing I need is you setting Galadriel on fire."

"Hey!" I wrinkled my nose. "I know how to use my powers better than that."

"You really don't. However, we can address that later."

I grunted, wishing Cloak would cease his incessant commentary.

"Number Four: Don't bring your work home either. I won't tolerate a bunch of supervillains hanging out here, and if superheroes attack our house, I'm divorcing you."

"Okay." All her objections were reasonable. "I can do that."

"Finally, I want you to wear this." My wife walked to the bedroom and brought back an earpiece.

"Pardon?"

"I want you to be available when I need you. No more of your usual leaving your cell phone in your car or not charging it. When I see you on the news battling the Ink Splotch or whoever, I want to be able to call you."

I was pretty sure Ink Splotch never battled anyone outside of Future City but that was a technicality. "I'm not sure how good an idea it is to talk to you in the middle of a battle, but you've got it."

I put the device in my ear and checked my cell phone to see if it was fully charged. It felt good to have the wife's approval, however grudging. I couldn't do this without her. I'd once read in a magazine most supervillains were unmarried loners. It made me wonder what was wrong with them.

A spouse was the absolute best thing a supervillain could have. It was the superheroes who struck me as the perpetual bachelors. I mean, come on, the whole 'it's not you, it's my enemies' thing is so they can stay single and get sex from the people they rescue. I have it on good authority the Silver Lightning uses it all the time to pick up guys. Admittedly, the good authority was my brother's old gang but if you couldn't trust them then who could you trust?

"You're a very strange man, Gary Karkofsky. You've obviously put far, far too much thought into this."

"Proudly so." I affixed the earpiece. "I come from a long line of criminals, lunatics, and insurance salesmen."

Which was about one-third true.

"Okay." Mandy looked at me. "I think that's it. Stay safe and don't get yourself killed."

"Thank you, baby." I leaned in to give her a short kiss on the lips. It turned into a much more passionate one, lasting over a minute. Breaking away, I stared into her eyes. "I'll try and make it back soon."

"Hurry," Mandy said, her voice softening. "And don't get killed."

"I won't."

Chapter Three

Where I Discover the Limits of My Powers

The Douglas Grand Hotel towered over Falconcrest City's skyline. Sixty-six stories high, its black stone edifice sported gargoyles along the sides of its windows. The Douglas family rejected the whole 'hotels are meant to be inviting and pleasant places' theory of design. Instead, they went with 'hotels should look scary as shit.' The place looked like a giant red eye should be hovering over it.

Staring up from the ground at the topmost floor of the building, I said to my cape, "You know, I have to wonder about the architects in Falconcrest City. It bothers me less the Douglas Grand Hotel looks like Dracula should be staying there than that it *fits in with the surrounding buildings.* It's like the city fathers decided to combine Art Deco with H.P Lovecraft."

"The city was designed by the Brotherhood of Infamy as a gigantic mystical amplifier to summon their demon-god, Zul-Barbas. They intend to offer the citizenry as a human sacrifice in order to bring about the end of the world."

"What?"

"One of the many random facts I know. You'd be surprised at how many horrible secrets lie hidden in this city. Don't worry, the Nightwalker hasn't heard from the Brotherhood in years." Cloak's voice was almost cheery.

"You're terrifying."

"Thank you."

Seeing the hotel was cordoned off by the police and

surrounded by hundreds of cop cars, I cursed my luck. I didn't want to announce my existence to the police, especially after robbing a bank less than three hours before. I needed a plan, not just for getting in, but for dealing with the Typewriter when I did.

I tried to remember what I knew about the supervillain. All I could recall was that he wore a stupid outfit and was supposedly a complete buffoon. When even civilians know you're a joke, your career is over.

"I need some info about this guy," I muttered aloud. "Something to build a battle strategy around."

"Yes, because a man who dresses up in an antiquated suit with a prop typewriter on his head is a man you need to out-think."

"It's always the kooky ones you have to watch out for." Pulling out my cell phone, I dialed Mandy. After she picked up, I spoke in my most charming voice, "Hey, Honey. It's your beloved husband, the world's greatest criminal mind."

"Have you rescued the girl yet? Also, have you been paid?"

I bit my lip. "No, I just got down here. Traffic is terrible. You'd think there was a crisis downtown or something. Do you have your computer?"

"Of course," my wife answered. "I was looking up information on the next Derek Hawthorne novel."

My wife loved urban fantasy novels; it was another of our shared interests. "How's that going?"

"It's available for pre-order! I'm also searching for signs you've been killed or maimed. Thankfully, there's none of that."

I shook my head. I hadn't intended to worry her like this. "Okay, I need you to look for information on the Typewriter. I don't need to go in there blind."

"Okay. Oh, by the way, could you pick up some yogurt on the way back?"

"Sure." I wondered if Tom Terror ever did grocery shopping for his wife. "No problem."

"Henpecked."

"What was that?" I glared at my cloak.

"Huh?" Mandy asked.

"Nothing. Just talking to my costume."

Mandy grimaced. "That's freaky. You know that, right?"

"He's an okay sort. His comments are starting to grate, though. Any luck with the Typewriter?"

"One second," Mandy said. It took more like five. "Okay. Got it."

"You hacked into his police file?"

"No. I'm checking out his Superpedia file."

"Oh." I realized that was probably the better resource. "That works. Lay it on me."

"The Typewriter, real name: Theodore Keyes," Mandy started. "With a name like that I suppose he was destined for supervillainy."

"Tell me about it."

"Theodore was a book editor at a major Belgian publishing house before murdering his entire staff with explosive computer keyboards. He had grown sick of all the typos sent to his office."

"A common enough story. The Belgians have always been twitchy about their grammar."

"No superpowers to speak of, the Typewriter possesses a genius intellect and a cane that possesses uncertain super-technological properties."

"Uncertain super-technological properties?" I asked, confused.

"That's what it says."

"It means the cane does stuff no one understands. Technology is like a grab bag. Sometimes, devices do random unexplainable things."

"Ah, super-science," I said, probably confusing Mandy. I was going to have to learn to respond to Cloak with my thoughts and thoughts alone.

"Oh, and he's cheap," Mandy added.

"Cheap," I repeated. "A *cheap* supervillain?"

That shocked me more than the fact the Typewriter told the police where he was. Good pay was one of the major draws for henchmen. If a supervillain didn't pay his goons well, why would they put up with his antics? What was *wrong* with this guy?

"Yeah, over here on the commentary page, one of his henchmen said so. He wrote some nasty stuff about him,"

Mandy said. "Be careful, Gary. This guy may act like an idiot, but he's killed a lot of people."

"Hey, I'm always careful." I smiled. "Take care of yourself, Mandy. I'll give you a call right after I'm done."

"I love you," Mandy whispered.

"I love you too." I tapped the side of the earpiece to hang up.

"That was simultaneously heartwarming and sickening. I don't think I've ever met a happily married supervillain before."

"There's no law against it," I said, smiling. "And if there was, I'd break it."

"Touché. May I ask how you intend to get to the top of the building where the hostage is held?"

"Can I just, uh...fly up there?" I was pretty sure Cloak had mentioned levitation.

"Levitation is not flight. There's a subtle difference. You can go up and down but not forward. You also move as fast as a rising balloon."

"The Nightwalker glided everywhere," I pointed out.

"He started from tall heights and moved down," Cloak countered. *"Unfortunately, the Douglas Grand Hotel is the tallest structure in the city with the exception of the Clock Tower and Warren Towers."*

Unfortunate indeed. Both structures were on the other side of town. "Maybe I could waltz through the police cars, blowing them up one by one, as I send the crowds scattering in awe of my terrifying visage. Then I can march into the hotel and call the Typewriter out."

"..."

"You think that's a bad idea?"

"I live to serve, Master."

"It's amazing how you managed to make that sound like you're telling me to fuck off."

"Thank you."

"Relax, I was joking." I didn't have enough skill with my fire powers to pull that off. "Okay, I have a plan but you're not going to like it."

"That's my opinion of most of your ideas, Master."

"Stop calling me that. We're partners in this. Whether you like it or not."

"*Yes, Master.*"

"You're saying that sarcastically, aren't you?"

"*Of course not.*"

"Jerk."

Closing my eyes, I concentrated on becoming intangible and proceeded to descend into the city's sewer system. Sewers were a lot smaller in real life than depicted on television. Intangibility made up for that problem, but I still had to pass through a bunch of pipes full of icky goop. None of the stuff could touch me but just passing through it made me feel unclean. I could feel that Cloak felt the same way, perhaps through some form of psychic feedback.

"*You're right, I don't like this plan.*"

"Oh be quiet, we're not *actually* traveling through sewer water," I grumbled before pausing. "Are we?"

"*Your complete lack of knowledge regarding my capacities is frightening.*"

"It's not too late to find a wizard to pull us apart. Then, I swear to you, I will set you on fire."

"*Where would you find a wizard?*"

"Superpedia."

"*I'll be quiet.*"

Eventually, we passed underneath the hotel entrance and levitated up into the laundry room. There, I was surrounded by hundreds of washing machines and dryers. The staff had been evacuated, and the room was empty. Checking my clothes, I was pleased to discover there was no raw sewage on them.

"Wow, my plan worked. You're pretty useful."

"*Don't sound so surprised.*"

Taking a deep breath, I prepared to levitate up the penthouse. "Now I'll levitate through the sixty or so floors above me. With the powers at my command, I will force the Typewriter to his knees!"

"*Not to trouble you, but have you considered taking the elevator?*"

I took a look at the elevator about three feet away from me. "I see. Are you sure I can't levitate the last thirty or so floors?"

"*You're mocking me.*"

"Yes. Yes, I am," Walking up to the elevator doors, I muttered, "I swear, you take all the fun out of superpowers. I'd also like to register a complaint about the general crappiness of my abilities, too. This whole 'no flying' and 'intangibility for thirty seconds' isn't doing anything for me. You said I could take more damage than a normal person. Am I at least bulletproof?"

"*Mostly.*"

"Do I want to know what you mean by that?"

"*No. Try not to get shot.*"

Well, no one said supervillainy was going to be easy. "I'll try to remember that."

After entering the service elevator I hit the button for the penthouse. The doors closed and I felt the elevator lurch and rumble as it started its way up. I wasn't certain where Typewriter was but everything I knew about supervillainy told me he would be above everyone else. Supervillains liked the rich and glitzy lifestyle, the higher priced the better. At least, that was what my brother had told me. Stingray, sadly, never quite managed to make it into the big leagues.

"*I must say, I am pleased by your efforts to help this young woman. It is a courageous use of your abilities to prevent an innocent from dying,*" Cloak said about the time we passed floor thirty. "*I believe, if you fight intelligently, you should be able to subdue the Typewriter without putting either her or him at risk.*"

"I don't intend to fight the guy."

"*Pardon?*"

"I'm going to make an offer to split the half million dollars with him. Then I'm going to offer to help him escape the building in exchange for his assistance in a *Supervillain Team Up* to rob Douglas blind."

"*That's...*"

"Ingenious? Diabolical?"

"*Stupid.*"

"Spoilsport," I said. I was about to say more when the doorway to the penthouse opened.

Preparing my dramatic entrance line, I turned intangible just in case they reacted to my presence with gunfire. I didn't expect trouble, but it was better to be safe than sorry. After all, there were plenty of old people and supervillains but very few old supervillains.

"Hi guys," I said. "I am Merci—"

Instead of gunfire, I was hit by a weird energy beam. The blast smashed me against the back of the elevator, knocking the air out of my lungs; I slid down, collapsing on the ground. A look down at my chest told me a hole hadn't been blown in it, which was good. Instead, it was like I'd been hit with a giant Taser.

"What...the hell...was that?" I coughed out, unable to move.

"Uncertain super-technological properties in action. Funny, that beam shouldn't have been able to hit you."

"No kidding!" I shouted, struggling to get up.

A hulking figure wearing an elaborate horned devil mask and a business suit pulled me out of the elevator and dragged me to the center of the penthouse. He was almost seven-feet-tall and possessed muscles on muscles.

Something about the manner the figure carried himself, however, told me that he was more than just dumb muscle. There was an elegance to him that contrasted to the simple kidnapping scheme I'd found myself caught up in.

"Hi." I waved, weakly.

"Be silent." The big man picked me up and slammed me down in one of the room's easy chairs.

"Kay," I answered, coughing. Clearing my throat, I looked up and got my first clear look at the penthouse and my opponents.

The room was creepy and archaic enough to be a supervillain lair. The curtains were drawn across the windows and the doors were barricaded with furniture. Everything had a pseudo-Victorian feel that made the place look like it had come straight out of a Gothic comic book. Someone needed to talk to Dudley Douglas about the décor for his hotels. This one was starting to spook me, and I was a bad guy.

The Typewriter's gang, by contrast, looked rather mundane. Except for the hulking man dressed like a demon, none of them were even in costume. They were just a bunch of generic thugs in suits. It seemed Typewriter was too cheap to spring for theme costumes. It made me wonder how he ever expected to make it in Falconcrest City.

The Typewriter himself, at least, tried to make up for their lack of showmanship by being dressed like a proper supervillain. I'd seen a picture of him once or twice in the papers, always being dragged into the police station by the Nightwalker, but none of the photos did him justice.

He was much, much, *much* sillier looking in person.

The aforementioned 1930s business suit wasn't so bad. He was wearing a pleasant looking pair of black slacks, a white silk shirt, and a red vest over the front with suspenders. However, topping the outfit was a typewriter. Literally, he'd arranged for a helmet made to look like an extra-large version of his namesake. It was the most impractical thing I'd ever seen.

Still, I couldn't complain about the man's competence too hard since he'd gotten the drop on me. His golden cane topped with a T was more than it seemed.

"Did you pay money for that outfit?" I couldn't help but ask. "If so, you need to ask for a refund."

The man in the demon mask pulled back his arm and slammed me in the chest with his fist, almost causing me to pass out from the pain.

"Oomph!" I eloquently replied. It seemed my superpowers weren't enough to make punches not hurt like hell.

"Hi-too-ho, we've got someone new! HA-ha-ha-ha-ha!" The Typewriter laughed, shaking as if in ecstasy. It was such a bizarre sight, I was distracted from the fact my plan to deal with the gang and rescue the girl had gone awry.

"Are you okay?" I asked, perplexed by the man's behavior.

The Typewriter jabbed me in the gut with the end of his cane.

Fool! You didn't realize my Power-Cane possessed a transdimensional matter disruptor and stun beam! Any and all superpowers from the Nightwalker's intangibility to Ultragod's invulnerability are *helpless* before its power!"

"Wow. So that's where your entire budget went. No wonder you couldn't afford a decent outfit."

The man in the demon mask gave me an uppercut across

the jaw, sending my head spiraling backward. If he'd hit me with any more force, he would have knocked my head clean off.

"Ow! I need those teeth!" My mouth was bleeding. Despite the pain, I grinned. "Where the hell did you learn to be a supervillain? You look like something out of the funny papers."

The Typewriter was so ridiculous I couldn't take him seriously even when he could kill me on a whim. Even the Typewriter's henchmen looked confounded by his behavior. The man in the demon mask looked as if he was embarrassed to be here.

I didn't blame him. He had a majesty the others lacked. In a way he looked as familiar as Cindy had, back at the bank. He wasn't one of my old high school associates, however. They had been more into Live Action Role-Play than looking like a demon-masked Mafia don.

"Silence! You are in the presence of the great and powerful Typewriter!" The flamboyant supervillain began pacing around in a circle, talking to himself. "They said I was mad, mad I tell you! Well, who is the mad one now?"

"Did he just say the 'who's the mad one now' line?" I asked, stunned by the man's complete lack of dignity. "Cloak, didn't that go out of fashion during the Forties?"

"I think it's even older than that," Cloak replied. *"I remember encountering it in 1932. Even then, it was stale."*

"Just checking."

The Typewriter kicked the air and spun around, pointing at me with his cane. "Do not think you can fool my genius-level intellect. Your youthful form does not fool me, foolish man! I'd recognize that costume anywhere: you're the *Nightwalker!*"

I rolled my eyes. "Is this going to be a running theme? I'm getting sick of being mistaken for him."

"Well, I was a rather important part of his costume."

"Shut up," I muttered at my costume. "I'm working an angle here."

The man in the demon mask interrupted our debate. "It is not the Nightwalker. I fought him many times."

The Typewriter wasn't listening. "Once I slay you, I shall be acknowledged as the greatest of all supervillains in Falconcrest City!"

"Hey!" I interrupted him, pissed off. "There's only going to be *one* 'greatest of all supervillains' in Falconcrest City, and that's me!"

Everyone looked at me.

"You're a supervillain?" the Typewriter asked, poking my stomach with the end of his cane.

"Damned straight!" I proclaimed, blood dripping down my chin. "I am *Merciless*! The supervillain without a shred of mercy!"

They all looked at me like I was out of my mind.

"Still redundant."

"Oh reeaaallly?" the Typewriter asked, snorting.

"The man dressed like...whatever the hell you're supposed to be dressed as...should not be questioning my credentials." I turned my nose up at him. "I mean, can you even see in that thing?"

One of the mobsters beside me looked nervous. "I think I saw this guy on the news. He killed the Ice Cream Man and robbed the First National Bank."

"Thank you!" I said, trying to think up an excuse. "Uh, I killed the Ice Cream Man because he was moseying in on my action."

"Moseying?" The Typewriter asked.

"Oh you are *not* going to comment on my way of speaking—after your intro," I snapped.

"He has a point," the man in the demon mask said.

"Silence!" The Typewriter turned to me. "You may be a supervillain, but you have removed one of the greats of supervillainy. For that, I sentence you *to death*!"

The man in the demon mask grabbed me by the cloak, pulling me up before wrapping his arms around my neck.

"Meep," I said, staring.

Chapter Four

Where I Recruit My First Henchpersons

The man in the demon mask lifted me up, intending to either strangle me or break my neck. I wasn't sure which. Remembering I could turn intangible, I slipped out of his hands and passed through the floor.

Levitating up behind him, I became physical long enough to punch the base of his spine...only to draw my hand back in agony. The man was pure muscle, not an ounce of fat on his body.

"Ow!" I hissed, shaking my fist in the air.

"You don't have super-strength, remember?"

"I remember!"

The man in the demon mask spun around and punched me, sending me flying backward into a nearby table. Thankfully, my quasi-invulnerability seemed strong enough so it just *felt* like every bone in my body was broken.

"Farewell, Sweet Prince!" the Typewriter shouted, aiming his cane at me.

"What the hell are you on?"

I jumped to the side the moment I saw him bringing the cane around. Its brilliant beam missed me by a hair's breadth, striking the ruined table instead. The damaged piece of furniture disappeared along with a substantial chunk of the floor, leaving a gaping hole instead.

"It is just *wrong* a doofus like the Typewriter has a weapon like that," I grunted, trying to find cover. A couple of the business suit wearing henchmen charged at me, perhaps intending to hold me down for their boss.

The Typewriter fired again, not bothering to aim, and hit one of his henchmen instead. The man disappeared in a flash of golden light, causing the other henchmen to back away. As I struggled to find a weapon that would give me an advantage against him, I remembered I had power over fire and cold.

"Idiot," I cursed myself.

Raising a hand to set the Typewriter on fire, my wrist was grabbed by the man in the demon mask who started punching me with my knuckles.

Yes, I was being forced to punch myself in the face.

Each blow felt like a mallet, making my head spin and my vision blur. I couldn't concentrate enough to use my powers. The pain was so intense. The man in the demon mask wrapped his arm underneath my neck and his palm over my forehead. The hold was so tight he'd just have to make the barest of motions to snap my neck.

"He's yours, Typewriter," the man in the demon mask said. "He fought well, give him a clean death."

I closed my eyes and focused on causing the interior of the cane to freeze over. Hopefully, the Typewriter wouldn't notice. If this didn't work, I was about to have the shortest supervillain career of all time.

The Typewriter aimed the cane at me a couple of times before shaking it. "Hell in a hand basket, I knew I shouldn't have bought this from the Electrifier without a guarantee!"

"I cannot believe I've been reduced to this," The man in the demon mask whispered.

It hit me who the devil-masked henchman was. "Holy crap! I know you! You're Diabloman!"

The man in the demon mask seemed surprised, twitching a bit. "I was...once."

"You were, like, the biggest supervillain ever!" I said, choosing to talk instead of fleeing. "God, I remember the fights between you and the Nightwalker in the Eighties. I was a kid, but you were a real inspiration. You even managed to have a few showdowns with Ultragod and the Society of Superheroes despite having no superpowers!"

Hell, he'd started the Grim and Gritty Era of Supervillains

vs. Superheroes by killing the Guitarist!

"The Guitarist was a good man. You should be ashamed for cheering his death."

"Hush you," I mentally said to Cloak.

"That was...a long time ago," Diabloman responded.

"What are you doing working for an idiot like the Typewriter?" I asked, feeling a fanboy glee at getting my ass kicked by one of the premiere supervillains of recent history.

Diabloman sounded regretful. "It is...complicated. I must kill you now."

"How much are you getting paid?" I asked, hoping to distract him from his current line of thought.

"Twenty-thousand." Diabloman paused from killing me. "Why?"

"You realize he's making, like, ten million dollars off this job, right?" I said. "I'll pay you double if you smash him and his henchmen to pieces."

"Kill him, you magic steroid-popping buffoon!" the Typewriter shouted, flinging his golden cane against Diabloman's head. The thing bounced against him, landing off to the side.

Diabloman tensed up; looking at the Typewriter with such hate I thought he might launch himself at him. Instead, Diabloman hoisted me up into the air and said, "I accept your offer."

Diabloman then tossed me at the Typewriter. I was sent crashing into the garish supervillain, and the two of us spiraled to the ground. All the while, I heard Diabloman grunting and the sound of painful grunts from the other henchmen. There was also the sound of gunfire.

I wasn't the best fighter in the world but even I could beat up a rail-thin idiot like the Typewriter. After punching him several times in the face, I grabbed a lamp from a nearby table and smashed it across his face.

"I think that got him," I said. "Is he dead?"

"No."

"Pity." I got up and started looking around. Across the room, I saw Diabloman had torn into the thugs with ruthless abandon. Their corpses were spread around the room in various unpleasant poses. I saw most of them had their legs and arms broken, a few had their spines shattered.

The fact Diabloman had done this despite being armed with nothing more than his fists, highlighted what a dangerous man he was. At the other end of the room, I saw him dusting off his hands.

"Wow, he took the 'smash them to pieces' thing a bit literally," I whispered before rubbing my head. I had a blinding headache from the earlier business of facing down Diabloman. "I need to handle this guy with a deft touch."

"Or you could set him on fire."

"Because that worked out so well earlier."

"Point taken."

Diabloman was over by my side in an instant, once more lifting me by the cape and hoisting me in the air. "If you are lying about the payment, I will break you."

"Nope, it's real," I said. I was about to say something else when Diabloman doubled over, clutching his chest. Concerned, I placed my hand on his shoulder. "Are you okay?"

"No!" Diabloman swatted away my hand. "I... I am sorry. I do not like people to see me like this."

The Typewriter started to get up behind me, reaching for his golden cane to beat me over the head. I snapped my fingers and he caught fire. The flamboyant supervillain screamed, making terrible sounds as he burned.

"Is this why you're no longer an A-list supervillain?" I asked, ignoring the Typewriter's plight.

Diabloman did the same, giving a short nod. "The demonic cult that raised me covered me in black magic tattoos as part of my training. The tattoos allow me to take more punishment than a normal human being and give me the strength of ten men, but such power comes at a price. Once I could battle my opponents for hours but now I cannot fight for more than a few minutes before crippling pain sets in. The human body withers when exposed to such evil power."

"Geez, that's rough," I was sympathetic to the mass murderer and evil mystic. "No wonder your supervillain career tanked."

"Indeed," Diabloman said. His voice was resigned, heavy with the burden he was carrying. "The drugs were expensive enough, wiping out my personal fortune. The treatments to keep me alive afterward? Those were even worse. Now, I am forced to trudge along as a shadow of my former self. I need to take ten pills an hour to feel anything close to normal."

"I'm sorry." I meant it too.

"You may want to put the Typewriter out before the apartment catches fire," Diabloman suggested.

"Sorry," I said, turning around and freezing the villain's body. Walking over to Diabloman, I gave him a pat on the back. "Listen, I'm just starting out this whole supervillain thing—"

"Obviously," Diabloman replied.

I ignored that. "I could use someone to show me the ropes. How about I throw in an extra ten thousand to your forty-thousand dollar fee as a retainer? You could be my number two and mentor!"

"Please tell me you did not suggest to a seasoned supervillain you want to hire him as a career counselor."

"He's Diabloman! The Monster from Mexico! The Genius Bruiser who can speak forty languages while throwing you just as many feet! He deserves respect!" I said to Cloak, revealing my habit of talking to him. Looking at Diabloman, I said, "There's an explanation for why I'm talking to myself."

I just needed to think of one.

"Your cloak is magical and sentient," Diabloman said. "You haven't learned to talk to it with your thoughts. Therefore, you speak to it aloud and look like a lunatic."

"Fair enough," I replied, giving a triumphant shake of my fist. "Glad to know we're on the same page. So, what do you think?"

"I think you have some very strange ideas about how supervillains work," Diabloman said. "However, it is the best offer I have heard in some time. I will share what little wisdom I've gained."

"Hell, yes!" I gave a fist pump. "Where's Miss Douglas?"

Diabloman gestured over to the bathroom, grunting as he got up from the floor. "She's in there, with the last remaining member of the Typewriter's gang."

I shouted to the bathroom. "Hey! Come on out! We're not going to kill you...probably!"

Seconds later, Cindy Wakowski walked out in a new outfit. This time she was wearing a woman's pin-striped suit, a cute beret with a tiny typewriter on top, and a flamethrower pack.

Cindy was escorting a twenty-something, almond-eyed girl with shining black hair I presumed to be Amanda Douglas. The latter was wearing clubbing attire that was way too short and way too low for a girl her age, or maybe I was just getting old.

Amanda Douglas wasn't beautiful but was pretty. She was also athletic-looking, being more substantial than the stick figures that passed for attractive nowadays. I suspected she either worked out or played heavy sports, not something you expected from a billionaire's daughter.

Amanda took one look at the corpses and said, "I see that the criminals here show their usual amount of loyalty. Just so you know, when I get out of here, I'm going to hire some people to train me in how to hunt your ass down."

"Charming," I said, turning to Cindy. "What the *hell* are you doing here? Don't you have tests to study for? I mean, I just saw you a few hours ago! In another supercrook's employ!"

"I was double booked for tonight." Cindy sniffed the air. "Anyway, I'm done with medical school. I'm shopping around for a good residency program. These jobs help pay off my enormous student loans."

"I take it you know this woman?" Diabloman asked.

"You could say that. I let her go after killing her last employer."

"He's killed two in a row!" Cindy kicked the Typewriter's still frame. "I haven't even been paid yet!"

"Are you sure he's dead?" I asked, looking between Cindy and the Typewriter.

Cindy responded by blasting the Typewriter's corpse with her flamethrower. There was no movement from the figure burning on the ground. "Yep."

I laughed.

"That was abominable."

I stopped laughing, still smiling. "It was, wasn't it?"

Diabloman looked at me, a strange expression on his mask-covered face. "Did you feel anything after killing these two people?"

I thought about it, gauging how I felt about killing two people. After a few seconds, I came to terms with how I felt. "No. Is that bad?"

"It means you might have a chance of becoming a supervillain." Diabloman pointed at my chest. "Conscience is the enemy of our profession."

"Oh good. Your praise fills my Grinch-sized heart with spiteful glee."

"Yay for sociopathy!" Cindy shouted, smiling like a lunatic.

I thought about that before saying, "Am I a sociopath if I only kill bad people?"

"It depends on your definition, I suppose," Diabloman said. "Sociopath is clinically meaningless, unlike psychopath."

"Well, that's reassuring," I said, not at all concerned. If I was a sociopath, I'd been one for my entire life. Besides, whatever it was that allowed me to kill with impunity didn't keep me from loving Mandy.

Amanda started to look afraid. "Oh Christ, this is bad. I'm in the hands of *actual* supervillains now."

"You're darn tooting. However, I'm not here to do you harm. Yet."

"You're not?" Amanda asked.

"Nope, sorry. I'm here to return you to your father in exchange for an insignificant part of his fortune, but a not-so-insignificant amount of money to me. Cindy, you work for me now."

"I do?" Cindy looked confused. She was doing a very good impression of a bubble-headed blonde, despite being a redhead. Of course, it was just an act to manipulate people. I spent most of my senior year wrapped around her finger before I figured that one out.

"Yes," I said. "You're getting ten thousand dollars for your services."

"Spiffy!" Cindy said. "Wait, this isn't one of those 'sexual favors for cash' things? I get a lot of those as a henchperson."

"No!" I said, repulsed. "I'm a married man!"

"Oh, good!" Cindy looked relieved. "Because those cost extra."

Diabloman snorted in amusement.

"So, you're here to rescue me?" Amanda said. "Dad didn't send any of his evil cultist henchmen?"

"What?" I asked, looking for both a fire extinguisher and a phone book.

"Nothing," Amanda said. "Forget I mentioned it."

"O-kay." I found a fire extinguisher in the bathroom behind the toilet and started putting the Typewriter out. I could have used my freeze powers but I wasn't going to overuse my abilities if they had a finite amount of power every night.

The phone book was much easier to find. Looking up Chief Watkins' number, his wife was kind enough to give me his cell phone number. Of course, unlike in movies, I *still* got a busy signal despite the important nature of the call. So I ended up texting him.

"Come in with the money. The situation is resolved," I said as I used my thumbs on my cell phone.

I got texted back within seconds. "I'm coming."

Ten minutes later, the elevator to the penthouse was coming up with what I presumed to bed Chief Watkins and Dudley Douglas with my money. Either that or a group of cops interested in shooting us to death for being, well, criminals attempting to profit from another criminal's crime.

I'd gotten Diabloman some bottled water from the penthouse fridge and he was taking his pills while Cindy sat beside him, watching HBO. Amanda Douglas was sitting beside me on a finely appointed couch, looking positively mystified at the insane situation she'd found herself in.

"So, let me get this straight. You're supervillains my father hired to rescue me from other supervillains?" Amanda asked, sipping her diet soda.

"That's about the size of it," I said.

"That's cool," Amanda Douglas said. "My dad is kinda supervillain-ish. He holds the black masses to his dark god on weekends. I never get to see them."

"You should ask about that," Cloak suggested.

"Someone else's problem," I muttered then clasped my hands together and spoke in a normal voice. "I hope you don't blame me for any trauma you may have suffered being surrounded by a half-dozen dead hoods." I gestured to the carnage around us. "I wanted to do this without violence."

"Oh, don't worry about it," Amanda said. "It gives me something to talk to my therapist about."

"This situation has gone so far past the point of insanity it's come around and become mundane again," Cloak observed.

"You noticed that too, huh?" I smiled. "I think she has an excellent career in supervillainy ahead of her...or corporate finance."

Seconds later, Chief Watkins and Dudley Douglas arrived with a trio of police officers behind them.

Chief of Police Watkins was a gray-haired man in his sixties who resembled Sean Connery. He was wearing a beige trench coat over a pair of brown pants and a white shirt with a brown tie. Chief Watkins looked a lot more dashing than he was, given the city was suffering its worst crime rate in eighty years.

Dudley, on the other hand, looked very much like a Japanese man trying to look like a Texas oil baron. He wore a ten-gallon hat, a ten-thousand-dollar suit, and a smile that looked like it came from a plastic surgeon. Dudley was carrying a duffel bag over his left shoulder, which I hoped contained half a million dollars.

"You do realize they're going to try and arrest you, right?"

"Don't worry. I have a plan." I raised my hands into the air as if surrendering. I had no intention of doing so, though.

"How reassuring."

I stood up, pointing my fingers at both. "I know what you're going to say, Chief. I didn't mention I robbed a bank earlier this morning and sort-of-kind-of killed someone. Then, of course, you walk into this hotel room and you discover about a half-dozen more bodies and you think you're dealing with a homicidal lunatic. Well, I'll have you know, you're incorrect. Homicidal lunatics kill for no reason. I kill people *for money.*"

Thank you, John Cusack.

Before they had a chance to respond, I continued, "The

important thing to understand is everyone here who died...*had it coming.* I know; who are we to play judge, jury, and executioner— but the answer is: the people who have to deal with these psychos. The Nightwalker did a great job; I'm starting to understand what the man went through, having a magical cape talking to him day-in and day-out. However, let's face facts, he's not coming back. You're now two supervillains down at the cost of a mere five-hundred-fifty-thousand or so dollars. How many supervillains are active in Falconcrest City, thirty? Forty? *One hundred?*"

"Four hundred and eighty-nine," Chief Watkins said before looking down at the corpse of the Typewriter and giving it a light kick. "Four hundred and eighty-eight."

"What do you people even *do* at police headquarters? Keep a tally of the dead?" I asked, looking at him sideways.

"Now see here—" Chief Watkins' eyes narrowed.

"Never mind, my wife loves you. We here on Team Villain™ wouldn't have you any other way."

And yes, I said the trade-mark initials.

"Go Team Villain!" Cindy jumped up and down while clapping. It was an impressive feat given she had a flamethrower on her back.

I continued, ignoring her, "Now let me paint you a picture: one supervillain in Falconcrest City, with maybe a half-dozen or so supervillain henchman. The Society of Superheroes is too busy fighting alien invasions and extra-dimensional tentacle monsters to help with the crime here. I don't like supervillains any more than you do, they cut into my business. Ponder the cost effectiveness of having someone willing to beat the psycho-killers of the city to death with a pipe."

"This is never going to work."

Chief Watkins stared at me for a long moment then narrowed his eyes. "Take your money and go, Merciless. Take your henchmen with you, too."

Dudley Douglas tossed me the duffel bag, which I grabbed in mid-air. His daughter then ran up to him and gave him a hug.

"Thank you," I said, almost disappointed. "Let's go guys."

Chief Watkins added under his breath, "We'll talk later."

Chapter Five

Where I Learn the Basics
of Effective Supervillainy

Diabloman stared at my getaway vehicle. "You have to be joking."

"I confess; it's not *traditional*..." I trailed off.

"You drove a minivan here," Cindy said, putting her hands on her hips. "A minivan, Gary."

"Merciless, please," I corrected. "And there's nothing wrong with minivans."

Okay, that was a big fat lie. My white minivan was anything but an appropriate transport for a supervillain. However, it's not like I'd purchased it as a getaway vehicle. Mandy and I had once planned on having children and nothing said family car quite like a minivan.

"Minivan, Gary." Cindy shook her head, tying her red hair into girlish bunches. "Minivan."

"Hush up," I said. "A half-million dollar payday should be enough to warrant me a little respect."

Diabloman snorted, hot air blowing out of the nostril slits of his mask. "I confess, it *is* nice to have an operation go off without a hitch. A year ago, this would be where the Nightwalker would show up to ruin our escape. Still, do not grow cocky. Once, I would not have been satisfied with anything less than a million dollars per heist."

"Yeah, well, I just started this gig. I'm willing to work my way up to the Devil of Durango standards." I unlocked the car. "I'm happy to drop you off anywhere you want before I return to my villainous lair."

"You mean your house in the suburbs?" Cindy asked, sliding on in. "I was at the after-wedding party, remember."

I winced before correcting her. "Yes, my *villainous lair*."

Diabloman gave a hearty chuckle before climbing in and strapping on his seatbelt. "Many an insidious and cruel villain has begun his career in the microcosm of suburbia."

"Thanks, Diablo," I said. Stepping into the driver's seat, I started up the car. "So where do you want me to drop you guys off?"

"Kane and Morrison," Diabloman said.

"Timm Blvd," Cindy said.

Both named obscure parts of town, I didn't at all mind driving to. It would add about an hour to my travel time, but I didn't feel right asking them to take a cab, there were people crazy enough to mug a supervillain in this town.

As we drove along the city streets, I asked Diabloman, "So, could you give me a little advice to start off our mentor-student relationship?"

"Don't eat yellow snow," Diabloman said, gruffly.

"I hired you to be my evil Obi-Wan. The least you could do is take your job seriously."

"Your first mistake was letting two known supervillains into your car while carrying half a million dollars. How do you know we're not going to steal it?" Cindy asked, crossing her arms.

I paused, thinking. "Well, first off, I have superpowers. You don't. Second, I'd take it personally."

Cindy bit her lip, looking deep in thought. "Right. Never mind."

"You have nothing to fear from me. It would be dishonorable to turn upon an employer before they have betrayed me."

Cindy looked annoyed more than anything. "I never understood the whole 'honorable supervillain' shtick. Wouldn't the fact alone that you're a thief make you dishonorable?"

"No," Diabloman said. "It would not."

"It's important for evil to have standards. Otherwise, nothing separates you from the common rabble," I explained, using my great knowledge of evil derived from comic books and movies.

"You have already learned the first two lessons I would impart," Diabloman said. "Show no fear to your enemies and never compromise whatever principles you choose to live by. These will make it so even your enemies respect you."

"Were you serious about killing every other supervillain in Falconcrest City?" Cindy asked, just now realizing she wasn't dealing with the harmless man she'd dated.

"If they get in my way, yeah," I said, watching the various foreboding buildings of downtown pass by. "There can be just one king of the hill, after all. Plus, I don't mind killing bad people. Is that a problem, Diablo?"

"No," Diabloman said. "That is Rule Three. Never trust another supervillain. Rule Number One is you must never kill a superhero."

"What?" Cindy asked, staring at Diabloman in shock. "You're kidding, right?"

"No," Diabloman replied. "If you kill a supervillain you will receive respect and praise. Better still, you will receive fear. If you kill a superhero you will receive condemnation and hatred. Every superhero in the world will consider it their personal duty to bring you to justice. Very often, you will not be taken alive, even by the greatest paragons amongst them. Believe me, I speak from experience on this."

"Is that why supervillains leave superheroes in easily escapable death traps?" I was only half-joking.

"Yes," Diabloman said, without irony.

Cindy was, however, still focused on my earlier words. "Hold on, back to this murder every other supervillain thing. Does this include the cute sexy ones?"

Looking in my rearview mirror, I saw her clutch her hair bunches and give me a pearly white smile.

Smirking at her transparent attempts to manipulate me, I said, "I don't know. I'll have to run that by my wife. I'm sure she'll ask me to spare one or two of them in the future."

"Eesh." Cindy blanched.

"Anything else?" I said, driving through the dark and dingy streets of Falconcrest City.

"You will need to spend most of the money you acquired on

this heist," Diabloman said.

"What?" I was tempted to hit the brakes. I'd been envisioning a certain amount of financial security from this point on.

"To be a supervillain, you must command respect from your henchmen. For that, you must display the wealth they are expected to have. You must be flashy and theatrical in a way that intimidates and inspires others to want to be around you."

"Uh-huh"

Cindy nodded, understanding. "It's why gangsters wear lots of gold rings and necklaces. I learned that in Super-Criminal Psychology 101."

I looked at Cindy in the rearview mirror. "You took that too?"

"It was one of my electives," Cindy said. "Didn't you switch out and get your Master's degree in History?"

"Yes. I thought it would be more useful than it's turned out to be. At least it's still useful as hypothetical toilet paper."

Diabloman ignored Cindy's digression. "In order to maintain cooperation from authorities, you must spread around the wealth. I haven't even mentioned the equipment costs. Freeze rays and giant robot labs do not pay for themselves."

"Well that, at least, makes sense," I said, thinking about his words for a second. "So, what you're telling me is as soon as I make a fortune due to super-crime, I'm going to end up blowing it?"

"Yes. It is the vicious cycle we exist in," Diabloman replied, giving a heavy sigh. "You will be required to make even bigger scores in order to break even."

"Then why am I doing it?" I asked the obvious question.

"To gain respect. A supervillain without respect does not live very long. Other villains will attack you, target your loved ones, and eliminate your henchmen." Diabloman's voice had a grave authoritativeness that reminded me of my grandfather.

I wasn't looking forward to explaining that to my wife. 'I'm sorry, Honey, I stole six million dollars in cash but we're still having trouble paying the bills' was going to go over like a ton of bricks.

"You could always retire."

"You be quiet!"

"What?" Cindy asked.

"Not you!" I said, almost getting sideswiped by a car running a red light. Talking with the forces in my head and driving was difficult.

"He's talking to his magical cloak," Diabloman said. "It belonged to the Nightwalker and is haunted by the spirits of all previous bearers."

"It is?"

"That would have been part of the orientation. You know if you'd bothered to listen to me for more than a few minutes."

"You bear a heavy curse." Diabloman spoke with a sage-like tone. "Being a supervillain will exact a heavy toll on you as well, but not as much as the Reaper's Cloak shall."

"You seem to know a lot about this."

"Yes," Diabloman said. "I researched the Nightwalker for a decade before I made my move against him."

"And you still weren't able to beat him," Cindy said. It was amazing, she'd *lost* tact since her high school years.

Diabloman, in an instant, had his hands around her neck.

"Merciless, may I break her neck?"

"No."

Cindy wasn't afraid. "Try it, Buster."

"No killing each other."

"All right," they both said at once.

"You are all insane."

"Probably," I said. "So, Diablo, Cindy, can you hook me up with a guy who can set me up with a lair? Maybe someone I can talk to about getting a better Merciless Mobile?"

"Please don't call it that," Cindy said. "It's bad enough I'm traveling in a minivan. You don't have to make it worse by giving it a name."

"No promises."

"I know someone who might be able to help you." Diabloman rubbed his chin. "Just a note, with the recent influx of supervillains into the city with the Nightwalker's death, it will be difficult to get the usual haunts."

"Usual haunts?" I asked, not having a clue as to what they were talking about.

"Amusement parks, toy factories, and so on. Abandoned warehouses are the pits, though," Cindy said. "Let's not get one of those. We should start a new trend of supervillains in luxury high-rises with live-in models."

"Man," I said, sighing. "Who knew being a supervillain was so damn *complicated*?"

"Everyone," Cindy said.

"It is a rather well-known bit of truth," Diabloman replied. "*Yes.*"

I was about to respond to them all with a rather stinging bit of sarcasm when I suddenly felt like my chest was about to explode. I had to pull over and park the car, my breath became ragged as I had to labor for every breath.

"Gary, are you having a heart attack?" Cindy sounded concerned, which was surprising. Since reuniting with her earlier today, I'd been under the impression she'd ingested the supervillain Kool-Aid wholeheartedly.

"I don't know. I've never had one before," I said, coughing.

"You're not having a heart attack. Believe me, I would know. Your death is marked on the Grim Reaper's calendar along with everyone else and so far, we've not been wrong yet."

"You know my..." I cleared my throat. "My death date?"

*"Do you **want** to know it?"*

"No!" I shouted at Cloak. "Life is depressing enough without knowing when I'm going to die."

"Do I even want to know?" Cindy looked at Diabloman.

"No," Diabloman said. "You do not."

After a few seconds the pain in my chest receded and my head cleared a bit.

"Okay, what the hell was that?" I asked.

"Bad chili fries?" Cindy asked, looking concerned. "Do you want us to take you to a hospital?"

"Not you." I waved her away. "I need to work on talking to my magical cloak in private."

"You detected a spirit. A very old spirit. One of the enemies of the Balance."

"I need to sit down for the full orientation it seems. I don't recall 'having heart attacks around old ghosts' mentioned amongst the downsides."

"This falls under 'you will see dead people,' Master. Don't worry. It will become easier over time."

Looking around to see where this sensation was coming from, I saw a little girl standing across the road. She looked no more than twelve and had long black hair that shined under the streetlights. Her attire was anachronistic, almost Edwardian. She held a single red balloon in her left hand.

"That's a ghost?" I asked.

"Who's a ghost?" Cindy questioned, looking frightened. "Oh God, are we getting haunted like in *The Shining*? Is it a pair of spooky twin girls?"

"The spooky girl part is right. There's just one of them, though." I unbuckled my seat belt. "You guys stay here; I'm going to go investigate."

"As you wish, Merciless," Diabloman said. "I shall meditate on my past victories."

"Uh, sure. Go right ahead." Stepping out of the car, I asked Cloak, "So, what do I do now?"

"Anything you want. You can sense the dead, but you do not have to do anything about them," Cloak sounded forlorn, as if the problem was too big even for him. *"The Lost are a problem far beyond the scope of mere mortals like yourself."*

"How long has she been standing there?" I inquired.

"Decades, in all likelihood."

"You never did anything about her?"

"There are a lot of ghosts, Gary. Sometimes, they just fall through the cracks."

That wasn't a good attitude for a superhero to have.

I liked kids, despite not having any of my own. Seeing a little girl, even a dead one, in distress made me want to help.

Walking across the street, I saw she was staring at a bloodstain on the ground. The child showed no recognition of my presence and stared at the blood with an impassive expression on her face.

"Hello," I said. "Can you hear me?"

"I'm afraid she's too far gone into her memories. You would need a name to call to her."

"Do you know it?"

"I possess many magical powers; omniscience is not one of them. As much as I regret doing so, I advise you to move on. There's nothing that can be done with your present resources."

"Screw that." I pulled out my cell phone and called Mandy. She was the person I could always depend on for information. "Hey, Honey. I need your help for something very important."

"You're alive?"

"Yes."

"Free?"

"Yes."

"Not fleeing the police?"

"Nope."

"How about the money?"

"Got it."

"Thank God. Did you get the yogurt I asked for?"

"I'll get it, I swear. However, I need you to look up a little girl's name on the internet. Use your '133t' internet skills to find any references, old time references, to a girl about twelve years old who died on Seventh Street."

"Why?"

"I'm trying to make contact with her restless spirit," I answered matter-of-factly.

"Oh, okay." Mandy took it in stride. "Okay, give me a minute."

"I know this is a lot to ask. It's probably imposs—" I started to say.

"Theresa Douglas. The same Douglas family you helped regain its lost heir," My wife explained. "She was murdered in 1942 by her father as part of some weird murder-suicide pact the Brotherhood of Infamy was involved in. Her mother killed herself a week later."

"Wow," I said. "That was fast."

"I'm magic."

"That you are. I'll call you right back after this. The mission went very well, and I got some henchmen. I'm only getting like a four hundred thousand dollars fee, though. I'll also have to spend a lot of my take in order to build up my street cred."

"What now?"

I was very grateful when the line cut out. I'd forgotten to charge the cell phone battery.

"Oh, I'm going to catch hell for that, later." I grimaced, staring at the phone. "I'd better call her back on someone else's cell on the way back. I should also pick up a few dozen roses too."

"I retract any doubt I may have had about you being a supervillain. You've taken part in the murder of half a dozen people and your chief concern is about how your wife is going to react to your phone dying on you."

"I have my priorities straight." I put my cell phone up. "It's why most marriages fail today. People don't put their spouses first."

"For once, I have no objections to your words."

"They have cloak marriage where you're from?"

"Let's move on."

Coughing into my fist, I stared at the girl. "Theresa, Theresa Douglas, can you hear me?"

Like a light bulb turning on, she became aware of my presence. "I can't talk. I'm waiting for my mommy. She was supposed to pick me up here, but my father came here instead. He...hurt me."

I wished I could raise her dad from the grave, so I could kill him. "Your mommy...is waiting for you elsewhere."

"She is?" Theresa asked. "Where?"

I didn't know how to talk to a dead child. "Help me out here, Cloak."

"The Place Beyond."

I whispered the name in her ear and she nodded. "I saw it... once. It was pretty."

Theresa faded away. Once she was gone, the bloodstain vanished as well. A clean sensation replaced the cold darkness that I hadn't even realized I'd been feeling until that moment.

"Will she be alright?" I asked, genuinely concerned.

"As much as anyone who is dead."

That wasn't very comforting.

"Merciless...Gary...Thank you." Cloak's display of emotion surprised me. He was more than just a magical artifact.

"Don't mention it."

I headed back to the car.

Chapter Six

My Motivations for Becoming a Supervillain

Mandy took the whole business regarding my new minions and my intention to spend most of my ill-gotten loot on supervillain overhead even better than she did the announcement I was a supervillain. She threatened to divorce me. I also wasn't allowed to bring any murderers into our house.

Fair enough.

"So, where *am* I allowed to bring murderers?" I asked, leaning up against the door.

It was close to midnight and the two of us were in the living room. We'd been arguing in a very polite fashion for the better part of an hour. Mandy was sitting in her comfy chair typing on her laptop. I could see the Foundation for World Harmony logo on her webpage from where I stood, which made me think she'd hacked into their database again.

"Did you *actually* ask me that?" Mandy asked, looking up. She had a pair of reading glasses on and they were sexy as hell.

"Yes."

"You don't see *anything* wrong with that question?" Mandy said.

I pretended to think before responding, "Nope!"

Mandy grumbled, continuing to work on her computer. "I believe you. Which is terrible. What is sparking this whole 'I want to be a supervillain' thing? I know you're taking advantage of an opportunity but tell me what's at the root."

"It's…complicated," I said. "Lots of children want to grow up to be supervillains. I never gave up the dream."

"Bullshit. Children also want to be pirates and I don't see you dressing up like Johnny Depp."

"Well I—" I started to make a crack.

"Please, Gary," Mandy interrupted. "Why are you doing this?"

I realized this deserved a serious response. Dropping my flippant attitude, which was *hard*, I gave her a straight answer. "My brother."

"Your brother?" Mandy looked surprised.

"Yeah. Remember what I told you?"

"He was the arch-nemesis of the Silver Lightning?" Mandy asked, sounding somewhat impressed. She shouldn't have been.

"Arch-nemesis may be too strong of a word. The Silver Lightning can turn into living electricity, my brother had a harpoon. There's not much comparison. I think he should have tried being the nemesis of an aquatically-themed superhero… but yeah, Keith's the reason."

Mandy put her computer aside and got up. She walked over to me and placed her hand on my shoulder. It was warm and made me feel better. "Tell me what you're thinking." She knew about Keith's death but not about how it related to my sudden, from her perspective, desire to become a costumed criminal.

"Sorry," I said, clenching my teeth at the memory. Even after a decade and a half, discussing my brother's death was painful. "I keep thinking about how he died. The papers celebrated his death. Celebrated, Mandy. My brother never killed anyone during his decade-long career and they *still* cheered when some wannabe shot him in the head."

I still had nightmares about Shoot-Em-Up. I always would. Some things never left you.

"So, you want to be like your brother? Is that it?" Mandy asked, looking at me in disbelief.

"No," I answered, turning back to her. "I don't intend to get killed, for instance."

"I doubt he did, either."

"Keith never made it to the big time." I ignored her jibe. "He was a B-list villain for an A-list superhero who I bet doesn't even remember his name. Still, it was the happiest time of his life. I figure, if I can be the supervillain he wasn't able to be, I can exorcise his ghost."

Mandy looked at me with a skeptical expression on her face. "That is the single dumbest thing I've ever heard in my entire life."

"Okay, it's because I want to be rich and famous," I said, shrugging my shoulders. "That better?"

"If people ask, go with that." I was about to say more when my cell phone rang. Voltaire's "When You're Evil" was my ringtone.

"Can you change that to something more upbeat?" Mandy asked, staring at my cell phone. "That creeps me out."

"Pet Shop Boys' 'It's a Sin'?"

"No." Mandy rolled her eyes.

"Michael Jackson's 'Bad'?" I smirked while suggesting.

Mandy threw up her hands. "Forget it. Answer the damned phone."

Pulling it out, I asked, "You want to get Chinese food tonight?"

"Sounds good," Mandy replied, switching gears, "as long as you aren't going to get *evil noodles*."

"No, that would be silly," I said, answering the phone and putting it to my ear. "Hello?"

There was nothing but an unearthly horrible static on the other line. Then there was a voice which sounded eerily like Mandy's own. "Gary...zzzzt...Gary...we...bzzt...need—"

I hung up.

"Who was it?" Mandy asked.

"Wrong number," I lied, shrugging.

"You really shouldn't have done that. That sounded like spirit world static."

"Is it a pressing issue?" I asked, mentally.

"Not now."

"Then hold off on it," I said. "I'm talking to my wife."

I started dialing the Chinese restaurant.

Mandy walked a bit away from me. "Gary, is this your dream?"

"Excuse me?" I asked, looking up.

"Your dream, the thing you want most in the world."

I was surprised at the direction the conversation was going but, I supposed, this is what I wanted, the chance to talk to Mandy about this seriously.

She walked over to the fireplace shelf. The fireplace, which we hadn't used in our entire marriage and wasn't even linked to a chimney, was purely a place to put pictures. Picking one up of her father, she looked at it. He was a slightly balding man wearing a blue military uniform with numerous patches indicating the various alien invasions, robot uprisings, and anti-terrorist operations he'd been involved in.

Colonel Summers hadn't liked me.

"I had a dream too once." Mandy said, surprising me.

I knew what my wife was referring to, but I also knew she wanted to talk about this. "I take it you don't mean your music career."

Mandy looked down. "No."

"You mean wanting to join the Foundation," I said, sighing. "Like your dad."

The Foundation for World Harmony was the institution that existed for the explicit purpose of cleaning up after the superhuman, supernatural, extraterrestrial, and ultraterrestrial so a modicum of sanity might prevail in this world. Its agents were outmatched by even low-level supervillains, but they did a bang-up job fighting P.H.A.N.T.O.M and the International Crime League.

Good guys.

Mandy got a little misty eyed. "Yeah."

Her father had passed last year from congenital heart failure. It had been rough on all of us.

"My father was never a liaison to the Society of Superheroes or even one of its members, but he was always there fighting the good fight," Mandy said. "I remember him pushing me from day one. Ballet, martial arts, gymnastics, linguistics, mathematics, criminology, gunplay, ethics, and computer programming. That was just my high school years."

"I still think he pushed you a little too hard."

Mandy put up the photo. "He did, and I was wound so tight, I snapped when I got to college. He'd wanted to make me into the perfect candidate for the Foundation for World Harmony or even a superhero myself."

"Lots of parents do."

"And lots of parents ruin their kids that way," Mandy said, looking back. "I came to Falconcrest U wanting to be the perfect student, only to end up smoking dope and screwing everyone I liked within a week."

"Oh, you monster," I said, heavily sarcastic. "They should just throw the book at you."

"You know where this leads, Gary."

"I'm sure I don't."

"The Black Witch."

Oh.

I bit my lip. "Then I guess I do know where it's going." We hadn't discussed that part of her life in detail. I knew my wife had been involved with her in the past, but aside from statements about 'The Black Witch's bleak poetry speaking to her', I didn't really know how close they were. "Sort of."

Mandy looked down. "Do we really want to go here?"

I also knew it was perhaps better to leave some things buried in the past. "I think we've been together long enough to share everything without judgment."

"Perhaps not without judgment." Mandy said, looking down. "But with love? Yes. Gary, I loved Selena Darkchilde."

"Loved?" I asked, wanting to make sure it was in the past tense. It was unfair of me since human emotions weren't so easily shut off. If you loved someone in the past, it didn't go away just because you wanted it to. God knows, my parents' lives would have been simpler if they could have just disinherited Keith and me.

Mandy nodded. "Yes, loved. I was never her henchwench, but I knew who she was, what she was doing, and what she planned to do. I was an accomplice because I never tried to stop her or even suggest she should."

I blinked, staring. "Wow. So, uh, you didn't just know about her crimes after she was finally captured by Ultragoddess."

Mandy crossed her arms. "No. I knew her when she was just a mousy occultist before her experiments with Professor Thule made her Hecate's champion. Which, in retrospect, yeah, with a name like that he was going to become a supervillain."

I pointed at her. "I *never* liked that guy. Swastikas being harmless Asian good luck sigils, my ass."

Mandy blinked. "I thought it was all good fun. Striking at the system, getting revenge on people who'd wronged us, and so on. I...perjured myself when I was brought to court as a witness. They found me guilty."

I blinked. "I see."

"I got my sentence reduced to community service because someone pulled strings. They even kept me in the program." Mandy looked back at her father's picture. "I had a criminal record, though, now. Worse, I'd been proven to be involved in a sexual relationship with a supervillainess. I might have gotten away with it if I was a man, but a woman? No. My father never said anything about it, but I could tell I'd disappointed him in a way he never forgave."

That was very much like the Colonel. He never stopped loving his daughter. He also never stopped judging her. I still hadn't told Mandy about his ever so delightful conversation with me about how I should convert to Christianity so I could help her back to the righteous path.

"*He sounds like a real ass,*" Cloak said.

"*Thanks,*" I said back. "*Now would you stop listening? This is private.*"

"*I wish I could.*"

I decided I needed to convince Mandy she wasn't the biggest fuck up in the room. "If it's any consolation, this isn't the first time I've tried to be a supervillain."

"What?" Mandy asked, eyes widening. "You did this before without telling me?"

I went to the fridge to get a beer. "No, this was before we started dating."

Mandy blinked. "When?"

"It was a phase in college," I said, using words that caused Mandy's eyes to narrow. "Not *that* kind of phase."

"I dislike bisexual erasure," Mandy said, shrugging. "What can I say? It's a pet peeve."

I unscrewed the beer bottle top and took a swig. "I was pretty idealistic during my Junior year. I was away from my parents and I thought I could honor Keith's memory by taking up his mantle."

"You became Stingray?" Mandy said, stunned. "Why didn't I hear about this?"

I took another drink of my beer. *"Because I was awful at it."*

"When has that ever stopped you before?" Mandy said, smirking.

"Ha-ha," I said, still smiling. "I decided I would take up the environmental cause of the oceans versus, you know, robbing banks and stuff."

"The oceans?" Mandy said.

I gestured with my half-empty beer bottle in hand. "Words cannot express what terrible horrors mankind has unleashed on the sentient porpoises, Atlanteans, Lemurians, Merrow, and transmigrated Space Whales."

"I had sex with a Merrow once," Mandy said. "It turns out the whole fish tail thing is a myth. Not that we needed that part. She was great in a hot tub."

I stared at her.

A minute passed.

"Gary," Mandy snapped her fingers.

"Hmm?" I said, finishing off my beer. "Sorry."

"Must you make that joke every time I mention my sex life?"

"Do you have any people not ridiculously hot you've dated other than me?"

Mandy paused. "No?"

"Then jokes I will continue to make," I said. "Anyway, I defaced corporate property. I got help from the computer department and whistleblowers to hack corporate records and expose the truth. I also sabotaged some Omega Corp dolphin nets during trips with my girlfriend at the time and her father."

"That sounds less like supervillainy and more like social activism," Mandy said.

"Yeah," I said, throwing away the bottle in the trash bin. "So I decided to blow up Omega Chemicals."

"Goddess."

"That may be a bit dramatic. I was going to set a bomb to blow up their pumping station on the weekend after hours and expose the fact they'd been leaking stuff into our groundwater for decades, causing gross mental illness and homicidal rages."

They'd settled the lawsuit last week.

Still in business.

Mandy said, "That's still terrorism."

"Maybe," I said, sighing. "In the end, I couldn't go through with it. A bomb wasn't my style. I might have been willing to go up to the CEO's office, put a bunch of pictures of dead children on his desk, and shoot him in the face but I wasn't going to risk bystanders. What if my *Anarchist's Cookbook Revised*-made bomb was found and someone died? No. After it happened, Gabrielle talked to me, and I agreed to hang up my wetsuit for good." I stared down at my outfit. "Until opportunity knocked. I owed her a lot for persuading me—but this feels different. It feels right."

Or maybe I was just a helluva lot angrier than I was back then.

And sicker of the system.

"Gabrielle Anders? She was your other girlfriend, right? The one aside from Cindy, I mean." Mandy always hesitated to bring her up, for much the same reason I didn't like bringing up Selena.

I tried to play it off. "I've had tons of girlfriends, Mandy. I mean aside from you three I can name off like thirty I've slep..." I noticed her stare. "Sle...S...okay I can't think of a good word I can substitute. Yeah, Gabby was my only other serious girlfriend."

Despite the fact I was an enormous nerd, I'd had a significant advantage over my socially challenged kin in both high school and college. A secret I had exploited to its fullest extent in dating: I treated women as human beings who probably wanted fun dates or satisfying sex as much as I did. It had worked staggeringly well until I'd met Gabrielle. As much fun as Cindy and I had on a regular basis, the two of us had always been more partners in crime than anything else. Well, literally so, now. Gabrielle had been different. My usual charms had worked like a spoon on a steak, leading me to become entirely focused on winning her over.

She'd worked as a reporter for the college newspaper and was more focused on her studies than anything else. I would have written her off as uninterested in dating and moved on if not for the fact we'd bonded over our shared love of superhuman battles as well as criminology. She'd always gotten the best shots of Ultragoddess pounding the Black Witch and her monsters. Which was amazing because she always seemed to disappear when those battles were happening on campus.

Probably getting the best shots she could.

"*Oh for Chrissakes,*" Cloak muttered.

"What?" I asked.

"*Nevermind,*" Cloak grumbled.

In the end, Gabrielle and I had fallen in love. It was the one secret I kept from my wife, as I did my best to pass off my relationship with her as over and done with. Which it was, but not emotionally. We'd gotten into all manner of wacky hijinks together, checked out all manner of strange leads, and even talked about moving to Atlas City together after graduation. Then she'd started disappearing for longer and longer periods, coming home with injuries she wouldn't explain, and flat out lying to me. Even living together for six months didn't bring us closer together. After the Cackler had kidnapped me out of some perverse belief I was related to Ultragoddess, she'd broken it off with me. I still had a fuzzy memory of her telling me something but every time I tried to recall it, it slipped away. I also felt like something was keeping me from reaching some sort of obvious conclusion.

"*Ultra-Mesmerism,*" Cloak said.

"*What?*" I asked, immediately forgetting what he said. "*What was I asking about?*"

"*It doesn't matter.*"

"We met at one of my concert's after-parties a week after you broke up, as I recall," Mandy said. "You were hitting on two of my exes and I'd heard you were a good lay. Strange how it managed to blossom into what it did."

"Yeah," I said, looking down. "Amazing how the brother of Stingray and girlfriend of the Black Witch ended up getting together at the same college."

"Eh, not really. Falconcrest City University has the best unusual criminology department in the country and doesn't discriminate on past associations or records. There were, like, seventy active superheroes and villains on campus while we were attending, according to my father."

I stared at her. "Huh. That explains so much." Like, why I was rejected for every college I applied to but Falconcrest U.

"Do you regret where your life ended up?" Mandy asked. "That you're the brother of Stingray and not Merciless ten years earlier?"

I looked at her. "Are you asking me if I regret marrying you?"

Mandy looked away. "If the shoe fits."

"Merciful Moses, no!" I said, staring at her. "God, no!"

"Then what are you saying?"

I looked at her. "Life has a way of going in directions we don't expect. I didn't like being kicked out of the Unusual Criminology program for getting kidnapped and missing finals. I didn't like trying and failing to get a teaching position anywhere decent for five years. I didn't like being forced to work at that damned bank while they cheated every single customer and hid money from the government. I may be a supervillain but that's just wrong. But you? You, Mandy? I regret *nothing* about our relationship. I would have gone *insane* without you."

Mandy looked at me.

I looked back.

"We're going to pretend you're not clearly insane, okay?" Mandy said.

I smiled. "For tonight at least."

"I'll support you in pursuing your dream," Mandy said, sighing. "Maybe it's time we both revisited the ways our life has gone off track—and how they've succeeded."

"I never had any doubt." I kissed my wife passionately and

the two of us began taking each other's clothes off.

It was a good night.

It would be the last for a while.

Chapter Seven

Bad Dreams and Memories.

The next hour was beautiful.

Exhausted, my wife and I fell asleep afterward, only for dreams to take me. I was a frequent sufferer of nightmares due to past events of my life. For all the fact I didn't have any sense of guilt for killing the Ice Cream Man or the Typewriter, I still saw their dead faces and other people's in my dreams.

My brother Keith.

Shoot-Em-Up.

Gabrielle.

My parents.

Mandy.

The dream coalesced out of the random imagery into a memory. It was a memory I'd revisited several hundred times over the past two decades. A memory that had continually repeated itself and wormed its way into my mind. It was one that haunted me, shaped me, and controlled me. It was an inescapable memory that defined the way I chose to live my life to this day.

It was the day my brother died.

The weather was hot in New Angeles, a heat wave having hit the city not long after the recent Atlantean invasion. It was incredibly humid, and most of the citizens were staying indoors until it passed. The Silver Lightning, Aquarius, and the rest of the city's superheroes were cooperating with the Foundation's Eco-Warriors in the cleanup but it wasn't going fast enough for most of our tastes.

I was lying on the couch wearing jean shorts and a t-shirt showing the words 'Superhumans Unite' around a D.N.A helix held by a fist. Half my head was shaved; the other dyed purple. I had two gold piercings in my ear and was wearing a pair of shades indoors. I was fourteen and quite the little hell-raiser. I was presently flipping through a copy of *Tights*, which had a nude pictorial of the newest Larceny Lass. I'd found it an excellent palette cleanser after finishing *Anarchism in a Post-Human World* by Emanuelle Goldenstein (pseudonym) and *The Spirit of the Laws* by Montesquieu.

The room had seen better days, with my family having to move into a worse house after Papa Karkofsky got fired from his job for having a supervillain son. Joel Karkofsky was currently watching Foxhound News from his easy chair and complaining about every little thing he thought I might be listening to, as well as plenty he didn't.

He was an overweight man in his late-forties wearing a button-down shirt and dress pants. Joel was missing his right eye and wore an eye-patch over it at home since we couldn't afford a decent cybernetic replacement since being dropped by our insurance provider. The wall had a framed picture of his medals from Vietnam II, showing how he'd lost it. I mentally vowed that when I became a supervillain, I wouldn't ever do any work for P.H.A.N.T.O.M after what they did to my dad.

"This is all that damned abominable new President's fault," Joel muttered, pointing at the television. "We never should have elected one of *them*."

"Dad, don't be racist," I didn't bother looking from my magazine.

My dad pointed back at me. "It's not racist if he's a robot. We should have elected Clinton."

"Android John was made in America, he can be President," Keith said, talking from the kitchen. "Besides, the economy has never been better."

"Not that we're seeing it," Joel said, over to the kitchen. "Also, you can't tell me you approve of humans marrying robots."

I looked up. "Ultramind II is pretty damned hot in her digital avatar."

"And about as touchable as your pornography," Joel said, shaking his head. "Don't tell your mother I said that."

I made a zip-it gesture over my mouth. "So, Keith is dinner almost ready?"

"You'll love what I'm doing. It's a seafood recipe that uses all organic ingredients plus a new flavoring," Keith said, walking out of the kitchen wearing an apron, jeans, and a Grateful Dead t-shirt. Aside from the scars on his face, arms, and New Angeles Highwaymen tattoos, you couldn't tell he'd ever been a supervillain.

It was disappointing.

"You're still trying to become a chef now," I said, looking at him.

"It's honest work," Keith said.

I tried not to roll my eyes. I didn't have much of an opinion of honest work given how the System worked. It was deliberately designed to prop up the one-percent and protect the establishment at the expense of social mobility, non-military superhumans, ethnic minorities, and non-capitalist systems. I'd tried explaining this to Keith, but he'd looked like, well, I was a fourteen-year-old trying to explain how the real world worked.

"Uh-huh. How's that working out for you?" I asked.

Keith looked away. "It's working out."

"Just remember, you have to look after your little girl," Joel said, getting up from his chair. "That's the most important part of your life now. A man is a breadwinner and it's his duty to provide for his family."

"Trust me, I know," Keith said, wiping his hands off with a cloth. "I thought I could make her a princess but all I did was let my shit roll down on my family."

Joel stared at him. "I've heard that speech before, Keith."

"Right before you tried to seize the Atlantean throne, which was fucking awesome!" I said, looking up. "You totally hit Aquarius' evil sister, right?"

"You shut up boy." Joel pointed at me.

Keith looked to one side, guilty. "This time, I promise you. It's different. I've got a clean slate from the government and—"

A wailing siren sounded, threatening to deafen everyone

in the house. Looking outside the window, I saw an NAPD cruiser tricked out with armor and machine guns flashing its lights outside. It had a pair of speakers attached to the top with the words 'Shoot-Em-Up' spraypainted on the side. I blinked, wondering what the fuck this was about.

Seconds later, AC/DC's "Thunderstruck" started playing on loudspeakers. I was confused as all get out before the door to our living room was kicked down and a man wearing riot gear spray-painted with an SEU in a diamond in the center stepped on in. The visor on his helmet was down and had been outfitted with a mirrored front. In his hands was a laser-sight equipped, advanced, hand-gun that looked like it had probably cost more money than most cops made in a year.

"THIS IS THE AGE OF PUNISHMENT!" Shoot-Em-Up shouted, lifting his gun at Keith's chest.

Everyone but Keith was too stunned by the anti-hero's sudden appearance.

Keith pushed Joel to the ground and shouted to me, "Get down!"

I started to move toward him, however three bursts of bullets came from Shoot-Em-Up's gun into Keith's chest and showered me with gore. Shoot-Em-Up stayed long enough to put an additional set of rounds in Keith's face before looking down at us both and saying, "Scum comes from scum."

The memory became fragmented and a swirl of imagery as I tried to keep my head clear of the gory remains of my brother.

They picked up Shoot-Em-Up, a disgruntled police officer named Theodore Whitman, about an hour later and it turned out he'd visited two other inactive supervillains' homes before Keith and was on his way to blow up a fourth's with a rocket launcher. That one had probably saved a lot of lives since the last target was attending his six-year-old daughter's birthday party.

Despite this, there was no changing the media reaction to Shoot-Em-Up. The police deliberately botched the investigation and he was let off with a technicality. Everyone across the country, seemingly, supported his actions and there had been promises of a book deal as well as promotional tours.

His actions helped trigger a slew of imitators ranging from Bloodscream the Retributive, to the Extreme. Many normal heroes grew a lot more comfortable with killing, too, even though the Society of Superheroes officially condemned their actions. But for my family, it was the end of everything.

I found my own way of coping.

I hated this next part.

And loved it.

Shoot-Em-Up didn't exactly keep a low profile after his initial murders were resolved and he was back on the streets in months. None of the gangs, crime lords, or supervillains would touch him because they were all too afraid of him.

They didn't realize he wasn't a superhero, just a cop in a cheap costume. I gave credit to the Silver Lightning, he attended my brother's funeral and tried to give his condolences. But the Silver Lightning didn't bring in Shoot-Em-Up and a lot of 'unsolved' murders started to pile up. I was wearing a hoodie and gloves, a backpack over my shoulders, walking up the stairs of a ratty hotel in the Southside of Falconcrest City. My parents had moved there in hopes of getting a fresh start, but they hadn't realized just how much worse things were there. It had, ironically, attracted the very bane of our existence.

I'd gotten a tweet about Shoot-Em-Up's location from a guy who'd caught him on his camera phone not ten miles from my location. I wasn't a great believer in divine intervention, but that seemed like it to me. The smell of the Rusty Scabbard, a lovely name for a hotel that charged by the hour, was horrible. It was like someone had combined vomit, a men's' bathroom, pot, and desperation into a single odor. I passed by a collection of passed-out drunks as well as prostitutes. A few of the latter said I'd have to wait in line, ignoring the fact I was fourteen or perhaps counting on it since some of them weren't too much older.

Reaching Room Fifty-Two, I took a deep breath and went over my escape plan in my head. The building was old and still had fire escapes with an exit just down the hall that led to a window. I knew this because I'd made sure to get a good look at the place first. I should have gone over the details with a fine-toothed comb, but I was still a kid.

And seething for revenge.

Looking at the red door with a pair of numbers painted on, I pulled off my backpack, unzipped the top, and looked in to see the gun with a silencer inside. It hadn't been difficult to acquire. This was Falconcrest City after all—the wretched hive that gave wretched hives a bad name. Holding the grip tightly with my right hand, the backpack's strap keeping it in place, I knocked on the door.

"Go away!" Shoot-Em-Up shouted. "I'm paid for the next three hours!"

"There's a guy who wants to see you about a television interview. He says you're on something called Superhero Watch."

"What?" Shoot-Em-Up said, and I heard him come to the door. It swung open and he looked down at me. He wasn't in uniform, wearing just a pair of boxers and a wife-beater t-shirt. He wasn't an impressive looking man, ginger hair and a receding hairline, but I'd recognize his face even if I were blind.

I pulled the trigger.

Shoot-Em-Up fell a step backward as a red hole appeared in his chest.

I pulled it again.

And again.

I just kept pulling the trigger and soaking up the recoil even as he fell on the ground. I ended up emptying the chamber into him.

And I kept pulling the trigger still.

It felt good.

And horrible.

But mostly good.

My hand shook as I held the gun; there was a big hole in my backpack from where the bullet had passed through. Shoot-Em-Up's uniform was lying strewn about the crappy hotel room along with a platoon's worth of guns. Either Shoot-Em-Up was a great believer in overkill, or most of the weapons were for show.

Then I saw the witness.

She was lying on the bed, her crimson hair tied in girlish

pig-tails, in a little pink dress. The girl was no older than I, her hands duct-taped together. The girl didn't look particularly upset by what had happened to Shoot-Em-Up and was currently chewing off her restraints.

"Crap." I debated what to do. The smart thing to do was to shoot her but I wasn't that sort of villain. "You didn't see anything!"

"We go to the same school, Gary," the girl said, chewing her restraints off.

I blinked, recognizing her as a girl from class. Which made this so much worse. "Uh, Cindy?"

"Yeah," Cindy said, stepping over Shoot-Em-Up's corpse and picking up his wallet from the desk and his watch. "Wow, there's like a thousand bucks in this. Not to mention credit cards with false names! Sweet!"

"Uh, keep it."

"Awesome," Cindy said, not looking up. "You're learning already. Pity about the average height thirty-something guy who shot him."

I blinked.

Cindy looked at me. "Oh, you should dump the gun in the dumpster at Seventh and O'Neill. The International Crime League processes the weapons put there. They've been making inroads in town recently."

I slowly nodded, stunned. "Uh, are you all right?"

"Eh, a girl has to make a living. At least according to my drug-addict mother," Cindy muttered. "This should take care of her for about a week, at least." She looked over to the nearby weapons. "Or maybe longer."

I slowly backed away.

"See you at school?" Cindy asked. She sounded hopeful, like she'd made a new friend.

Which she had. Just not for any bonding we'd done over my recent murder. I needed to befriend her to keep her quiet. I admit, though, my fourteen-year-old-self was impressed by her attitude. She was handling the murder far better than I was. I wanted to find a toilet and throw up, which I would in a few minutes. "Sure, I guess. That sounds great. See you Monday."

"Awesome!" Cindy's enthusiasm was sincere, and we'd go on to be good friends. Albeit, ones who would drift apart as she sank farther into crime and I tried to get out of it. Apparently, she'd had a better idea of where she wanted to go with her life than I had.

Still, I couldn't help but remember Shoot-Em-Up's bullet-ridden corpse. The image was burned into my memory. I remembered it whenever I went to sleep and sometimes when I was just daydreaming. I didn't feel guilt, per se, but I felt *something*. Acknowledgment that I wasn't a normal person anymore perhaps. It hadn't been as satisfying as I'd hoped, but it had left me feeling a sense of, closure I guess.

They never did find out the cause of Shoot-Em-Up's death. Otherwise, I'd have been in jail. Cindy sold his weapons and costume on Crimebay and managed to pull herself out of the worst of Southside's poverty. The Society of Superheroes did an investigation but never managed to find out the truth, perhaps because some of them didn't want to.

Or maybe I just got lucky.

Either way, I got away with it.

For what it was worth.

Thrashing in my slumber, I woke up, covered in a cold sweat. Cloak had receded into my skin so he wasn't present anymore. Yet, I could feel him in my head still.

"*The Nightwalker handled the investigation of Shoot-Em-Up*," Cloak said, "*He interrogated his ghost for an hour.*"

"Why didn't you arrest me?" I asked him, mentally.

"Whitman didn't remember who you were," Cloak whispered. "*The Nightwalker should have sought you out, made sure you got help. You were turned into a killer at an age you should have been playing or noticing girls.*"

"Superheroes should have stopped Shoot-Em-Up from happening in the first place," I muttered. I looked over to see Mandy's naked form on the other side of the bed, sleeping peacefully. I got up to get a drink of water.

"*Are you so different from him?*" Cloak asked. "*Can you truly say you are walking a different path?*"

"Yes. I can."

Chapter Eight

The Ethics of Being a Supervillain

Staring into the bathroom mirror, I tried to see if there were any signs of my nightmares on my face. I'd worked for years to get rid of the signs of stress and worry about getting caught, pushing down the emotions until they were nonexistent. I wondered if I was a sociopath like Cindy had suggested, or if I was simply very good at fooling myself.

"*I don't think it's that simple,*" Cloak said, invisible but still inside me. "*I think I have a better understanding of you now.*"

"Yeah, I'm a cold-blooded killer. Ever since I was a teen. Quite the step down for the Nightwalker's cloak."

"*The Nightwalker had his own secrets. Other heroes may judge you for your actions, but I won't be one of them.*"

I turned on the hot water to splash some on my face. "You just said I was as bad as Shoot-Em-Up. You could have been more sensitive, you could have compared me to *Hitler.*"

"*I'm sorry.*"

That surprised me. I hadn't expected Cloak to show such a humanlike reaction. Then again, he'd done that at the sight of the little girl's exorcism too. "Apology accepted."

"*I would, however, like to discuss your choice of pursuits to use our powers.*"

"Ah-ha, so there's the judgment."

"*You don't seem to be a supervillain for reasons of insanity, though I questioned that a few times. You do not need the money—*"

"Mandy's family had money. We're not rich but there's

enough of a cushion we don't need to worry about losing everything like so many of the bastards in this thirty-percent unemployment city. At least until—"

"*You get a job?*"

I paused. "Yeah, I just realized I don't have to do that now."

"*I don't think you've fully internalized being a supervillain, dream or not.*"

"Do you understand why I want to be Merciless?"

Cloak was silent.

"Tell me," I said, daring the Reaper's Cloak to deny he did.

He didn't. "*Yes, I do. If there's one thing I understand, it's exorcising the ghosts of the past.*"

"You know all my secrets now."

"*I am privy to everything you think, feel, and see. I am not privy to those secrets you hide from yourself.*"

A thought occurred to me. "Uhm…were you watching when, uh?" I was referring to what Mandy and I had just done.

"*Do you really want me to answer?*"

I shook my head.

"*Good.*"

I splashed some water on my face. "This city has the highest crime rate in America for a reason. It is riddled from top to bottom with predators. While some of them are damned obvious, I'm not worried about the guys dealing drugs or selling themselves or even stealing to survive out there. I'm more concerned about the guys who have driven this city into the ground since before I moved here. The guys who steal a thousand families' savings and never see a day in court because the system is designed to prop them up. I don't have anything against superheroes in-general, Cloak. The only ones I hate are like Shoot-Em-Up and I know they're a minority."

Thank God.

"*We call them anti-heroes, Gary. They're not part of the team even if we must work with them. The government demands it.*"

I ignored Cloak, not bothering to dignify the hypocrisy. "The fact is—superheroes are tools of the establishment. They prop up the system with super-planes, super-tech, super-powers, and super-justice even though that's what they should be tearing down."

"*As bad as the system is. It's better than the alternative. I've seen lands where the system gets torn down.*"

"And that's because they were allowed to run screaming into the wall." I turned off the faucet. "So, if you're asking me if I should use my powers to be a superhero then no. No, I'm not. I don't know what I'm going to do with my powers just yet but I'm pretty sure it's going to involve robbing people as well as putting the scare into the people who piss me off about the world."

"*How noble.*" I could tell Cloak was being sarcastic.

"There's nothing noble about it," I said. "I intend to do this because it's going to make me feel better. I'm probably going to throw a lot of the money I take back out into the world but I'm also going to keep plenty. I don't have to justify myself or my actions. That's the fun part about being a supervillain. You don't have to justify yourself. You do what you want, and what I want is to make some noise."

"*That is a remarkably juvenile view of the world.*"

"Out of the mouth of babes. The only billionaire who was ever worth a damn in this city was Arthur Warren and he died last week, not long before the Nightwalker. It took like fifteen minutes for his heirs to shut down his Foundation and divert the money to golden parachutes for the disadvantaged Ivy League fratboys they hired to replace his social workers."

"*...yes.*" There was genuine anger in his mental voice, which surprised me.

That was when the lights all over the house went out, plunging the house into darkness. "Oh, for crying out loud. What now?"

"*Well, it could be one of the Nightwalker's countless supernatural foes. He was Dimensional Guardian of Earth in addition to being an opponent of street crime. The Fear Lord, Mammaloth the Eternal, and so on could all be coming to kill you and steal his cloak.*" Cloak paused. "*Or you could have a short in your wiring.*"

"I'll choose option two."

"Wise decision," Cloak replied. *"I'd suggest you study magic, but I somehow think the humility and enlightenment necessary to successfully navigate such things is beyond you."*

"I can't sell my soul to something for those?"

"I'm really hoping that was sarcasm."

"Probably."

Turning around in the dark and stumbling around my bedroom, I heard Mandy was still snoring gently in the night. While it was likely the Omega Energy Company was just shutting down again to drive up energy prices like they did every couple of years, I decided to check the circuit breaker anyway. It was unusually cold, which was strange given it was a hot summer outside. I felt like all the warmth had gone out of the place.

"Why did the Nightwalker fight so many mystic supervillains anyway? Did they just come here to Falconcrest City to take a shot at him? I never understood how so many superheroes ended up getting villains who followed their theme."

"I can't speak for the others, but Falconcrest City is a massive convergence of negative energy both in its architecture and ley lines. Those who practice evil magic find it a better place than anywhere on Earth to work their rituals. It's why Diabloman was so dangerous despite being a relatively minor tattoo mage."

"We're on a frigging portal to hell?"

"Essentially."

"Is that why this town is such a shithole?"

"More like this city's misery led to it becoming a convergence for everything bad in the universe. It's why Arthur and Lancel were so determined to fight human evil as well as foster goodwill around the city. They hoped to weaken the malevolent occult forces gathered here to prey on the helpless."

"I just thought it was because they were nice." I searched the kitchen drawers for a flashlight and found it. Turning it on, no beam came out. "Great."

"Arthur was a good person. Lancel…was complicated."

Deciding it was more likely the batteries were dead than demons from hell were coming to kill me, I headed to the basement door, passing by Galadriel who'd woken up and was moving around in the dark.

They were as close to kids as I'd likely ever have.

"Should I ask about that?"

"No," I said, heading down the stairs with one hand on the banister. "Don't ever ask again."

"Alright."

It was blacker than the already dark house upstairs, verging on pitch black. The stairs were unusually creaky, too. If not for the fact I didn't think it was within his powers, I'd say Cloak was trying to scare me.

Which was a lost cause. Nothing scared me since Keith.

"That disturbs me because it seems to be true."

"I'm scared of losing Mandy and my friends, but death? No, that doesn't scare me. I made peace with that a while ago."

"May I offer you a piece of advice?"

"Can you not?" I asked, wondering if I was going to be stuck with a surrogate dad in Cloak for the rest of my life.

"I advise you to be wary of Diabloman and Ms. Wakowski. Diabloman is affable enough to his friends and those who treat him with respect, but responsible for many deaths. Cindy is a broken woman like so many others who survived the south of Falconcrest City. Anything good in her died a long time ago."

"And maybe you're a judgmental prick."

"Perhaps."

That was when I felt my costume *slither* over my body as if it was a bottle of ink poured over me. It wasn't an unpleasant feeling and I enjoyed Cloak's presence in physical form. Uh, for some measure of the term.

However, I *didn't* summon him.

"Did you do that?" I asked aloud.

"No."

"Uh-oh."

Lifting my right hand, I conjured a ball of flame to illuminate my surroundings. Instead of its normal golden-orange color, though.the flame burned a brilliant white. For the most part, what I saw was nothing more than the usual stuff I found in my basement: washing machine, dryer, polybagged comic book collection, unused gym equipment, Mandy's highly illegal arsenal of weapons in case of P.H.A.N.T.O.M attack or alien invasion, and boxed Hanukah decorations.

Then I turned around.

Greeting me on the other side of the room was a naked blood-soaked Mandy or a woman who looked identical to her except for the eyes that reminded me strongly of Gabrielle's. Her fingernails were like talons and she reached out to me.

Her voice was like the voice of Hell itself.

"Oh, my Samael," the bloody figure whispered in the dark. "God sent you to me to be my *gevurah.*"

I retracted my earlier statement about never feeling fear. I screamed like a little girl. Actually, no, my sister Kerri was a little girl once, and she never screamed like this. I screamed like a very scared shrieky person.

"Soooooooon." The bloody figure vanished.

I swore for the next minute. I was still doing so when the basement lights switched back on.

"*Calm yourself,*" Cloak said. "*It is over.*"

"What the bleep was that?" I asked, actually using the word bleep since fuck had lost its power after the sixteenth time I'd used it.

"*Death,*" Cloak said. "*The Master of the Reaper's Cloak. She's trying to contact you.*"

"Death as a concept, angel, goddess, force, or anthropomorphized entity?"

"*Yes.*"

"Thank you, so very much," I muttered. "*Did the Nightwalker deal with her much?*"

"*No, he did not. This could be very good or very bad. Probably the latter.*"

I cursed again. "I was fine with ghosts who look like little girls and bankers. It's cheating when they look like loved ones."

Cloak was not sympathetic. "*Oh boo hoo.*"

I cursed at Cloak and dismissed the attire. Taking a moment to calm myself, I sighed. "Okay, this is just one more of the many-many surprises I'm finding out is involved with owning the Reaper's cloak. I'll deal with it like I've dealt with the others."

"Good," Cloak said. *"She used a word to describe you. Gevurah. Do you know what that means?"*

"You don't know something?" I asked.

"It happens, surprisingly enough. Judaism is one of the few areas I'm wholly unfamiliar. The Rabbis of Falconcrest refused to teach Master Warren anything due to his past involvement in matters best left unspoken of."

"His loss. It's some Kabbalistic stuff I'm not too certain on but Kerri is into. It is God's mode of punishing the wicked and judging humanity in general. It is the foundation of stringency, absolute adherence to the letter of the law, and strict meting out of justice."

"An odd thing to ascribe to you."

I frowned. "Perhaps not."

"Oh?"

"Samael is the name of the Accuser in Judaism. The corruptor, the tempter, the seducer, and destroyer. He's also the Angel of Death who works for God rather than opposes him like Lucifer. He's both good and evil."

"Death never says anything without purpose. If she chooses those names to describe you. I'd be very afraid."

I was.

But I'd never admit that.

I'd had enough of being afraid to last a lifetime.

Chapter Nine

Promises are Made to be Broken (or Destined)

Icouldn't sleep after my sudden encounter with Death and her mysterious words. As much as I'd wanted this, I was starting to think maybe, just maybe, I'd bitten off a little more than I could chew.

"*You don't say,*" Cloak said.

"Don't be a wiseass," I muttered, heading to the kitchen to prepare Mandy's breakfast. "That's what I'm for."

It was almost sunrise anyway, and by the time I had the eggs, bacon, and toast made, it was the start of a brand-new day in Falconcrest City. According to the morning news on the kitchen television, there had been eighteen reported murders last night and one terrorist attack. They barely touched on Amanda Douglas being kidnapped but did mention she'd been seen in the company of a boy band member who used to be popular ten years ago.

"Huh," I said, setting out full plates for both me and Mandy. "That's a surprisingly slow day."

"*The city is tearing itself apart without the Nightwalker,*" Cloak muttered, his voice low and gravelly.

"When the cat's away, the mice will play," I said, pouring myself a glass of orange juice. "Except, the cat is dead, and the mice are mutant cannibal rats."

"*You are very blasé about this.*"

"The Nightwalker was always a release valve on this city.

He, Arthur Warren, Ultragoddess—for the brief time she was here—and the Sunlights, kept the city from exploding. The thing is, they couldn't do enough to fix things. Maybe things getting so bad the Society of Superheroes, government, or god forbid, the *actual citizenry* stepping up will be a good thing. Things sometimes have to fall down to be built back up."

"*Your anarchist sentiments are noted. But no one gives much thought to just what falling will look like versus reform. The people in power will not turn to gentle measures to preserve their position. They will turn to the harshest measures they can get away with and the public will let them. They will call monsters who call themselves heroes and give them free reign. They will test children for superpowers then those children who have them, and their families, will disappear. Cops will stop carrying guns and start carrying death rays. Power will be given to those who promise changes and never surrendered.* **Then** *it will have to be burned to the ground. I have seen it happen before.*"

I took a long drink of orange juice. "And I thought *I* was the tin-foil hat wearing crazy person out there."

"The difference between a superhero and a supervillain is often only that one knows when to stop."

"Nope," I said, finishing my drink. "The difference between a superhero and a supervillain is one has *style.*"

Cloak wasn't entirely talking out of his ass, well if he had an ass. As much as I envisioned myself as a budding counter-culture icon in the making, superheroes were often in the middle of any argument between the right and the left. They were always counseling moderation, empathy, and half-measures. While I wasn't a big fan of it, there were plenty of times when the public seemed ready to hand the country over to folks like Tom Terror or General Venom if they got rid of the superhumans.

People would burn the Mona Lisa to get rid of a smudge on it.

"*Those who would give up essential Liberty, to purchase a little temporary Safety, deserve neither Liberty nor Safety.*"

"Ben Franklin," I said, recognizing the quote. "It was also about taxation to build a militia."

Cloak sounded frustrated. "*Be that as it may—*"

"Yo, Mandy!" I called to my wife as she was getting out of bed.

Mandy was dressed in an extra-large black and white Hello Kitty T-shirt. Kitty had a pair of batwings sticking out of her head and a pair of fangs. She was wearing a pair of fuzzy Chewbacca slippers on her feet and rubbing her eyes. "I had the strangest dream about dragons, vampires, and death."

I grimaced. "Yeah, Death came to visit me last night."

"Eh?"

"Long story," I said, handing her a cup of coffee.

"It can wait," Mandy said, blinking; still shaking off her sleepiness. "So, anything in the papers about your exploits?"

"Not a bit," I said, shaking my head. "Apparently, I'll have to raise a bigger stink if I'm going to make it famous."

Mandy went to give the dogs treats. She then picked up the paper and unfolded it in front of the refrigerator. "The gang wars are heating up, it seems, and way too many costumed criminals are suspiciously out on parole. Maybe they'll do us all a favor and kill each other off."

I stared at her, looking up from the Keurig. "Really, Mandy?"

"How many criminals have you killed since you started all this?"

"Not…that many."

"Since *yesterday*?"

She had a point. "Well, in any case, I'm going to be out most of this week. I'd like your help in making sure I don't screw up."

Mandy didn't look up from her paper. "So, now you want me to be an accessory to your crimes?"

"What if my crimes are limited to very bad people?" I suggested.

Mandy paused. I could hear the wheels turning in her head. "I'm listening."

"Marriage is a compromise. Why don't you help keep me on the crooked and narrow?" I said, starting to cut up my eggs. "We can work together to keep me from doing anything so heinous you'll divorce me, and I'll have access to your wonderful expertise in figuring out how to screw over people who stand in my way of being the best supervillain in town."

"Gary, what *is* your definition of a supervillain, anyway?"

I paused, thinking carefully. "A person who commits crimes for their own benefit, ego, and self-interest. Which frankly, let's be honest, I am."

"Alright." Mandy said. "I suppose I might be willing to work with you on this. You need to understand, though, Gary, I don't think this is a game. You were almost killed fighting the Ice Cream Man and Typewriter and they don't even have superpowers. You're also hanging out with very dangerous people."

I gave her a sly look. "Worried about me straying?"

"With Cindy? No." Mandy paused. "But that's because I'm not sure I have enough acid to dispose of both your bodies."

I smirked.

Mandy lowered her paper, glaring.

I grimaced, taking another bite. Chewing, I said, "Come on, we did good work there, Mandy. We killed a domestic terrorist and saved a celebrity. The police seem willing to look the other way, too. We can do some real good in this town. Maybe we can even get some of the chaos under control."

"That's what I'm worried about."

"What's that?"

"The easy justifications. You've killed people, already, Gary. First, it's robbing a bank after saving it, then it's blackmailing the Douglases for more money. How long until you're trying to take over the city's underworld for the greater good?"

"That you don't have to worry about," I said, continuing to eat my breakfast.

"How's that?" Mandy asked.

"I make no pretense of this being for the greater good. It's for mine and mine alone."

Mandy looked at me. "Gary?"

"Yeah."

"If you hurt anyone innocent. A kid or an innocent bystander or someone who is in your way—like a witness—I'll stop you. Permanently, if I have to."

Wow, that went dark quickly.

"What did you expect when you embarked on a life of crime?"

Cloak had me there.

I looked up at her, meeting her gaze. I then spoke from the heart. "If I start doing that, I'll want you to. I want to honor Keith's legacy, not drag it through the mud to become the kind of man Shoot-Em-Up claimed him to be."

Mandy and I were silent for a long time.

Finally, she said, "I'll hold you to that."

That was when the kitchen landline rang. It was the first call we'd received on there in years. Picking it up, I said, "I really hope this isn't another phone call from Hell."

"What now?" Mandy asked.

A thick Mexican accented voice spoke on the other end. "It is I, Diabloman."

"Oh, hey, Diablo."

"You're talking to *the Devil* now?" Mandy asked, her eyes widening.

"Not yet," I answered her. Turning back to the mouthpiece, I asked, "What's up?"

"I have located suitable lodgings for you," Diabloman said, his voice all business.

"Suitable lodgings?" I asked.

"Si," Diabloman said. "You cannot be a proper supervillain without a lair. A place where you can conduct business, store stolen goods, keep weapons and equipment. A location that impresses potential employees with your power and influence. Truly, these sorts of places are a vital part of the process."

I hadn't really given much thought to the whole thing, but I supposed he was right. I was more surprised he was taking his whole "supervillain consultant" thing so seriously. "Okay, tell me about the place."

"It is better that you see it for yourself. Big Ben and I have been in negotiations for the past hour and a half."

Ah, Big Ben, now there was a name that had serious pull in the Falconcrest City Underworld. He'd been at this whole supervillain thing since the Forties, being there when gangsters had started to be replaced with more serious criminals.

Caught by the Nightwalker hundreds of times, he'd managed, to almost always avoid getting convicted of anything serious. He'd served jail time once for an extended period but ended up back on the streets in the Nineties. I hoped I was still in the game when I was almost a hundred. I wondered what health foods the guy ate.

"This isn't going to turn out to be an abandoned warehouse somewhere, is it?" I asked, hoping to God it wasn't. "I really don't want to start at the bottom."

"No amusement parks, abandoned factories, fun houses, or warehouses," Diabloman said, surprising me with his thoroughness. "I also avoided any buildings with giant M's on them. I thought that might be a bit ostentatious until you've developed a legitimate front to market your image."

"I'll have to ask you about branding. Supervillain culture is a big thing now in rap music," I replied, looking over at my wife. Mandy was frowning at me. Clearly, we still had a long way to go in coming to an understanding regarding my dream. "So, Diablo, where should I go to check out my new digs?"

"The Falconcrest City Clock Tower. It's yours now."

"Mine?" I wasn't sure I liked that. It was expensive-sounding and I hadn't made *that* much money. The Clock Tower was the largest building in town and I was pretty sure I couldn't afford a down payment on a down payment.

Mandy looked over from her computer. "What's going on?"

"I own the Falconcrest City Clock Tower."

Mandy looked at me sideways, blinking. "Can you buy landmarks?"

"Either that or I'm buying the rights to use it. This is my first time buying a secret headquarters."

"You are purchasing the secret compartment behind the clock face," Diabloman explained.

"Ah, that makes more sense," I said. "How much will it cost?"

"Ten million dollars," Diabloman said, calmly.

"Ten *million* dollars?" I choked out, needing a second to catch my breath.

"What!" Mandy sounded even more shocked than I.

Dammit, that was going to be a conversation.

"Will that be a problem?" Diabloman asked, concerned.

"No!" I replied. "Not at all. See you there in an hour."

"*Si,*" Diabloman said.

"Gary!" Mandy's mouth was hanging open. "Tell me you're not serious."

"I'm not serious."

"Gary..." Mandy whispered, her eyes narrowing.

"I know what I'm doing," I lied.

"*You will have enough money to purchase the Clock Tower.*"

"I will?" I asked, confused.

"*What's inside that place must not fall into the hands of anyone but me.*"

"Are you talking to your magic hoodie again?" Mandy looked at me sideways.

"It's a hooded costume, not a hoodie. There's a big difference. Muggers wear hoodies. Supervillains wear costumes," I said. "But yes, Cloak says I should be able to afford it."

"You're taking financial advice from a piece of sackcloth," my wife grumbled, rolling her eyes. "This keeps getting better and better."

"Hey, it can't get any worse than taking advice from the so-called experts," I replied, smiling. "Remember what shape they got the country in."

"Oh, God, more of your class warfare bull..." Mandy started to speak before Diabloman coughed in the receiver.

"Oh, are you still there?"

"*Si,*" Diabloman said.

I was surprised he hadn't hung up. "Something wrong?"

"The Clock Tower appears to have been the Nightwalker's former headquarters," Diabloman said.

"I'll be right there." I hung up.

Diabloman's description changed everything. Possessing that would be enough to change my status in the Underworld forever. I could skip over all the parts about building a reputation right to declaring myself a major player. That didn't include any potential loot, trophies, or information I might get from the place.

"*It's really not as impressive as you might think. More of a workshop than anything else.*"

"Did he say the Nightwalker's headquarters?" Mandy asked.

"Yes."

"I'm coming with you," Mandy said.

"I'm not sure..." I trailed off.

Mandy's eyes narrowed.

"All right," I said, giving her two thumbs up. "Let's wolf down our breakfasts, put up the dogs, and get this show on the road."

Chapter Ten

Where I Get My Supervillain Digs

The Falconcrest City Clock Tower was the single most impressive building in the city. It was the sort of building you expected King Kong to climb to the top of or the Ghostbusters to banish Gozer from. If the Douglas Grand Hotel was creepy-disturbing, the Falconcrest City Clock Tower was creepy-magnificent. Constructed at the turn of the century, it was a monument to the founders' desire to create the weirdest city in America.

It wasn't even the fact it was a clock tower larger than the one in London, it was the fact that it rose like a spire from the center of the city and seemed a focus for all the weird, offbeat energy that permeated our metropolis.

Pulling our minivan into the tower's underground garage, I drove thirteen stories down to the empty bottom level. There, Diabloman and Cindy were waiting for us. Both were in full costume, though Cindy's had changed yet again. This time, she wore a cloak very similar to my own except dyed red.

Complementing the outfit was a cleavage-displaying black corset and miniskirt. It was a poor choice for a henchwoman's outfit. She looked like she was auditioning for the adult film version of Little Red Riding Hood. I don't know, maybe that was the look she was going for.

Parking the car, I stepped out and waved. "Great choice, Diablo. I can't think of any place I'd rather have as my hideout."

"I can. Maybe someplace that's *not* a local tourist attraction?" Mandy was disguised, wearing a blue trench coat, red wide-brimmed hat, and sunglasses. She was beautiful but looked a trifle out of place.

"Carmen Sandiego?" Cindy inquired.

Mandy glared at Cindy. *"Hello,* Cindy." Her voice was frosty.

I winced. "Is her presence going to be a problem? Cindy is an excellent henchwench. She'll keep me from being killed."

"Hench*person,"* Cindy corrected. "And probably! Don't look at my past track record with bosses."

"Ugh." Mandy ignored Cindy's statement. She then looked up and down her somewhat lingerie-esque costume. "I will say it makes a great deal more sense why you're interested in becoming a supervillain now. If you wanted a hot girl to wear sexy costumes around you, you could have just asked me."

I had a response for that, but it was lost in going through various memories of Mandy's outfits at FalconCon.

"Are you a supervillain now too?" Cindy asked Mandy.

"No," Mandy responded.

"It's too bad," Cindy said. "Supervillain parties are the best. There's this one kind where everyone puts their keys in a bowl—"

Diabloman bowed his head to me, clapping his hands together. "Big Ben will be arriving shortly."

"Great, I want the ten-million-dollar tour before I pay full price." I turned around to look at the lot's entrance.

Diabloman was about to say something when his cell phone started playing "Sympathy for the Devil." Looking surprised, he said, "Excuse me, it's either the satanic cult that raised me or my daughter. Either way, I have to take this."

"Sure, go ahead." I waved him off. "Say hello to your daughter for me."

It's important to keep good employee relations after all, even when you're evil.

Diabloman answered his phone. "Hello, Pookie. What can Daddy do for you?"

Meanwhile, Mandy was still staring daggers at Cindy. I had no idea what they were discussing, but I suspected it had gone farther south than the neighborhood where we'd gone to school together.

"Gary, fire her." Mandy glared at me.

"Hey!" Cindy said, putting a hand on her hip. "Just because I got drunk and told inappropriate stories at your wedding is no reason to hold a grudge."

"That and half of those stories involved unsolved felonies," Mandy said. "That and attempting to invite yourself on the honeymoon."

"Oh, was that not welcome?" Cindy asked.

Mandy shot me a nasty look. "I mean it, Gary."

I grimaced. I'd forgotten about that. There had been a time when Mandy and Cindy had been friendly, back when she'd been cleaning up her act to go to medical school. I couldn't help but wonder what had happened to that. I wasn't one to pry but I had the sneaking suspicion she wasn't in the program anymore.

"Oh, you think?" Cloak asked.

The wedding, though, had been an unmitigated disaster and I wonder if she'd been backsliding since. She might even be using Happy Gas again. That wasn't my problem, though, and a choice between her and Mandy wasn't a choice at all. Sighing, I stared down at my feet before looking back up. "I'm sorry, Cindy, but if my wife doesn't want you here—"

Cindy clasped her hands together in a pleading gesture. "Mandy, can I *please* work for your husband? Pretty-please with sugar on top? He pays well and hasn't tried to kill me once. You have no idea how rare that is in the supervillain business."

"No," Mandy said.

"I'll be your best friend," Cindy said, cheerfully leaning up against her.

Mandy pulled away. "No!"

Cindy then leaned up and whispered something in Mandy's ear. My wife did a double take, staring at my henchwench. "That was you?"

"Uh-huh!" Cindy smiled.

Mandy sighed, slumping her shoulders in defeat. "Okay, then, I guess you can work for him."

"Really?" I asked, confused. "Do I want to know?"

"No." Mandy sighed. "Just know I owe her. I still don't like her, though. Not by a long shot."

"Oh, you'll like me. I'm infectious like that!" Cindy said,

jumping up and down. She did the whole adult 'woman-child' thing well. I suppose it was a blessing she'd given up her medical residency dreams. Could you imagine her dealing with patients?

"Know there will be no flirting with my husband," Mandy said, "or killing people for him."

"That don't deserve it," I added.

"No flirting with you or your husband, gotcha. I forget the next one." Cindy shouted, giving Mandy a hug from behind. "We're going to be like sexy-sisters! Or co-henchpersons! Beautiful assistants! Bi and Bi-Curious Life Mates! The four of us can go on quadruple dates with fellow sexy supervillains!"

Mandy sighed, holding her face with the palm of her hand. "She's not listening to a word I say, is she?"

"Not a bit." I shook my head in amusement. "I wouldn't worry, though. That's how she treats everybody."

"That's...terrifying," Mandy said.

Further discussion was prevented by the arrival of Big Ben's distinctive car—a stretched limousine with a Union Jack color scheme. The car pulled in at about ninety miles per hour and spun around into a nearby parking spot.

"Why does he drive a car like that if he's a criminal? Isn't it just announcing to the police he's inside?" my wife asked, distracted from Cindy's presence.

"It's a supervillain thing. Big Ben was a trendsetter for a lot of classic tropes. Whenever you think of bad guys who have a specific theme, you're thinking of him. Before Big Ben, most superhero foes were gangsters and mad scientists. He's also the guy who invented the razor-sharp throwable bowler hat. He had it *decades* before Oddjob used it in *Goldfinger*. He and Tom Terror practically *invented* supervillainy."

"Stop hugging me," Mandy said.

"Oh, right." Cindy let go.

Seconds later, a group of henchmen dressed as chimney sweeps stepped out of Big Ben's car. Yes, like in *Mary Poppins*. The chimney sweeps formed a protective circle around the limousine before the tallest one opened the door to the back seat. The distinctive figure of Big Ben stepped out, looking every inch the supervillain.

He was about four foot two and he cut a memorable figure with his bowler hat, silver-tipped cane, and U.K. flag-colored suit. Even in his mid-nineties, Big Ben looked scary, projecting the menace only a criminal who had outlasted generations of younger rivals, could pull off.

Speaking in an exaggerated Cockney accent, Big Ben addressed me, "Greetings Gov'ner, glad to make your acquaintance. You've been making big waves. I've been lookin' forward to this meeting since your debut."

"Which means you've been looking forward to it for all of twenty-four hours?" Mandy asked.

"Shh," Cindy said. "He's supervillain royalty."

"Save it for the tourists, Ben," I said, exaggerating my natural Southside accent. "I came here to do business."

Big Ben's accent vanished. "Fair enough, Merciless. I understand you're in the market for a secret headquarters."

"You could say that. You could also say..." I trailed off when I realized I had nothing to say, blowing my cover as a smooth operator. "Yeah, yeah I am."

Big Ben ignored my idiocy. "Then I think you'll like the location we've found."

"I bet I will." I glanced over at Diabloman. "Diablo, time to go up."

"No, Pookie, all the girls are not doing it." Diabloman was still talking on the phone. To his daughter, I hoped. "Yes, I'm quite sure. Your boyfriend is feeding you a line. Oh, and tell him if he touches you, I'll rip out his spine."

I paused. "Do you need a minute?"

Diabloman raised his palm to me. *"Uno momento."*

"No sweat. We'll wait."

If Diabloman needed a few minutes to talk to his daughter, I wouldn't begrudge him it. It would be healthier for me in the long run.

"Yeah, yeah, yeah. Okay, I'll see you next weekend when it's my turn for custody. Remember, no summoning demons and don't do drugs. I learned both lessons the hard way. Bye-bye." Diabloman hung up, putting away his cellphone. "Kids."

"She sounds like a lovely girl," I said. "Shall we go?"

Diabloman nodded. "I think you will be impressed. The Night Tower has been sought after by supervillains since its existence first became known in the Forties."

I looked over to Big Ben and raised an eyebrow before asking, "Just so we're clear, this is the Night Tower, correct? The headquarters of the Nightwalker?"

"Master Warren never called it that. That was an invention of the radio show adaptation of our adventures. We also never named half of the gadgets his brother bought for us. Hell, we never even used a third of them. I mean, what possible use could we have for a spray to ward off dinosaurs?"

"Shh," I whispered, wanting to hear what Big Ben had to say.

"So it would appear. I've fought the Nightwalker since before you were born and never thought I'd see the day when he was dead and gone. I won though, by outliving him." Big Ben cackled before degenerating into a series of violent coughs.

One of Big Ben's henchmen brought out an oxygen tank and mask from that the elderly supervillain took several long breaths. Wheezing, he put it aside and said, "You didn't see that."

"Of course not," I said. "To what do you attribute your longevity to, anyway?"

"An often-asked question." Big Ben took deep breaths between words. "Hate, regular sex, and carrot juice."

Eww. "Good advice!"

Mandy leaned into my side and whispered, "You do realize these guys are all lunatics, right?"

"Trust me; I know what I'm doing."

"You have no idea what you're doing, do you?"

I shook my head and muttered, "Not at all."

Mandy glared at me. "I heard that."

Thinking at my cloak, instead of talking, I said, *"You were with the Nightwalker for eighty years. You must have known about this place. However, you didn't think to mention it. Anything else you're keeping from me?"*

"Not deliberately. We haven't had time to sit down and chat. There're a million possible things that might get you killed that I haven't had time to tell you about."

Wow, that was reassuring.

I gave my wife a quick peck on the cheek. "It's cool"

Mandy shook her head and gestured for us to go. I appreciated her trust, even if I hadn't done much to earn it. "Just don't get us killed."

"I'll try."

Allowing Big Ben's gang to go up the elevator first, my group followed. Something about the situation set my teeth on edge and I found myself becoming paranoid.

Would Big Ben sell this place for a mere ten million dollars? Even assuming it was nothing more than a finder's fee, there were still a lot of unanswered questions. If it was the Night Tower, the equipment alone would be worth a hundred million dollars or more. What did Big Ben *really* hope to gain from all this?

"You're learning. I'm surprised. You can't trust Big Ben."

"No shit," I mentally replied. *"Really?"*

"No need to be sarcastic."

*"There's **always** a need to be sarcastic,"* I snapped back.

"I'm getting that feeling…with you."

My hesitation vanished when the doors opened to reveal the Night Tower. It was a mixture of retro and ultra-modern, embodying what a well-equipped badass the Nightwalker had been. There was a huge wall of monitors, a giant computer, a brachiosaur skeleton, a disassembled giant robot, and of course the massive clock-face behind everything. Scattered between these items were multiple platforms filled with the Nightwalker's equipment, vehicles, and trophies.

Weirdly, most of the place looked unused. The one part that looked used was a large section to the back. There, two dozen plain wooden bookshelves were covered in spellbooks and other occult paraphernalia. There was also a small table nearby with a map of the city and a big black scrying orb beside it. I knew what the latter was because it looked like the crystal ball the Wicked Witch of the West had in the *Wizard of Oz*. The incongruity between the two sides of the Nightwalker's hideout didn't keep me from being awed by the place, though.

"I am *totally* buying this joint."

"Where did the Nightwalker get the idea for something like this?" My wife asked, sounding impressed.

"Comics. *That's where all the big names got their ideas. You know, back when they were still about fictional characters.*"

"It explains a lot," I muttered, still stunned by the place.

"*Don't be too impressed. Master Warren's brother tried to give us a proper secret lair and equipment but it's all for show. There's no point in driving around a super-car if you want to sneak up on a subject. Plus, it'd be easy to follow back to your headquarters. The Nightwalker drove around the city in an anonymous white van and turned into his costume form whenever he wanted to make an entrance. I never had the heart to tell Arthur—*"

"Does the car come with the place?" I asked, having stopped listening around the word 'super-car.'

"Absolutely!" Big Ben flashed a salesman-like grin.

"Sweet!"

Big Ben had already begun the ten-million-dollar tour, gesturing with his cane as he walked. "As you can see, he was a well-prepared little twerp. From what I could tell from his notes, he started fighting crime after his wife and child were killed, and he somehow got his magical cloak from...someone. Local legend says he made a pact with the Devil."

"*The Grim Reaper, actually.*"

"Shush," I told Cloak. "I want to hear this."

It's impossible for a cape to roll its eyes, but I sensed Cloak was doing the closest approximation he could.

"This place has been untouched ever since," Big Ben said.

Except for whoever gave me the cloak. I wondered who it was. It clearly wasn't Big Ben.

"*You're only now just wondering that?*"

"*I've been busy,*" I said back.

We passed a row of mannequins in display cases. These held a Nightwalker costume for every day of the week. They were all lacking his trademark cape, however. That didn't make any sense, though. The cloaks permanently bonded with a person. If he had these, then that meant he never wore them and must have gotten them from someone dead.

"Good. We'll make a detective out of you, yet. This was where I stored the other cloaks to keep them out of the hands of evildoers."

Big Ben pointed to the display case with his cane. "Here was where the Nightwalker stored his uniforms. Sadly, when I recovered this place, all his spare magical cloaks were missing. There are still many benefits to be had, though."

Spare magical cloaks?

"It's a long story," Cloak said. *"There are seven Reaper's Cloaks. The Nightwalker stored them, though, rather than wear them."*

"Someone took them?" I said, suddenly feeling very anxious. I didn't like to think about the possibility of six or seven other Merciless-es out there. I could stand another Nightwalker, but I had an image to maintain.

"This is unfortunate. If the Reaper's Cloaks have fallen into evil hands...well evil-er hands... the entire world could be in danger," Cloak said, sounding concerned.

I paused a second, looking down at my attire. "Listen, you're going to have to give me the whole story now. This is a pretty big bombshell you're dropping on me."

"Yes, I'm afraid we don't know who acquired them," Big Ben answered, assuming I was talking to him. "All seven cloaks were present when one of my informants found the place. Admittedly, one was on dear old Lancel Warren's back. Who'd have ever thought that old coot was the Nightwalker? His brother didn't last much longer after him. Still, when I came up here, they were all gone along with a few other knick-knacks. Very strange."

That's when I decided to switch subjects. "Tell me, Ben, why such a low price?"

"What do you mean?" Big Ben coughed, one of his henchmen giving him a whiff off an oxygen mask.

"Even if you could access his files, which I doubt you could. The equipment alone is worth many times the mere ten-million dollar asking price. What is your game?"

Before Big Ben could respond, we were interrupted by an indistinct figure in a bright yellow and white costume who leaped down in front of me from one of the platforms above us.

"For the shining rays of justice!" the figure cried out, giving me a roundhouse kick to the face. It didn't hurt at all.

Big Ben's henchmen didn't hesitate to defend their boss, however. Since I was right next to him, they were also aiming right at me. Thankfully, my assailant threw a set of smoke pellets at their feet.

These spewed forth noxious black smoke and sent the chimney sweeps down to the ground gasping for air. Big Ben was the only one to remain standing due to his oxygen mask being within easy reach.

Ironic.

"You shall not defile the Nightwalker's tower of nobility, fiend!" the man assaulting me said. He punched me in the chest and face, the blows feeling like light taps against my skin. To be fair, I suspected that they would have been devastating attacks to a man who didn't have limited invulnerability. It took someone like Diabloman to kick my ass.

"Do you want me to handle this?" Diabloman asked, as unconcerned as I was.

"No, I think I can deal with this guy." I caught the man's next blow and head-butted him. It hurt like hell, but it sent the guy to the ground with a thud. It didn't knock him out, which surprised me, but it allowed me to get a good look at my attacker.

The first thing I noticed was the man was old, not quite as old as Big Ben, but still showing his years. My father was sixty-five and they looked roughly the same age. The next was he was dressed up in a bright superheroes' outfit, complete with a big sun symbol on his chest and a little white domino mask.

I recognized the attire as a Sunlight costume. It was one of the less regarded parts of the Nightwalker legend he once had a series of rivals for the position of top superhero in Falconcrest City. The Sunlights used flash-bangs holograms, smoke pellets, and gadgets in place of the supernatural. For whatever reason, perhaps because no one liked bright and airy heroes in

Falconcrest, they'd never achieved the same level of popularity as Lancel Warren.

"Dude, why are you dressed up as Nightwalker's old rival?" I couldn't help but ask. "I mean, the guy retired when I was still watching cartoons."

"You *still* watch cartoons," Mandy said.

"Shh! No one else needs to know that."

"That **is** *Sunlight. One of them at least."*

I stared at the old man who was already back on his feet. "You have got to be kidding me."

"Specifically, Robert Warren, Arthur's grandson. He developed a serious drug problem in the Eighties after failing to save a school bus of children and had a nervous breakdown. Master Warren had to have him committed. His two sons briefly took up the mantle. Up until a month ago, he was living in a Canadian retirement community under an assumed name."

The sexagenarian superhero pointed at me with a sun-shaped shuriken. He shouted in a high somewhat boyish voice, "Now, evil doer, I arrest you for trespassing, consorting with criminal trash, and defiling the cloak of the greatest superhero of them all!"

One of the chimney sweeps on the ground pulled out a sword from his broom handle and swung at Sunlight from behind. The aged champion of justice smashed the man's face in with the back of his fist, broke the man's knee with the reverse kick, and head-butted him unconscious, all without ever turning around.

"Pretty spry for an old guy." For whatever reason, I wasn't frightened of Sunlight. Maybe it was the fact the guy was one of the old school superheroes who helped people and not the sort who gunned down people's brothers. "How does he keep in shape?"

"Ancient Tibetan calisthenics Robert learned in Shambhala from the Iron Dragon while studying for a way to match the Reaper's Cloak. I…Master Warren never approved of his family following him into the superhero business, but that didn't mean they were incompetent."

"Uh-huh. Listen, Sunlight—"

I was about to ask what the hell Sunlight was talking about when Cindy interrupted me. "You want me to kill him? You know; if your wife is okay with it?"

"I am *not*," Mandy said, her tone withering.

"I think it's bad karma to kill geriatric superheroes," I said. "Even if they are still kicking ass. Diabloman advised me not to kill any good guys."

"That's what's stopping you?" Mandy asked.

Sunlight aimed another shuriken at me. "Surrender now or face the scourge of the Underworld!"

"Uh, okay." I raised my hands up for the second time this week. "I surrender."

"What?" Cindy said, staring. "You can't be serious. We can take him! He's just one guy."

"A statement made by many a supervillain before getting their asses kicked," Diabloman said, raising his own hands. "Though, Red Riding Hood is correct, we could at least give a token resistance."

"I'm not hitting Sunlight!" I replied. "Merciful Moses, I used to wear Underoos with his picture on them!"

"Too much information."

Before Cindy could reply, I heard Big Ben's men cocking their guns at us again. The smoke had cleared, and they were ready to start shooting. Sunlight turned around, only to be almost decapitated by Big Ben's bowler hat. During the distraction, one of the men ran up and clobbered him on the head, forcing him to the ground.

"Make sure he's dead!" Big Ben coughed between words. He made no apologies for almost gunning us down earlier and seemed focused on killing Sunlight. Probably because the later had been a thorn in his side since before I was born.

Mandy looked at me, clearly not happy about Sunlight's imminent execution. "Gary, we need to do something!"

"Applaud?" I asked. Yeah, it was hypocritical, but there was a difference between killing a hero yourself and letting someone else do it.

Mandy glared.

"Fine," I muttered, sighing. If I didn't do something, then

Mandy would, and God knew how many bodies that would lead to. "I'll save the superhero's life. But only because I'm under the impression Big Ben is going to betray us."

Not at *all* because I thought the old guy seemed like a decent fellow who deserved to be protected. Geez, if that got out, I'd never be able to show my face at a supervillain bar again. Not that I'd ever visited one.

How the hell did I keep getting into these situations?

Chapter Eleven

Where I Learn My Secret Origin

Big Ben had never read the Evil Overlord's List and was taking time to gloat. "Sunlight! Ha! Now this is a red-letter day! I just thought I'd lure a bunch of rubes to waste a fortune buying the Night Tower."

A couple of Big Ben's goons turned their guns on my group. Their weapons were an M16 and Uzi both shaped like chimneybrushes. Being held hostage by a bunch of Dick Van Dyke look-a-likes was a new experience for me.

I didn't like it.

"Huh," I muttered. "I guess I was right."

"Curse your sudden but inevitable betrayal!" Cindy shouted, shaking a fist at Big Ben's gang.

"Then I'd kill them," Big Ben continued to monologue, "but this! This, I never expected! I spent *decades* in prison thanks to this nincompoop. The forties to the nineties, languishing in and out of jail because of the Nightwalker's idiot sidekicks! Well, I didn't get to kill the Nightwalker, but I'll at least get to kill... Argh!"

That was when Big Ben burst into flames, his suit going up like a piece of dry kindling. He seemed surprised, yelping in shock as his men watched the sight in confusion. It looked like word hadn't gotten around yet that I had the power to set people on fire with my mind.

Amidst the crime lord's screams, I iced over the guns of the henchmen threatening me before Diabloman charged, tackling the thugs to the ground.

"Shall I kill them, Boss?" Diabloman asked, holding two of the thugs up by their necks.

"Yes. Do that thing you do."

"With pleasure." Diabloman crushed the necks of both before tossing their bodies to the side.

I didn't think Sunlight would approve of us villains slaughtering the bad guys about to kill him but that was one of the benefits of being a bad guy. We didn't have a higher standard to aspire to.

Grabbing both Cindy and Mandy, I turned intangible as the remaining henchmen fired upon us. Their bullets passed harmlessly through our forms before I froze the wire suspended platform above their heads.

The metal cracked and shattered before dumping its contents on their heads. Unfortunately for them, its contents included the Nightcar: a customized black vehicle as much tank as it was sports car. Two henchmen and the still-burning Big Ben were crushed.

Sunlight, on the other hand, escaped unharmed. He was standing over one of the bad guys who'd been prepared to kill him. Said villain was the only one to survive our attack. "Alas, poor Big Ben. He never realized that it was the cold hand of death that awaited his life of evil and not the fortunes of ill-gotten loot he envisioned."

"Are you on drugs?" Cindy asked, staring at Sunlight.

"Clean for decades!" Sunlight giving a thumbs up. "I have to arrest you for murder. I will, however, argue it was in self-defense."

"I killed Big Ben too?"

I looked over at the Nightcar and saw a bloody mess leaking out from under it.

"Yeah, people are going to start thinking you're a good guy the way you're knocking off bad guys!" Cindy pointed and laughed.

"Oh, I doubt that." I wondered if there was a limit to the number of people you could kill before self-defense stopped being a defense. I was about to make another crack when I noticed one of Big Ben's henchmen was missing from the body-count I was compiling. Turning around, I saw he was behind me and carrying a futuristic-looking gun he had to have looted from the Nightwalker's various trophies.

"*Death's scythe, he's got the Solar Devastator!*" Cloak shouted, stunning me with his tone of genuine horror.

"The what?" I asked.

Mandy moved before anyone else, doing a roll on the ground to grab one of the late henchmen's guns, lifted it up, and shot my attacker repeatedly in the chest. It was magnificently executed, just the way her father had trained her, even as I could see the look of dawning horror in his eyes as the figure fell.

"*Gary, stop the weapon from hitting the ground!*" Cloak shouted again.

I froze the futuristic gun and the resulting snowball landed on the ground, nothing happening as it did.

"What would have that done, Cloak?" I asked, wondering what all the fuss was about.

"*Tom Terror miniaturized the power of a nuclear explosion into handgun form during the Fifties.*"

"Why *the hell* would you keep something around like that?"

"*Kaiju. I could never get the cloak to generate enough power to destroy them outright.*"

I blinked. "Ask a stupid question, get a stupid—"

I noticed Mandy was shaking, staring at the corpse, her gun, and then me. I immediately went to her side and wrapped her in a hug. She pushed the safety on the gun then returned my embrace.

"It's all right, Gary," Mandy said, taking a deep breath and returning my embrace. "I just never hurt anyone before."

"You did wonderfully!" Diabloman said, nodding in approval.

"Bravo!" Cindy enthusiastically applauded.

Mandy stared at them both then narrowed her eyes.

Both of them blanched as if terrified.

I continued hugging Mandy. "I am sorry. I did not mean to get you into this situation."

"Eh, it's okay," Mandy said, sucking in her breath. "I don't think this is your fault, actually."

"Ahem." Sunlight cleared his throat. "You're all under arrest."

"Yeah, we heard you the first time," I said, unconcerned. "I think you should realize this was all in self-defense."

"Three of you have outstanding warrants," Sunlight pointed out. "The woman dressed like it's the Forties is innocent, though."

"I have a warrant on me?" I asked, shaking my head. "I thought the Chief and I had an understanding."

"Never trust the cops in this town," Cindy said, starting to look through the Nightwalker's stuff, presumably for something to steal. "They'll disappoint you every time."

"I can assure you that the judge will take in your attempts to help me during sentencing," Sunlight said.

I ignored him, not really caring. It wasn't like he could seriously threaten us. He hadn't exactly been kicking ass out there. "Could you give me a minute with my wife?"

"Of course," Sunlight said.

"Do you want me to beat him, Boss?" Diabloman asked.

"No," I said. "Not yet."

"Not ever. We're going to work this out peacefully," Mandy said before sniffing the air. "What smells like pork?"

"That's just burning human flesh." I gestured to where Big Ben had been crushed. "You get used to it."

Mandy scrunched up her face.

"I probably should have kept that part a secret."

Mandy nodded, slowly.

Cindy, meanwhile, was holding an armful of stolen weapons and supervillain memorabilia. Walking over to a nearby crate where I presumed she'd store them, she passed by the unconscious thug who'd shot her.

"You know, I just realized you saved my life." Cindy gave the unconscious thug a swift kick. "None of my previous bosses would have done that."

"Uh-yeah," I said. "They were all assholes. Try and keep up. A little gratitude would be nice too."

Cindy jumped in my arms, wrapped her arms around my neck, and kissed me. "Thank you!"

"Off my husband." Mandy's voice was low and dangerous. Cindy jumped off me like I'd shocked her.

Taking one look at Big Ben's henchmen, or what was left of them, Sunlight said, "Thank you for your assistance. Perhaps you are not a complete disgrace to the Nightwalker name. Now, are you going to come along quietly, or do I have to thrash you?"

Diabloman glared at him. "Even I am beginning to wonder if it might not be a good idea to make an exception to the 'no killing heroes' rule."

"That won't be necessary, I hope." I really wanted to beat this guy up but I wanted to forestall an argument with my wife. "Sunny, show some gratitude for saving your ass! If not for my wife, you'd be Swiss cheese."

"Swiss cheese?" Cindy said.

"I'm still working on my supervillainous dialogue," I said, "it's supervillainously difficult."

"Please, stop using supervillain as an adjective," Mandy said.

"Why?"

Sunlight looked chagrined. His next words confused the hell out of me. "You're correct; I owe you a debt of honor. From this day forth, until the day I return the favor, I pledge to teach you the path of justice!"

I looked between my henchmen and Mandy. "Is he serious?"

"*I'm afraid so,*" Cloak said. "*Then again, he may be right. Sunlight has a surprisingly good skill at rehabilitating supervillains. Since recovering from his breakdown he's delivered sixteen back to the path of righteousness. That's not including all the various superheroes and delinquents he mentored.*"

"Never use the words path of righteousness in a non-ironic context again," I said to Cloak.

"Sunlight sounds about as serious as you do," Mandy said. "Which is pretty serious about some pretty ridiculous stuff."

"There's nothing ridiculous about supervillainy. In any case, Sunlight, what are you doing here?"

"I confess...I tend to let nostalgia color my actions. At times like this I forget it's not the Sixties. I do owe you my life, and I also know you rescued the Douglas girl last night. So when

I speak about rehabilitation, I'm quite serious. I also suspect I know more about you, Mister and Mrs. Karkofsky, than you know about yourselves." Sunlight removed his mask, looking serious.

"Wow," I said. "My secret identity didn't last long."

"It rarely does for supervillains," Diabloman said. "One of the hazards of frequent arrests."

"You know us?" Mandy asked.

"I do," Sunlight said, putting away his mask. "I've been watching you, along with other exceptional civilians of note, for a long time. It's part of the duties I do for the S.O.S as a retired superhero. It helps keep me sane, knowing I'm doing at least some small part to fight evil."

"This sounds ominous," Cindy said, checking her stolen loot. "Do you get your kicks off spying on Jewish couples?"

"Mandy's Wiccan," I corrected. "And about as gentile as they come."

Mandy clutched me tight, making a 'zip it' gesture with her fingers. "Let Sunlight finish."

"I heard about the death of the Nightwalker the day it happened," Sunlight said, sounding regretful. "He and I didn't always see eye-to-eye, but he was a great warrior against evil. Some days, I might have even called him friend. All of them I think,, I called him family. So, I came down here to guard his legacy. Falconcrest City was always a den of inequity and predators who made lives miserable for the common folk. However, the Nightwalker was a symbol that evil didn't always prosper. He was a torch in the night and it wasn't right for him to fall with no one to pick it up."

For a moment, a *very brief* moment, I regretted that I, instead of a superhero, was the one wearing the Reaper's Cloak. Still, if he was going to ask me to join the Boy Scouts, I wasn't biting. "Yeah, he was all sorts of awesome. Listen, Sunlight, I'm a supervillain. It wouldn't work out, you trying to teach me to be a good guy. So, if you don't mind, I'm going to help myself to your friend's secret headquarters and equipment. Show yourself out and we'll call it even."

"*Oh yes, that's going to convince him,*" Cloak muttered. "*Brilliant.*"

"Hush you," I snapped. "I'm trying to avoid setting the old guy on fire. I have a 'kill only one senior citizen a day' rule, at least as of today. Now, are you going to leave me alone or not?" There was no way I could continue to use the Nightwalker's base, not with the fact Big Ben's goons knew where it was and however many other people he'd sold it to, but I could take everything here to a secure location and repurpose it.

"I'm afraid I can't do that," Sunlight said. "All of this equipment belongs to the chosen heir to the Reaper's Cloak."

"What?" I asked, shocked out of my fantasy. "I didn't know there was a chosen heir."

"There isn't," Cloak said. *"I'd know."*

Sunlight nodded, heading over to the huge computer in the middle of the room. "According to the Night Computer, there was one person in the whole of Falconcrest City worthy of receiving the power of my mentor's mystical cape. By feeding all personal data about the citizenry into the computer, I was able to deduce an appropriate heir and send them a disguised set of packages. These packages would give them everything they'd need to know to begin their superheroic careers."

A cold chill ran up my spine as I realized where this was going. There was only one reason someone would drop a package containing the Nightwalker's cloak on Mandy and my front doorstep. "Oh, really?"

"Gary?" Mandy looked to me.

Sunlight started typing away at the keyboard before several flashing lights blinked. The whole thing looked more like a movie prop than an actual supercomputer, which tended to be on the small and unimpressive side if my trips to Washington D.C. were any indication. A second later, a small white card popped out of the machine's side.

"Behold!" Sunlight said. "The identity of the Reaper's Cloak's heir!"

"Yeah," I said, looking at my feet. I felt gut sick. "We already know who it is."

"We do?" Cindy asked.

"Mandy Summers Karkofsky!" Sunlight declared, holding the card up in the air.

"Oh, for Death's sake. You have got to be kidding me."

"Tell me about it!" I said.

Diabloman, who had been watching the entire discussion with a faint aura of amusement, burst out laughing. "By the Seven Lords of Nightmare, that's hilarious! The husband takes the wife's mantle! Brilliant!"

"Alright, it's time for you to leave," I gestured to Diabloman. "Get him out of here."

"Listen here—" Sunlight started to say.

"Out." Diabloman walked up to Sunlight and grabbed him by the back of his tights.

Dragging him to the elevator, as Sunlight struggled against the super-strong warrior, Diabloman summoned it and proceeded to toss the superhero at the moment the doors opened. Reaching in, Diabloman hit the button for the basement and I watched the doors close before Sunlight could get to his feet.

"Thanks, D." I felt a headache coming on.

"Gary?" Mandy asked.

I didn't respond. Instead, I headed to the center of the Night Tower and plopped down on the throne-like chair. Placing my elbows on the arm rest, I held my head and stared at my feet.

"God, I can't believe this. I ended up stealing my wife's destiny as a superhero," I said. "I am worse than scum. I am… something worse than scum."

"The scum of scum!" Cindy said, trying to help.

"Thank you," I said, sullen. "I am the scum of scum."

The initial shock of Sunlight's revelation, surreal as the circumstances of it may have been, had worn off. Now, the horrifying implications of what he was saying were sinking in. I'd stolen my wife's destiny as a hero.

All three of my companions looked unsure about what to say or do. Mandy, of course, was the one who approached me. "Gary, I—"

I looked up and into the eyes of my beautiful wife. "I think you would make a tremendous superhero."

Mandy looked down. "Thank you. I mean that."

My wife and I kissed, our lips pressing together for close to a minute. It was the best kiss we'd had since our honeymoon.

"Geez, guys, get a room," Cindy said.

"There is nothing more pleasing than two people in love united by the sanctity of marriage." Diabloman sniffed. "Well, except perhaps the sacrifice of an enemy to the Lords of Nightmare. Married love may still edge it out, however."

My henchmen, people. You gotta love'em.

"Cloak, is there any way to, I don't know…transfer my powers to my wife?" I thought towards my cape.

"You'd do that?"

"Yes," I said, waving to the side. "She's the most important thing in my life. Besides, I do think she'd be a better superhero than I could ever be a supervillain."

"I'm afraid the transformation is permanent. However, you're more…complex than other supervillains. You're not the **worst** *person the Reaper's Cloak could have fallen to."*

"I'll take that as a compliment, but it doesn't make me feel better."

"You have managed to acquire yourself a new headquarters and a significant amount of new equipment, Lord Merciless. May I ask what you intend to do now?" Diabloman said, curious.

I contemplated acquiring one of the Reaper's Cloaks for Mandy. "I have a few ideas."

Cindy, meanwhile, was playing with an aerosol can marked 'Memory Erasing Gas' as she stood over the body of the unconscious hood. "Yeah, we're still going to be bad guys, right?"

"Yes, yes we are," I said, smiling.

Mandy coughed. "Yeah, about that. Could we have a moment?"

Uh-oh.

Chapter Twelve

Where My Wife Reveals Her Dream

Mandy took me by the hand toward the back of the Clock Tower to a set of shelves devoted to the occult arts. It was out of hearing range for Cindy and Diabloman, which bothered me to no end.

What was it that she wanted to discuss they couldn't hear?

I hoped she didn't want me to turn on them.

I owed them too much.

"You really don't," Cloak said.

"Gary, how are you feeling?" Mandy asked.

I blinked. "Fine. Why?"

"You just killed people."

I stared at her. "That's really not bothering me."

Mandy looked at me. "It doesn't bother you, does it?" I couldn't tell if she was disappointed or not. Saddened, definitely, but I'm not sure if she was disappointed.

"They were bad," I said, saying it like it justified everything. "Really bad."

Mandy looked down. "I suppose they were."

I blinked. "They were?"

"They came here to murder us, Gary," Mandy said. "Have you ever read *The Ethics of Post-Humanism*?"

I had actually. "Yeah, it's that book by Ultragod where he spells out his artificial and nonsensical rules for being a superhero."

Mandy glared.

"Which I suspect you really ascribe to," I said, grimacing.

"Superhumans shouldn't execute criminals who fall into their hands," Mandy said, removing her hat and putting it on a shelf next to a skull with glowing eyes. "They also shouldn't casually kill those they could use their powers to safely apprehend. Life is precious, even that of criminals."

"Even," I muttered.

Mandy continued, "But exceptions can and should be made in the context of whether a subject is deliberately endangering the life or lives of innocents or in self-defense. There's also a wartime proviso. This is all spelled out in the Society of Superheroes charter, even though they go out of their way to save supervillain and enemy combatant lives whenever possible."

"Still too cop-like for my taste."

"Is that so bad?"

I thought of Shoot-Em-Up. "I am not the greatest fan of cops."

Mandy blinked. "I suppose you wouldn't be."

"What's this about?"

"I'm not going to lose any sleep over Big Ben's death or the man I killed," Mandy said, pausing. "Or, if I do, I shouldn't."

"That's the spirit," I said, half-heartedly. I had a feeling a shoe was about to drop.

"That doesn't mean Sunlight isn't right."

"Any sentence that involves Sunlight and right automatically gets my skepticism. Did you see that lunatic?"

Mandy nodded. "I saw a man trying to help. A man who believed I had the potential to help this city."

Aw crap. "Yeah, a destiny I stole from you. I'm sorry."

"Gary, you didn't steal anything," Mandy said. "Who leaves a powerful magical artifact and equipment on someone's front doorstep with no instructions?"

"*Those who believe in destiny,*" Cloak said, grumbling. "*He doesn't realize the cloak answers to Death and she has a sense of humor.*"

"Well you certainly don't," I muttered.

"What?" Mandy asked.

"Sorry, talking to the hoodie," I said. I then grimaced. Dammit, now I was doing it. "I mean hooded cloak."

Mandy grinned, her expression turning serious. "Gary, I'd like to be a superhero."

I blinked. "Could you repeat that?"

Mandy looked around the Clock Tower. "This place is full of devices with uncertain super-technological properties taken from supervillains, plus the Nightwalker's own equipment. That's not counting all the books on arcana and mystical bric-a-brac lying about. I'm a religious Wiccan, rather than the sorceress kind but I know the latter who could arrange for me to get training in it. Combined with my childhood training and a refresher course, I could defend this city."

I stared at her. "You want to be *the Nightwalker?*"

Mandy stared at me. "There's only one Nightwalker."

I opened my mouth to speak.

"I would be the torch in the night Sunlight spoke of. The one who burns away the darkness and pursues the criminals who afflict this land," Mandy said. "I would be the Nighthuntress."

"Nighthuntress?" I asked.

"What's wrong with Nighthuntress?" Mandy said, frowning.

I made a wavy gesture with my hand. "It's not really doing anything for me."

"Says Merciless of the Redundant Sobriquet."

"Hey, hey, let's not get nasty."

"*I like it,*" Cloak said.

I took a deep breath. "Are you really comfortable being married to an unredeemed supervillain?"

"Like we'd be the first superhero and supervillain in love." Mandy smirked.

She had me there.

I was surprised she continued, though. "I won't lie to you, Gary. I'm not as morally upstanding as this city perhaps needs. My father was a spy and he worked with criminals, murderers, terrorists, and worse in order to make sure worse didn't destroy civilization. The Ice Cream Man, Typewriter, and Big Ben deserved to die but they didn't emerge in a vacuum either. Supervillains arise because people need them, want them to exist, or can't stop them. Who do you intend to target when you start your career?"

I looked to one side and scratched the back of my neck, through the cloak. "I *may* have a list of about one hundred and thirty-two businessmen, politicians, and so on who need a swift kick in the ass as well as removal of worldly assets. Assets I intend to redistribute with a healthy collector's fee."

Mandy raised her eyebrows at the collector's fee. "I won't try and stop you. This city also needs its organized crime, if for no other reason than someone needs to negotiate a truce for the people the city turns to because the cops are worse than the mafia. You remember what they found outside the city limits in Savage Swamp."

I nodded. "You'd think the police would be better at their job if they were killing people who bugged them and dumping their bodies." And people wondered why only the rich called the police in this town.

"*Watkins is a good man,*" the Nightwalker said.

"*I'm not so sure,*" I said back, telepathically.

"You really need to work on thinking to yourself," Mandy said. "You realize once we both start to have success in our respective endeavors, neither the Society of Superheroes or the criminals of this town will understand."

"I'm not married to them."

"Nor am I married to the other heroes," Mandy said, taking my hands. "Then we'll go down together."

I shook my head. "We'll triumph, over the entire world if we have to. Falconcrest City is just the beginning. We're going to FIX this planet."

"I agree," Mandy said.

"*That's not an unsettling promise,*" Cloak muttered.

I raised a fist. "Soon, the world will tremble at the mere mention of the name MERCILESS: HUSBAND WITHOUT MERCY!"

Mandy raised a finger in the air. "And Nighthuntress: Huntress of the Night!"

I frowned. "Yours sounds cooler."

Mandy gave me another kiss. "Ultragoddess doesn't know what she's missing letting you slip away."

I blinked, confused. "What do you mean?"

Mandy stared at me. "Really, Gary? You *never* figured it out? The Black Witch found out her secret identity like six times. Ultragoddess just kept brainwashing it out of her. She never thought her girlfriend would know."

I stared at her, stunned. "You mean you know Ultragoddess' identity? *Who?*"

Mandy's mouth hung open.

"Yeah, who?" Cindy said, popping her head through one of the shelves.

Mandy jolted backward. "What the hell?!"

"Oh, sorry," Cindy said. "I was eavesdropping."

There were some days I really wanted to strangle Cindy. "You really shouldn't do that."

Mandy's face went through various emotions. "You're okay with me being a superhero?"

"Absolutely," Cindy said. "We need superheroes. If you're not there to punch Entropicus in the face, then he might destroy the world and then where would we live? Worse, without superheroes, we might have to do something about it."

I'd never thought about it that way. "You raise a good point."

"Anyway, I'm just glad to be a part of this group." Cindy smiled. "Gary is the best boss I've ever worked for."

"Surely, you exaggerate," I said.

"Gary, do you want sexual favors?" Cindy asked.

"No," I said, offended.

"See? BEST BOSS EVER."

"I am actually kind of horrified," I said, looking at her. "And worried."

"You do have a rather glamourized view of the superhuman underworld," Cloak said. *"But I think we all knew that."*

"It's only glamourized because I'm seeing how I'm going to be running it in five years," I said, smiling. "I've already got my whole plan for after the world's governments are torn down for socially free and economically prosperous communes. With blackjack, hookers of both sexes, and superpowers for all."

"I approve!" Cindy said.

"My husband, the King of Anarcho-Communist Vegas."

Mandy chuckled. "Well, as long as you don't shoot anyone in it just to watch them die."

"No promises." I then sighed. "Well, we should probably get back to the control room. It's not going to take long for Sunlight to climb back up the elevator shaft even if Diabloman has locked down the controls."

"I don't think he's going to bother us anymore," Mandy said. She looked over at the fallen Nightcar and the dead bodies underneath. "I think he's made his point. This town is suffering badly."

"When has it not been suffering badly?" Cindy shrugged, picking an occult tome off the shelf and flipping through it. She paused on some illustrations of a naked witch's Sabbath and turned the book to one side. "Hope is for people who live in other towns. I prefer money."

Mandy put her hand on Cindy's shoulder. "Help keep my husband safe."

"Sure," Cindy said. "Whatever you say."

I was interrupted from having to answer by the Night Computer starting to blare like it was a fire alarm. Mandy ran over to it and started working the controls.

"What's wrong?" I asked, jogging up behind her.

Mandy stared at the screen, which was an unrecognizable stream of ones and zeroes mixed in with little free-floating boxes containing all manner of events across the city. I was amazed at how quickly she'd adapted to using such an advanced piece of equipment.

My wife *was* magic.

"A group of bank robbers rose from the Falconcrest City morgue and ate the attendant. They're now robbing the First National Bank...again." Mandy scrunched up her nose as if she couldn't quite believe what she'd said.

"It begins. The dead are rising from the grave to take their revenge upon the living. Whoever has the other six cloaks is not using them correctly. Perhaps deliberately."

"I guess asking you about your history will have to wait," I said, sighing. "Okay guys, I'm going to go burn some zombies in honor of my should-have-been-a-superhero-wife. Then I'm going to rob the First National Bank… again!"

Both Cindy and Diabloman cheered, Mandy sighed.

Yeah, it was good to be a bad guy.

I had to keep telling myself that.

Chapter Thirteen

Where I Encounter My First Zombies

The Falconcrest City First National Bank had been having a bad two days. If it wasn't insane killer ice cream men, it was insane killer *zombie* ice cream men. The Ice Cream Man had returned from the grave and was now robbing the bank with the same five or six henchmen I'd fought earlier. I was watching them through the lobby glass doors, doing a bit of solo reconnaissance.

The Ice Cream Man was standing over the bodies of a couple of dead half-eaten employees with a huge mallet in his hands. Which offended me since that was out of his theme. Maybe if it was ice-cream-cone shaped, it'd be appropriate, but this was just wrong.

Having only been dead for a day, the Ice Cream Man didn't look too different. Well, except for the fact he was missing a number of teeth and half his head was caved in.

"I want everyone to know being dead hasn't changed my rosy attitude! Ha! I'm going to kill and eat you all! Then I'm going to find your children and eat them! Hehehe. If you don't find that funny, well, I guess you have to be dead to get it."

During this disturbing display, the Malt Shop Gang was once more attempting to empty out the vault. All of them had been transformed into zombies with parts of their heads or necks missing from where someone had bitten them. I presumed the Ice Cream Man was the party responsible, but, for all I knew, a host of zombies was running around Falconcrest City.

Still, according to Cloak, the bulk of Falconcrest City's

zombie problems were a few months away. It would take time for the other Reaper's Cloaks, once merged with hosts, to create an army of the dead. Right now, it was just the Ice Cream Man and his crew, and I was certain I could handle them.

Walking in through the front door, I addressed the crowd, "Hey, Cream Puff. We've got to stop meeting like this."

"Watch the revolving door. You don't want to get me caught in it."

"Good point," I said, pulling my cape close behind me.

"You!" the Ice Cream Man hissed at me, his voice lisping from where I'd knocked out his front teeth. "You killed me!"

"Yes, yes I did."

"Thanks!" The Ice Cream Man replied, swinging his mallet at me. "Allow me to return the favor."

"Sorry, Chuckles, not happening," I turned insubstantial to avoid the blow before conjuring a free-floating fiery 'M' behind me to signal my henchmen. "I suggest you duck now."

Diabloman drove a stolen armored car through the lobby entrance, shattering the glass windows and sending their fragments flying in every direction. The vehicle smashed into our foes, crushing the first two of the Ice Cream Man's thugs under its wheels. The other four were thrown up against the wall like rag dolls, much to the screaming horror of the hostages around them.

Cindy stepped out of the armored car's passenger's side, carrying a fire ax marked with the inscription, "How's My Hacking?" and a phone number underneath it.

"Wow, Boss, that was a great entrance!" Cindy said, chipper as always. "You timed it perfectly!"

"Thank you," I said, magically stepping through the armored car and picking up a pistol.

"Cloak, shooting a zombie in the head will kill it, right?" I asked.

"That or decapitation. I recommend you tell the police to cremate the bodies, however."

"Thanks," I said. "Headshots only, guys, please."

"Yeah, I know. I've seen a zombie movie before." Cindy proceeded to strike every downed zombiefied (Is that even a word?) member of the gang in the head with her fire ax while I searched for their leader. I caught sight of the Ice Cream Man's mallet but there was no sign of the psychopath himself. "Oh, you've got to be kidding me." I tossed aside my pistol. "How did he escape? He's not inconspicuous!"

"Out the door in all likelihood." Diabloman shrugged. "I was driving the car and Cindy dealing with his henchmen. You were doing your theatrics. It's nobody's fault. Take comfort in the fact you managed to get him to retreat."

I wasn't at all comforted. "God, he's going to become my archenemy, isn't he? Deranged childhood icons should be restricted to KISS albums, dammit."

"Do we go after him?" Cindy said, pulling her ax up from where she'd disposed of the last of the zombies.

"Nah, we have better things to do. Okay, Cindy, Diablo, let's start loading up the cash!"

"You're robbing us, again?" the same overweight woman from earlier asked.

"Yep," I said. "Try not to take this personally. Banking in Falconcrest City is about as hazardous as aid work in a war zone. You should think about finding a new job."

"Wise counsel. I suggest you follow it," Diabloman began picking up the cash on the ground. "What will you be doing during all of this?"

"Supervising!" I shouted before surveying the crowd. "Does anyone need medical attention? My henchmen drove an armored car through the front window and I don't want a murder rap on my police record. At least, not one for people who didn't have it coming. Do any of you have it coming?"

In unison, all of the bank employees and patrons shook their heads.

"Good. Now, back to the medical attention issue," I said, sighing. "Anybody hurt?"

"One of the zombies bit me!" One of the employees said, holding his neck.

Cindy lifted her fire ax over her head. "He's becoming one of them! We have to kill it now!"

"Hold on!" I raised a hand to stop her. "Uh, Cloak, is that true?"

"Only if they die from it."

"Okay, Zombie Victim Number Three, you can go. Someone take this guy to the hospital. In the meantime, I'm drafting..." I started picking out employees at random. "You, you, you, and you go help load the money on the back of the truck."

Oddly, the employees were quite willing to help out once the injured man was escorted away. I was about to comment on their 'service with a smile' policy when my cell phone rang, again.

Picking up my cell phone from my belt, I saw it was Mandy. Tapping my earpiece, I said, "Hello?"

I'd just barely managed to persuade Mandy to stay behind as support. Frankly, in retrospect, I wasn't sure that was the best decision. My wife could kick ass better than me. It was just I didn't want her tainted by my crimes when she was about to embark on a fantastic career of saving the world.

Or at least the city.

"You've stepped in it this time." Mandy grumbled.

"I love you too, Mandy. What's wrong?"

"The Night Computer is linked to all the police reports and news broadcasts in the city," Mandy explained. "This—"

"Impressive, most impressive," I interrupted. "How's that work?"

"I could try explaining it to you, Gary, but your computers skills suck. Now do you want my help or not?"

"All right," I decided she wouldn't have called me unless it was urgent. "What's wrong? I'm not afraid of the Falconcrest City police...at all. Besides, I think I have a deal with the Chief of Police. I take care of rival supervillains and he doesn't send me to jail."

At least, that was how I *thought* it was supposed to work.

"The Chief of Police was overruled by Mayor Jackson. He's called in superheroes to deal with you."

I was now far less confident. "Superheroes? Ones who aren't ancient?"

"Master Warren fought crime past the point he was a hundred." Cloak sounded offended.

"And we saw how that worked out for him," I replied, sniffing. "I plan to retire before I'm ninety like a rational person."

"The Mayor called in the Extreme," Mandy said the words like a Marine might say terrorists.

"Those aren't superheroes," I said, sick to my stomach. "They aren't superheroes at all."

"Antiheroes," Mandy said, using the universally accepted word for those superheroes who went off the reservation. Those heroes who decided killing, torture, and collateral damage were justified as long as they got a few pick-pockets or pot-dealers along the way.

The Extreme were the worst of the bunch.

Every Falconcrest City citizen over the age of twenty remembered their rampage through the city's underworld during the height of the Nineties. Everyone thought they were a better solution to the city's supervillains than Sunlight or the Nightwalker. Right up until they collapsed the Falconcrest City Bridge trying to deal with one of the Toy King's robots.

Forty-nine people had died.

The Extreme received probation and a revocation of their license to operate in the city limits.

A license that had apparently been restored.

"The police have cordoned off the area," Mandy said. "Try and get yourself out of there."

"I will," I said. "I love you."

I worried it might be the last time I ever said those words. Putting two fingers in my mouth, I whistled for my henchmen's attention.

"Diablo, Cindy," I said, pointing at the piles of money already loaded in the armored car. "Take as much cash as you can and try to lose yourself in the surrounding buildings. I'll distract them so you can get away."

Cindy looked confused. "What's wrong?"

"The Extreme."

"The Extreme?" Cindy's already pale skin turning almost white. "You're kidding."

"As much as we've all come to cherish my wonderful sense of humor as I rob and kill people, no I'm not kidding."

"Oh, thank God!" one of the bank patrons said. "The superheroes are here to save us!"

"Diabloman, break his leg."

"As you wish," Diabloman said, kicking the man in the kneecap so he went down screaming.

"Thank you," I said, sighing. "Hurting idiots helps me think."

"Just about every supervillain I've talked to paints these guys as the angels of death," Cindy said, clutching her fists together as she looked furtively around.

Diabloman agreed. "As the Dark Lord spoke when he saw the Archangel Michael descending upon him: *We are in some serious shit.*"

"No kidding. What we need to do is assemble what we know about these guys and use it to discover their weakness. Then we need to run the hell away and pay someone to exploit it."

"I fought them and barely survived," Diabloman grunted, crossing his arms. "Afterward, I did a great deal of research on them. The Extreme were part of the President's answer to the rising tide of supervillainy. They had special authority to execute supervillains on behalf of the government. The military armed them with specialized weapons and guns."

"Wait, superheroes who kill…and carry guns?" one of the bank tellers said. "That's just wrong!"

"I know!" I threw my hands out in disgust. "It violates the 'superhero catches villain, puts him in jail, villain breaks out, superhero catches him again' social contract. I swear they might as well be cops. In any case, these guys kill."

"Can superheroes *do* that?" Cindy asked, horrified.

"Antiheroes can," Diabloman said, "After the Great Crash of 97, the government disavowed all knowledge of the Extreme's activities and shut down the American super-soldier program. Its members were cut loose to act as mercenaries for cities and countries who could afford their services. The fact the Mayor has called them in means he's desperate."

"I heard they're reviving that," Mandy said in my earpiece.

"Even the government wouldn't be that stupid," I said.

Cloak made a noncommittal noise in my head.

The Mayor calling in the Extreme was flattering in a disproportionate response sort of way. After all, I'd only been a supervillain for twenty-four hours. The Ice Cream Man had terrorized the city for years. Of course, it also meant that these guys weren't going to be satisfied with driving us away from the bank. They were here for my head. I did, however, wonder why they were being called in against me rather than the hundreds of other supervillains in the city. Mandy had said they were here for me, specifically, which made no damned sense.

"Yeah," I said. "I've killed three and there's been no civilian casual...well, not counting all the people who died today and the bank president. Well, okay, the Ice Cream Man came back so it's technically two so...never mind. The point is the Extreme are bad guys!"

"*We're* bad guys." Cindy pointed out the hole in my logic.

"Bad*er* guys!" I corrected her. "Gun-toting lunatics! Now get your asses going so you can get away safely. I'll deal with these guys myself."

"Gary, I don't think you're getting the whole henchman-supervillain dynamic. I'm pretty sure you're not supposed to protect us but the other way around," Cindy said, a concerned look on her face. "Besides, I'd be very upset if you died. You're kind of screwy but I like you. I also like Mandy. We should make her your second-in-command."

"I'm *her* second in command." I grinned in spite of our situation. "It's why our marriage works."

"I will not abandon you," Diabloman said. "You are a man worthy of following. Sort of."

"Just go!" I shouted, hearing the grinding noise of tank treads rolling up. "You can repay me by giving me your shares of the loot."

"Like hell!" Cindy said, her demeanor changing in an instant.

"Let us focus on survival first and profit later," Diabloman said, grabbing her by the shoulder and dragging her off.

"*Do you have any idea how you're going to deal with this situation?*" Cloak asked.

"I don't know; I'm making this up as I go along."

Turning around to the gigantic hole in the bank's front entrance, I saw a monstrous tank-like vehicle that had pulled up sixty feet away. The thing had four different sets of treads made of three different sets of smaller treads, seemingly just for aesthetics' sake. Really, who sees a tank and says, 'this needs more treads?'

The vehicle was armored like a tank, possessing multiple laser emplacements and one gigantic central gun. It was about the size of a motor home, having ample room for a team of seven. Spray-painted along the vehicle's side were the words, "This Machine Kills Supervillains."

I bet Cindy felt unoriginal now.

A loudspeaker popped out of the vehicle's top before a harsh male voice said, "Merciless, by the authority invested in us by the Mayor of Falconcrest City, you are ordered to come out with your hands up. If you do not surrender within ten seconds, we will open fire and destroy you!"

I held up my hands and exited through the front door. "Okay, okay, no need to get huffy about it."

"I am surprised by your actions. You have a spark of nobility underneath your glory-seeking immaturity."

"Thank you." The beginnings of a plan formulated in my head.

"You're going to fake surrender and kill them when their guard is down, aren't you?"

"Yep," I said. "That's the plan."

"Of course." Cloak didn't even bother to sound disappointed this time.

"I surrender!" I shouted to the tank, lifting my hands up over my head. "I'm unarmed! I'm a poor innocent misguided youth in a costume. No superpowers whatsoever."

"Good," The voice on the loudspeaker said. "That makes things much easier."

The vehicle's central gun turned around and aimed at me. Taking a hint, I turned insubstantial. A huge cannon blast passed through me, hitting the bank instead. A shower of glass and flame washed over me.

As the sparks died down, I tried to fathom what had happened. "Cloak, did they kill everyone in the bank trying to get to me?"

"*Yes. Yes, they did.*"

"Including Cindy and Diabloman?" I bit my lip, feeling their loss. There was just a small chance they'd made it out alive.

"*Apparently.*"

"Fuck."

Chapter Fourteen

Where I Discover the Problem with Killing Superheroes

"You damned psychos!" I screamed at the Extreme's mobile headquarters. I had never been so mad in my entire life. Spitting and kicking the air, I screamed, "You're fucking cowards! Every last one of you!"

I didn't care too much about the people inside the bank, at least the bystanders. I wasn't going to go out of my way to mourn a bunch of people I didn't know. Diabloman and Cindy were a different story.

Diabloman almost certainly deserved it after all the stuff he'd done over the years—to people both innocent and otherwise—but he was my friend. Cindy meant a lot more to me. She'd been my first kiss, first sexual experience, and first henchwench. Sure, she was a sociopathic money-hound but who wasn't nowadays?

Either way, the Extreme was going to pay for what they'd done, every last one of them.

"Come on out and fight you bastards!" I shouted, expecting them to fire again from the safety of their tank.

Instead, a hatch on the top of the vehicle popped open and a trio of figures exited onto its roof, one by one. The first was a muscle-bound soldier with cybernetic arms and more guns than a Sylvester Stallone movie.

The second was an attractive but anorexic-looking woman wearing a bikini, a pair of swords on her back, and kinky boots. The third was either a robot or a man in a suit of armor, a Germanic iron cross emblazoned his chest.

"Huh," the woman said. "He's still alive."

The guy in the suit of armor said with a metallic voice, "That's easy enough to fix."

"Great, more comedians." I was infuriated by their attitude. The hulking cyborg pulled out a massive gun, twice as big as an AK-47, and aimed it at me. His voice was low and gruff, like you'd expect a mercenary's to be. "I guess this is going to be more interesting than I thought."

"Yeah. Cause murdering innocent people is oh so entertaining."

"Prepare to die scumbag," the man with the assault rifle said.

"Hold on!" I waved to him, pulling out my cell phone. "Assume I'm going to rat out my friends while I'm on the phone, which will give you more...people to kill, I guess. Before you kill me...that I'm hoping to avoid. Give me a second, though, so I can call them and give you someone to track down and kill." All the while, I was trying to buy time to think of a way to kill them.

"You might have rehearsed this better. Do you need any advice?"

"How can you be so callous?" I asked without a trace of self-awareness.

"A century of witnessing the worst crimes man has been capable of doing to one another," Cloak said. *"To be honest, though, I am behind any plan to deal with these people. Master Warren was against the taking of human life, but it may save lives here."*

"Thanks."

The Extreme, uniformly, looked confused by my actions.

"Do we shoot him?" the woman said.

The man in the armor shrugged. "I guess."

"Fire!" the cyborg cried, pointing.

I took that moment to turn insubstantial and zoom underneath the pavement, temporarily putting me out of harm's way. These tunnels were slightly larger than the earlier ones and contained a maintenance tunnel large enough to walk down underneath a large section of pipes and electrical wires.

Pulling out my cell phone and hitting the speed dial, I called Mandy. "Honey, are you there?"

"Gary, are you all right?" Mandy asked, her voice wavering. "I've redirected Arthur Warren's satellite to get a feed on the place. Goddess, did they destroy the bank?"

"Yes, yes they did, and for once, I'm not lying to cover up my mistakes."

"I see," Mandy said, her tone concerned but professional. "I've got Lancel Warren's complete files on the Extreme. They're a lot more detailed than Superpedia."

"Give me the info," I said, comforted by my wife's voice. "I don't have much time before they start blowing up the pavement. I don't suppose they have a secret vulnerability to water or something equally close by?"

"I'm afraid real life doesn't work like that," Mandy whispered. "I'll keep looking though."

"Tell me what you've got."

I thought about using my brief respite to run away. I didn't want to. The Extreme's actions made me so pissed off, I wanted to stay and make them pay. It wasn't a smart attitude to have, especially given how many people got killed every year because they couldn't put aside their personal feelings, but I couldn't help how I felt.

"The big one is Captain Disaster," Mandy explained, speaking twice as fast as normal. "The woman with the swords is Ninjess. The third one is Iron Cross. They're all that remains of the original team. It seems killing supervillains encourages the next ones to try harder."

"Killing all those people certainly increased my motivation." I said into the phone, looking at the surrounding pipes and sewer water. "Give me a short rundown on what I'm fighting here."

"I'll start with the woman. Ninjess is a genetically-modified super soldier with a pair of mystical blades that can shoot transdimensional energy across multiple spectrums of existence," Mandy explained. "She can endure about any amount of damage."

"Can you repeat that in English?" I asked. I could already see tracer rounds being shot through the pavement above me. The Extreme weren't wasting any time coming after me.

"She's tough and can hurt you. Be careful around those blades of hers," Mandy said. "Iron Cross is a genetically-modified super soldier with a suit of armor that can fly, shoot transdimensional energy across multiple spectrums of existence, and endure about any amount of damage."

"I'm starting to notice a theme. I take it Captain Disaster is a genetically-modified super soldier who can shoot whatchamajiggers across whozits while enduring any amount of damage?"

"No, but he's telekinetic," Mandy replied. "He can hurl objects weighing up to fifty tons at you."

Great, just what I needed, a guy who could throw trucks with his mind. "Do they have any weaknesses at all?"

"They're theatrical costumed heroes," Mandy said, making the biggest redundancy since my name. "They like to make a big impression for the news crews. It comes with the fact they're trying to prove they're heroes. If you go in all big and bad, you might be able to get them to posture and pose instead of shooting you."

That was interesting. "Drama Queens, huh? I can use that."

"Plus, they're normal humans aside from their equipment and modifications. You have to think past their defenses," Mandy explained, her voice urgent. "That doesn't mean they're not extremely dangerous."

"Don't worry." I heard energy blasts firing into the ground above my head. If I didn't move soon, the entire roof would collapse on top of me. "I've got a plan."

"*Oh no,*" Mandy and Cloak said simultaneously.

Levitating, I conjured a ball of flames in my hand as I floated a foot in the air before lowering my voice to an animal-like tone. "Extreme, I'm going to tear your throats out! You psycho-killer disgrace to superheroes everywhere will end up decorating my wall with your hides!"

"God, that's awful. You need to work on your monologues," Mandy spoke in my headpiece.

"I'm better at banter," I whispered. "They seem to be buying it, though."

"We're not the psychos here." Ninjess postured with a pair

of katana like she was posing for a magazine cover. "You are."

"How *the hell* do you figure that!"

"We're heroes," Ninjess said, unrepentant. "You're a supervillain."

I narrowed my eyes. "Maybe *I am* a supervillain. Maybe I *do* rob people. Maybe I break legs and kill anyone who gets in my way. Maybe...okay, I'm a bad example. However, *I didn't blow up a bank full of innocent people.* I'm not toting around an arsenal of guns like its NRA Appreciation Day. I'm not the guy with a freaking Nazi in his group. A freaking Nazi! That trumps everything!"

The guy in the metal armor said, "I'm not a Nazi. I'm a member of Fascists for a Non-Racist Future."

"Shut up!" I pointed at him, staring. "I feel stupider for having heard that."

I noticed it was suddenly very dark. Turning intangible, I managed to avoid having a car telekinetically dropped on my head by Captain Disaster.

Levitating onto its roof, I stared at him. "Okay, that was just dirty pool."

Captain Disaster pointed at me. "Extreme, blast him!"

Wow, I was dealing with a military mind equal to Patton. Of course, I still jumped to the side when Iron Cross and Ninjess aimed their weapons at me. Seconds later, the hood of the car detonated as weird green energy reduced it to little more than charred embers. Even intangible, I could feel the heat brushing against my skin.

"Are they handing out those transdimensional thingies like candy, now?" I said.

"It's a common enough modification for a super weapon." Cloak sounded bored. *"You'd be surprised."*

"Dammit!" I dodged around as the Extreme members continued firing at me. I threw a few fireballs at them, but the flame harmlessly splattered against both. Ninjess' skin was apparently invulnerable to flames, since it sure as hell wasn't her clothing protecting her.

"Run all you like, supervillain!" Captain Disaster shouted,

firing his assault rifle for the hell of it. "The Extreme will go to any extreme to get their man!"

"God, that's even more redundant than my slogan," I grumbled before leaping down into the sewer system below them. "Cloak, how much juice do I have left?"

"*Juice?*"

"Mojo! Energy! Whatever fuels my powers!" I snapped, waving my hands around. "I need to know how much more time I have before my powers give out."

"*Oh. Thirty seconds.*"

"Goddammit."

"*Twenty-eight.*"

The Extreme didn't give me any time to think as they started blasting through the sewers to get at me. They were persistent, I'll give them that.

"Time to get creative," I whispered.

Levitating behind Captain Disaster, I grabbed the cyborg underneath the shoulders and continued into the sky. The guy weighed over three hundred pounds with his cybernetic enhancements, so I had to focus everything on thinking 'up.'

Captain Disaster laughed at me. "Do you think you can just lift me up into the sky and drop me? I'm telekinetic, you idiot."

"No," I growled, sticking my intangible hand through his chest. My hand was holding my car keys. "I only wanted some alone time."

I was originally going to remove his heart like in a video game but decided they didn't deserve such a dignified end. Sticking my keys in his heart, I pulled out my hand and let the keys materialize inside said organ. "Oops, lost my keys."

"*How are they even supposed to get that?*" Cloak asked.

I blinked. "Okay, but he's still dead."

Captain Disaster had but a moment to react before he choked on his own blood and died.

"*That was vicious. I'm not sure whether to be appalled or impressed.*"

"Pay evil unto evil." I smiled "That's my motto. That and

'Goth girls are the best.' I came up with that one after meeting Mandy."

I didn't have time to say more because Iron Cross was in the air beside me within seconds.

"Murderer!" Iron Cross screamed, his armor making him sound like he was talking into a microphone.

"That's only literally true!"

The Not-Neo-Nazi proceeded to blast me in the face with his transdimensional whatever blasts, which felt like being hit with an industrial-strength taser. I wasn't killed, thankfully, but my body went into convulsions.

Falling from the sky, I struggled to regain control of my powers as I managed to turn intangible once more, landing with a thud against the interior floor of the Extreme's armored vehicle. The place was filled with all manner of weird high-tech controls and a bizarre 1950s-esque living room with a flat screen on the wall.

"I'm not dead," I said, looking at my raw, burned hands.

"*Obviously*," Cloak said. "*You do have limited invulnerability. Albeit, a few degrees higher and it wouldn't have helped you much. I'm better at absorbing energy than ballistics.*"

"Gee thanks Mister Wizard," I said. "How much juice do I have left?"

"*Ten seconds.*"

"Shit."

In the center of the room I noticed there was a periscope-like device with a pair of triggers built into its handles. Assuming it was the control for the vehicle's main gun; I ran up to it and stared through it. There, I saw Iron Cross blasting away at the exterior of the vehicle. The Not-Neo-Nazi was looking very irritated at my escape, continuing to fire despite the fact I couldn't even hear his blasts inside the transport's thick armor. Taking aim with the periscope's crosshairs, I pulled down on both triggers. A second later, Iron Cross disappeared in an explosion of flame and metal.

"Two extremists down, one to go."

"*Have you considered a less violent career?*"

"Why would I? It's not the job I mind, it's the working conditions."

That was when Ninjess slashed through the side of the vehicle with her katana, the side of it peeling open like a can opener. In seconds, she'd cut open a pyramid-shaped hole large enough for her to walk through.

"I'm going to kill you," Ninjess called at me, tears streaming down her eyes. "Kill you and everyone you've ever loved!"

"Meep."

"*You were saying?*"

I made a run for the wall, hoping to pass through it. A second later, I was on the ground after smashing my head against the wall.

"*Oh, I'm out of power now. Sorry.*"

"I noticed!"

The bikini-clad assassin advanced upon me, drawing her second sword as both started glowing with other dimensional energy. Yesterday, if you'd told me I was going to die at the hands of a crazed ninja supermodel, I would have told you there were worse ways to go. Now, experiencing it? I thought it was something to avoid.

"Mandy, I want you to know I love you," I breathed into the machine. "You were the best thing to ever happen to me and I'm sorry I got wrapped in all of this. It's been a blast."

"Gary..." Mandy's voice whispered.

I closed my eyes, waiting to be impaled by the psychopathic superheroine. A second later, I heard a body hitting the floor. Opening one eye, I saw Cindy standing over Ninjess's body with her ax buried between the cyborg's shoulder blades. Cindy was covered in soot but looked none the worse for wear from being blown up. Somehow, she'd managed to hit a spot that wasn't reinforced by subdermal armor.

"You...bitch," Ninjess said on the ground, trying to get back up.

"Language! Kids look up to superheroes!" Cindy clobbered her again, and again, displaying a level of cartoon violence I would have found funny if not for my relief at her arrival.

"Hey!" I told Mandy. "Good news! I'm not dead."

"I heard!" Mandy said, relieved. "Thank God. Listen, Gary, I need to talk to you about this whole supervillain thing. It's not..."

The cellphone cut out, the sound of static interrupting her. Picking up the cellphone, I tapped it a few times. "I need to get some better cellphone service. Cindy, it's wonderful you're alive." Cindy leaned on the handle of the ax, grinning. "Turns out your whole spiel about leaving the bank was a good idea."

"Yeah. Those poor people. I'm going to catch such hell for this with the police."

"All that money, gone." Cindy sniffled. "Such a senseless waste."

Smiling at Cindy's priorities, I asked, "Is Diabloman all right?"

Diabloman popped his head through the hole Ninjess made. "Yes, for the time being at least. While I am grateful for your sacrifice, you broke the first rule of supervillainy."

"Yeah. Don't kill superheroes." I stared down at Ninjess' cold body. "I didn't have much of a choice, though."

"That will not matter to the Society of Superheroes," Diabloman said. "They depend on government support that means anti-heroes like the Extreme are accepted as auxiliary members due to political contacts."

"How bad is it?" I said. "The Extreme weren't exemplars of their kind."

"Bad enough. Not all agree with Ultragod's strictures against in-field executions and prohibition against collateral damage either."

"Great."

"I suggest you go to ground," Diabloman said. "It will make less of a splash than the entire team being wiped out."

I leaned down and picked up Ninjess' arm, checking her pulse. She was gone. While I leaned down, I saw the ax had buried itself into a group of live electrical wires in her spine, explaining why the attack had killed her. "I wouldn't count on it."

Cindy hefted up her fire ax, looking pleased with herself. "I think I've graduated from being a henchperson. I think I'd like to be known as Red Riding Hood."

Diabloman felt his head. "All three are dead? This is not good."

I walked out of the hole and threw up my hands. "Okay, I'll head back to the Night Tower and get some equipment together. We'll change our identities and start over as supervillains of a different stripe. Hopefully, everyone will lose interest in about a month. What's the worst they could do? Send Ultragod after me?"

That was when I heard a clap of thunder and saw the entire sky had clouded over, lightning bouncing around across the air as if it were caught in one of Nikola Tesla's science experiments.

Descending from the sky was an Olympian-proportioned African American man in a skin-tight white and gold outfit with a similarly colored golden cape flowing behind him. Otherworldly electricity moved through and around his body, circling his eyes especially. Unlike most superheroes, he wore no crests or symbols, but everyone in the world knew who he was.

"Ultragod," I said, awed. "The Lord of Light."

Ultragod was the greatest superhero on Earth. He was the leader of the Society of Superheroes. An inspiration for billions of people who had defeated gods, demigods, monsters, and dictators in the name of justice.

Eighty years ago, an African American astronomer had stumbled upon a glowing meteorite during his studies and found out it contained the spirit of an alien god called the Ultra. Bonding with that entity, he'd gained unimaginable power to manipulate the cosmic energies of the universe that permeated everything. The rechristened Ultragod had an aura of energy called the Ultraforce that could protect him from virtually anything and be manipulated to create any object he wanted. All of this was common knowledge, as was the fact those supervillains who went up against him lost.

Every single time.

I was *fucked*.

"Merciless: The Supervillain without Mercy," he said with a deep fatherly Keith David-esque voice. "We need to talk."

"Wow, you know my name and catchphrase," I said, starstruck. "That's flattering...and terrifying."

Cindy pointed at me. "It was all his idea!"

I would have glared at her but a second later, Ultragod had me by the scruff of my cape. The two of us took off, flying up high into the sky.

Dammit.

Chapter Fifteen

Meeting the Society of Superheroes

Falconcrest City grew smaller and smaller as Ultragod and I soared higher into the air.

"I think there's a lesson to be learned here," Cloak said. "Perhaps, 'do not tempt fate' or the simpler 'do not be a supervillain'?"

"Cloak, shut up," I snapped. "I need to think. If comics have taught me anything, there's a contrived way for the supervillain to escape custody."

"You should listen to your friend," Ultragod said in a strong fatherly voice. "It strikes me you could have avoided a lot of the trouble you were in with an ounce of foresight."

"Yeah, well," I said, pausing. "Wait, you can hear him?"

"Yes," the legendary superhero said. "With my Ultrahearing I can hear everything said on the planet at will. I see everything with my Ultravision. They're a secondary mutation from my ability to manipulate the Ultraforce."

"Do you refer to all of your superpowers with the word Ultra in front of what they do?" I asked, wondering if that was for trademark purposes or what.

"Yes," Ultragod said, without irony. "What else would you call them?"

He had a point. "Fair enough."

"I confess a little more originality by the newspapers would have been nice. I was stuck with the name once they assigned it. Do you want me to tell your wife about your situation?"

"That'd be nice, thank you." I did a double take. "Wait, you know about my wife too?"

"I know everything there is to know about you," Ultragod said, sounding paternal instead of creepy. "I started investigating Falconcrest City when I heard about Nightwalker's death. It was my hope his cloaks would fall into the hands of citizens desiring to be superheroes."

"Sorry to disappoint you." I was saddened by the situation myself. The thought of Mandy fighting alongside Ultragod and the rest of the SOS made my career choice feel hollow.

"Call me Moses," Ultragod said. "Please."

Ultragod reminded me a lot of Gabrielle's father in a way I couldn't quite put into words. Mostly in the fact they looked exactly alike and shared the same name. Yet, for some reason, my mind couldn't make any connection between those facts. Instead, for whatever reason, I just put it down to coincidence.

"Of *course* the world's greatest superhero is named Moses," I muttered, watching the Earth disappear beneath our feet. "How much trouble am I in?"

"Quite a bit. I know you killed the Extreme in self-defense, but other heroes won't see it that way. There's also the matter of the numerous other crimes you've committed."

"Wow, that's not good." I was still trying to wrap my head around the fact he knew everything. "Hold on, Moses, if you knew this entire time why didn't you...I don't know...*stop me* earlier?"

"I can't be everywhere at once. I was stopping a flood in Madagascar until about an hour ago. I am going to be serving as a witness in your trial, however."

"Great, you might as well find me guilty now." I tried not to look down. "No one in the world is going to take my word over the world's most beloved energy manipulator."

"Well, you *are* guilty." Ultragod chuckled.

"Touché," I replied, thinking about my chances. This was a bad, bad situation. I hadn't expected to be caught *quite* so early in my career. "I need to call my lawyer too or well...get a lawyer."

"We'll see you receive proper representation."

"We?"

"The Society of Superheroes," Ultragod answered, generating a giant Ultraforce hand to move a cloud out of the way. "According to the United States Superhuman Act, supervillains capable of killing superheroes can be tried by legally recognized superheroes on the moon."

I needed a second to process that. "Hold on, Super Duper Guy, we're going to *the moon?!*"

"Yes," Ultragod said, before reassuring me, "but don't worry, the S.O.S doesn't believe in torture. You'll just be incarcerated until your sentence is up."

"In *space?*" I choked out.

"We're all in space," Ultragod replied, a broad smile on his face. "Humans travel on Starship Earth."

"Why thank you, Super Hippie. I can't breathe in space, you know!" Panic overwhelmed any sense of wonder I might feel at my impending space travel. If I didn't die of asphyxiation, I was going to be judged by a superhero star chamber.

"I've extended my Ultrafield around you," Ultragod replied, looking down. "You should be able to draw all your necessary physiological requirements from it until we reach New Avalon."

"New Avalon, huh? Catchy title."

"It's the name for our headquarters. We figured the place to imprison supervillains should be far away from populated areas and surrounded by a thousand or so superheroes."

"A thous..." I started to speak before trailing off. "Well, there goes any chance of an easy escape."

"That's sort of the point, Gary."

"Merciless, please."

As Ultragod picked up speed, I saw we had already passed through the upper atmosphere and we were now overlooking planet Earth. It was a majestic sight; one reserved for astronauts, superheroes, and supervillains incarcerated on the moon. For a moment, I forgot all my troubles and took a moment to appreciate Mother Earth.

"I understand why so many supervillains want to conquer the planet now," I said, despite the lack of oxygen in space. "I must have it."

"Everyone has to have their dreams, I suppose. I don't think you're going to be able to do it, though."

"Why?"

"Remember, you're going to be incarcerated for the rest of your life."

"Oh right. Way to spoil my mood, Cloak."

"Sorry."

Minutes later, the moon came into view. Once we were a few miles away from the rocky barren surface of the satellite, I caught a glimpse of New Avalon. It was the size of a small city underneath a clear environmental dome.

The interior looked like something out of Flash Gordon with big, beautiful, spiraling towers and vast gardens filled with plant life from across the cosmos. I guessed there had to be at least ten thousand or more inhabitants in the small city.

"Wow."

"Home, sweet home. A monument to humankind's capacity for engineering and the benefits superheroes have brought to the world. I helped design this place with Nightwalker. It incorporates elements of Fairy, Mu, and Venusian technology."

"Venus is inhabited?"

"Oh yes, pleasant bunch. They're all red and have six-arms," Ultragod said, flying up to the side of the dome and knocking.

A tiny wormhole appeared and the two of us flew in. We emerged in a tranquil rainforest-like park in the middle of the city, the wormhole sealed up behind us. I didn't know much about physics, but it staggered me—the kind of technological effort that must have gone into creating a wormhole generator as opposed to installing an airlock.

"Cloak, how many laws of physics did we just break?" I asked, stunned by what had just happened.

"You can't break the laws of physics. Whenever you seem to violate one, it only means your understanding of them is incomplete. To answer your question, though, three hundred and forty-seven."

"I thought so." I was amazed at the power on display. It made everything I could do look like cheap tricks.

"It's not the level of your power but what you do with it."

"Keep telling yourself that," I said, staring at New Avalon in wonder.

Ultragod flew up the largest building in the city, a palatial-like structure resembling the Taj Mahal crossed with the Jedi

Temple. Around it was a beautiful park, almost Eden-like in its beauty. Once we were above a nice soft cushion of grass, Ultragod dropped me and the energy cage I was in popped like a soap bubble.

There, I saw many of the world's greatest heroes lounging around. There was Ink Splotch, the Prismatic Commando, Frankenstein's Monster, the Trenchcoat Magician, Succubus, the Silver Lightning, and more.

Now I was going to get the chance to outwit them all.

"You realize I'm going to try and escape."

"I understand you'll try." Ultragod hovered a foot above the ground. "Your kind never learns."

"Hey-hey," I said, pointing at him. "Can the racism."

Ultragod looked down at me. He raised an eyebrow.

"Sorry." I stared down at the floor. "That was funnier in my head."

"Gary..." Ultragod said, his voice pitying, "you're not like most of the criminals I've put away. You haven't been ruined by the lifestyle yet. Is there *anything* you can tell me that might mitigate your sentence? I know...people...who would be greatly upset to find out about your incarceration."

I found that to be a strange comment. "Even if I knew anything, I wouldn't rat out my friends. Honor amongst thieves and all."

"I've never encountered that. I think you'll find it's an extremely rare quality."

I'm sorry to say I didn't possess that quality either. If it meant being reunited with Mandy, I'd sell out everyone. Even Diabloman and Cindy, despite the fact they were my friends. I wasn't going to betray them, though, unless it was a last resort. "I'm sorry, that's my answer and I'm sticking to it."

"Oh, for the God's sake."

Then the   superheroes Robin Hood and Maid Marian walked by. "I will never understand people who use bows as weapons. It's the 21st century, people."

"Your attention span remains as consistent as always," Cloak said. *"I hope you know what you're doing."*

"Not a clue."

Ultragod's wristwatch, a thing straight out of the Fortieth century, started blinking. "Excuse me; I'm needed on the planet Rigel in the Orion Cluster. Pyronnus the Galaxy Destroyer is at it again. Guinevere will escort you to your trial."

"Wait, what? My trial is happening *now*?" I asked, watching Ultragod zoom away through a portal he conjured.

I was about to say more when Guinevere walked in. Dressed in a decorative suit of armor with a white-tabard, she had white-blonde hair which she kept up in a ponytail that stretched down to her neck. Her ears were elongated and pointed and her eyes the shape of almonds. Guinevere's face was thin and angular with racial features of the entire spectrum of the globe contrasted with golden brown skin. Despite the fact she wasn't my type, there was something about her that made me think she was the most beautiful woman on Earth.

Well, except for my wife.

Guinevere was a literal fairy princess, a descendant of King Arthur and Morgana Le Fey who'd grown up in the Otherworld. Aside from her ability to spellbind both sexes, she was one of the greatest warriors who ever lived. A lot of people shipped her with Ultragod, though Mandy held out hope she played for the other team.

Which I found annoying.

Also, hot.

"Hello, Merciless," Guinevere said, her voice was like crushed silk and made me feel weak in the knees.

"Duhhh…" I fumbled for something to say, my mouth hanging open.

She gave me a light slap on the cheek, snapping me out of it. "Merciless?"

I jolted like I'd been shocked. "I'm awake now."

Guinevere, who now looked like a gorgeous Anglo-Saxon woman with long blond hair and pointed ears, looked at me intently. "That's impressive. Very few people can break my glamour so easily. You must be either strong-willed or in love."

"Can I be both?"

"No," Guinevere said. "It's one or the other. True love requires one's heart to be flexible."

"Then I'm in love."

Wow, she was gorgeous. I looked away, feeling guilty.

"An admirable choice. However, it's not going to help you very much. The evidence against you has been gathered and it's pretty damning."

"What am I accused of?" I asked. "Exactly?"

Guinevere gestured for me to walk forward. "Multiple counts of arson, murder, robbery, and conspiracy to take over the world."

"I dispute the last one. I *just* decided to do that."

"*Gary...*"

"What? I might as well be honest. They have telepathy and goodness knows how many other methods of extracting the truth. A fair trial would screw me, so I want an unfair one."

"I'm afraid we're all out of unfair trials." Guinevere smiled, filling me with a sense of warmth and self-respect. "You'll be judged by a panel of seven superheroes selected on the basis of moral fiber and sound judgment."

"So much for a jury of my peers, huh?" I was offended. "Can't I get a bunch of supervillains to judge my innocence or guilt? Preferably ones I haven't killed? Cause, they seem to be coming back."

"I'm sorry, Mister Karkofsky, but no," Guinevere replied, shaking her head. Her voice was like a vocal brownie, making me feel warm and relaxed.

"Figures." I asked Cloak, "*Are you recharged yet?*"

"*Yes.*"

"Good," I muttered. "Sorry, Gwen, I need to make my escape."

I tipped my head and made a break for it, running for a nearby wall. Once more, I slammed headfirst into it and landed on the ground.

"Cloak, does God hate me?" I said.

"*It depends which god you mean. I've met several.*"

"The Jewish one."

"*Yes.*"

Guinevere put her hand on the receiver. "Queen Isis put an enchantment on New Avalon. As a result, no one but a member of the Society of Superheroes can use their magic here."

"Great," I muttered, getting up. "No wonder you guys are so calm around me."

"I'm sorry but this means we have to add attempting to escape to the charges against you." Guinevere shook her head. "Let us get you sentenced."

"You mean, judged, right?" I asked, feeling weak.

"Sure. If you like."

Chapter Sixteen

Where I Get the Book Thrown at Me

Well, I couldn't argue with the quality of the trial itself. An hour after it began, I was acquitted for every murder except the Typewriter and one of the Ice Cream Man's henchmen. It was the breaking of the guy's leg at the bank that got me worst; they considered that *malicious and unwarranted*. I argued it was warranted because the guy was a smartass.

That didn't win me any points with the judges.

Those crimes, combined with the two robberies I'd committed, meant I was sentenced to a 'relatively light' hundred and forty-three years of imprisonment. I was up for parole in thirty-three years. I was being escorted through the Minor Supervillains Wing, which contained several people I recognized. There was Amplitude, Mister and Mrs. Chillingsworth, Dreadmaster, Psychoslinger, and even the Black Witch. I said hello to the last one.

She brushed me off.

"How long is everyone here for?" I asked.

"Life. Each supervillain here has accumulated enough to sentence them to spend the rest of their existence behind bars. The Society of Superheroes decided to step in when it was clear regular prisons weren't equipped to handle supervillains. It's our hope to correct the whole revolving door of incarceration. Unfortunately, it was too late to serve as a deterrent."

"Moon justice is harsh."

I had to say, the prison level was different than I expected. Unlike the dark and dreary prisons of Falconcrest City, New

Avalon's prison was bright and well-lit. Most of the rooms were filled with furniture and amenities.

The Society of Superheroes didn't seem to be *punishing* their prisoners; they just seemed to be locking them away from the rest of society. It was like Guantanamo Bay crossed with *Good Housekeeping*. That didn't change my desire to leave. The thought of being separated from Mandy for the rest of my life was terrifying. I'd been in the Society of Superheroes' custody for just a few hours, but I was ready to do anything to get out.

"Really, I think the trial went well." Guinevere's good cheer was starting to irritate me.

"I think it could have gone better. You could have *shot* me."

"Oh, you're just upset you were found guilty."

"You *think?*"

Guinevere gave me a reassuring pat on the shoulder. "You've been a good sport, Merciless. Maybe we can find some way to shave off time from your sentence. You could start by making ice cream for kids or lighting campfires for the Boy Scouts."

"Or killing supervillains. I was good at that."

"Unlikely," Guinevere said, treating my suggestion as a serious one. "We prefer our inmates not get involved in violent professions. The Society of Superheroes doesn't believe in the death penalty. Permanent incarceration is much more humane."

"I don't suppose I could persuade you I've turned over a new leaf?" I gave a fake smile. "I'll spend the rest of my life fighting crime instead of committing it. I swear on my mother's grave."

"Your mother is alive."

"That's the point!" I said back to him.

Guinevere stared into my eyes, her dazzling beauty once more mesmerizing me. "Would your reformation be the truth?"

I started to drool again, speaking in a dull voice, "No, I'm telling you this because I want to get out. My mother is also alive. She is deeply ashamed of the fact I didn't amount to anything."

Guinevere lightly slapped me across the face again.

"Dammit!" I said, snapping out of it. "Stop doing that!"

Guinevere shrugged. "You're not the first villain to try that, Merciless. In any case, I think you'll like your living conditions. We've run out of space in the Minor Supervillains Ward so we're putting you in the Archvillains Wing. The quarters are much larger there."

"The Archvillains Wing?" I wasn't sure I'd heard that right.

"General Venom, Mister Chaos, Professor Skeleton, the Red King, Soviet Ape, Tom Terror," Guinevere said. "The big world-destroying evils."

While flattering, this unnerved me. I was being lumped with them. "Could you do me a favor and make sure my wife visits me in a place other than the ones surrounded by the world's worst psychopaths?"

A few of them weren't *too* bad but most were less 'rob banks' and more 'conquer the world.' Never mind the hypocrisy of my earlier vow to do so.

"Visits? What an interesting idea. We'll have to implement it."

"We have to get out of here."

"No kidding! I always thought visiting the moon would be cool. This, this is horrible."

"No, that's not what I mean."

"They're so…friendly while they're tramping over my rights," I thought at Cloak, *"I bet they drink nothing but milk while they debate how to reform people via brain surgery. Doc Savage used to do that in the old pulp magazines. It freaked me out when I read about it."*

"Master, if you don't use your powers for a week or more the dead will start to rise en masse. We've already got enough of a problem with those missing six cloaks. Master Warren went to elaborate lengths to get them from the Brotherhood of Infamy. Who knows who has them now?"

"Oh right." I remembered Cloak's warning. "Speaking of zombies—"

"We weren't."

The two of us arrived at a massive vault door marked, "A-Wing."

The door was made of reinforced steel and looked like it could resist a nuclear blast while a pair of guards in futuristic armor stood watch. They had laser guns in place of regular firearms, possibly because we were in space.

Clearing my throat, I said, "Gwen, if I don't use my powers on a regular basis the dead will rise to devour the living. There's also a bunch of cloaks the Nightwalker owned that need to be found, too. If not, it'll be like me not using my powers times seven. So, it would be a *very* good idea to release me. That way, I can go take care of it. It's for the greater good."

"*Smooth.*"

"Thank you."

"*I was being sarcastic.*"

Guinevere looked at me with pity in her eyes. "That's a nice story, Merciless, but you already tried persuading me to release you."

"No, wait, I—" I started to argue before the big vault door opened and the guards grabbed me by the arms, dragging me away. Seconds later, I was behind a translucent steel cell door.

"This could be a problem." I looked at my cell. It was a fair reproduction of my living room (which was just creepy). "I'm not sure which disturbs me more, the lengths they went to make me comfortable or the surveillance they had to put me under in order to do it."

"*They never would have done this before my death. I always believed superheroes should avoid getting involved in the legal process. It effectively restores feudalism.*"

"Yeah. An inquisition run by the Brady Bunch with eyebeams. I need to get back to Falconcrest City. This isn't my genre. It's way too science-fiction meets four-color comic book. I'm more of a gritty urban supernatural detective guy."

"*Bizarre as it may sound, I concur.*"

"Once I get back, I will never ever kill a superhero again. I'll restrict myself to bloodless crimes, unless I'm fighting communists, Nazis, rapists, or people who rub me the wrong way."

"*Have you learned nothing from this experience?*"

"I learned not to get caught."

"Ahem," I heard a voice coming from across the hall. "Hello, neighbor."

Looking up, I saw a middle-aged man in the cell next door.

He was bald, had a goatee, and was wearing tinted goggles from the 1940s. Completing the look was his outfit, which looked like a militarized version of a white laboratory coat. He couldn't have been more villainous-looking if he tried. Then I recognized him. My breath caught in my throat as I realized I was standing five feet away from Tom Terror, World's Greatest Criminal Mind.

"Wow," I said, staring. "Sir..."

I felt a mixture of admiration and fear. On one hand, you had to give kudos to the man who fought Ultragod on a regular basis with no powers—for eighty years. He looked good for his age, too. On the other, he was also the guy who blew up the Afghanistan-Pakistan border for shits and giggles.

"If I may debase myself to common correctional facility vernacular, may I inquire as to why you have found yourself in the deplorable state of incarceration?" Tom Terror asked.

"He said..."

"I understood what he said, Cloak." I rolled my eyes. "I'm here for killing the Extreme."

It was half-true, anyway. I never would have been arrested if not for them.

"Ah." Tom Terror smiled a mouth full of shark-like teeth. "A more troublesome gang of ruffians and thugs has never existed in the so-called superhero world. Your Darwinian elimination of them from the gene pool has gone a long way to correcting the imbalance of power and violence which exists between our captors and myself."

"Excuse me?"

"I said, good job."

"Thanks. I guess."

Tom adjusted his purple tie, dropping his disturbing smile. "Tell me, fellow victim of the exploitative superhero penal system, do you have any abilities above and beyond those of normal men?"

"Yes. However, they're being blocked by magic."

"Ah, so your powers rely on strange dimensional energy invoked by either incantations or application of will," Tom said, smiling. He certainly liked to hear himself talk.

"Yeah, my cloak is magic."

"Your lack of supernatural abilities can be rectified." Tom tapped the translucent steel of his cell door with his cane. "If I were to, say, offer you a chance to do such a thing, would you be willing to assist me in a large-scale relocation of the prison's population?"

"Tom—" I started to say.

"Thomas or Professor, please," the mad scientist interrupted. "Though please do *not* call me Professor. I know it's accurate, but I had to execute a dozen newspaper reporters before they stopped printing my name that way. I still haven't gotten them to stop shortening my name to Tom. Do they call him Tom Jefferson? Do they call him Tom Payne? I think not."

Wow, I was dealing with a real nutcase for formality.

"You know, you can say breakout if you want. It's not going to lower your IQ if you do. Also, there's nothing wrong with Tom or Professor Terror." I looked at him incredulously, putting my hands behind my back. "Mark Twain saw nothing wrong with the former and Professor Terror has a nice old school villainy feel."

"Don't lecture me on old school villainy, boy. I *invented* most of the tropes that come with it." Tom clasped his hands together, grinning. "As for the rest, well, the debasing of the English language is something I've made it a point to correct. When I take over the world, every child will be forced to speak properly. Television will be outlawed. Except for the educational channels, of course."

"I'll be sure to get all my favorite shows downloaded by then."

"I am asking if you want to assist in my breakout. I know most of the archvillains here, but I'm not familiar with you," Tom Terror said.

"Have you performed any other feats of criminal activity of which I might have heard?"

"I'm the architect of countless evils across the centuries, of which you know nothing because I'm *that* good at covering my tracks." I crossed my fingers behind my back.

"Uh-huh." Tom's voice dripped with disdain.

"Yes," I said. "You know the Black Death? That was me. Genghis Khan? Me again."

"I see" Tom said. "This is your first time in prison, isn't it?"

"Am I that obvious?"

"Yes. I believe you about the Extreme, however. My offer stands. I need someone who can be trusted to serve as my right hand."

I looked around, spotting Soviet Ape throwing darts at the Prismatic Commando's picture while Mister Chaos had decorated his room with headless dolls. "Wow, did you come to the wrong place."

"Tell me about it. Now are you in or not?"

"I'm listening."

"Do you know anything about parallel worlds?"

"Just what I learned from *Doctor Who* and *Star Trek*," I replied, not sure what he was suggesting. "Infinite realities, blah-blah, quantum physics, yakity-smackity."

"That's close enough for our purposes," Tom said. Something about his voice made me feel sick to my stomach, as if I was listening to audible evil. "I've discovered a parallel reality where superheroes never existed. Most of the pop culture is still the same, though, for reasons I cannot yet fathom."

"Huh," I said, suddenly interested. "If there were no superheroes then who killed Hitler?"

"Suicide, oddly enough. I confess it's a much less satisfying ending than Ultragod dragging him and Stalin before the World Court. I say that as Ultragod's worst enemy."

"What is it with you and Ultragod, anyway?" I said, trying to distract Tom while I thought about what to do. I didn't like the idea of helping the world's most dangerous man escape. Tom had broken out of prison at least a hundred times in the past, though. If I didn't help him, he'd eventually do it on his own. Still, this was eviler than I was prepared to be.

"It was the Thirties. I was a white mad scientist. He was a black superhero. It seemed natural we'd fight. I saw the light around the Fifties or so. I no longer hate him for his race. Now I hate him because he's standing in the way of my dominating the planet."

"I'm glad you've embraced equal-opportunity evil. So what's this parallel universe got to do with us?"

Tom's smile broadened to the point it covered half of his face. "The guards don't search for parallel dimensions."

He proceeded to pull a hole out of his pocket. Yes, the kind of portable-hole that Wile-E-Coyote would move around in the Looney Toons shorts. Placing it against the wall, Tom reached in and pulled out a flask containing a golden liquid.

"Okay. I'm not a skeptic or anything but that's insane."

"Any science sufficiently advanced is indistinguishable from magic," Tom Terror said. "Arthur C. Clark got that quote from me but never gave me credit. I may have to travel back in time to kill him...again."

"This conversation is both frightening and fascinating all at once. It's like listening to Professor Moriarty talk to Bugs Bunny."

"Thank you," I said to my costume, while looking at Tom Terror. "So what's the potion do?"

"It is my latest variant on my Elixir-X formula!" Tom said with all the relish you'd expect of a villain from the Golden Age of Superheroism. "Once I imbibe this potion, it will bestow Ultragod's powers upon me for twenty-four hours!"

"Classic supervillain plotline."

"I know, because *I invented it*. This version won't make my hair fall out and require me to get eye replacements like the last few dozen did either."

"The perils of self-experimentation," I replied, leaning up against my transparent cell wall. "What about the guards? Aren't you worried about them hearing your dastardly scheme?"

"I have bent all of the guards in the prison through an ancient brainwashing technique," Tom said, chuckling.

"Mind-Control Waves?"

"Cash."

"Damn," I said, both impressed and disappointed. "I wish I had a pen and paper to write all this down."

Tom Terror downed his elixir in one gulp, throwing the flask to one side. Seconds later, he was levitating a foot off the ground with miniature lightning bolts crackling up and down his body. It reminded me of the Quickening from the *Highlander* movies. A moment later, a glowing white aura surrounded Tom Terror.

Pointing at his cell door, Tom conjured a glowing chainsaw energy construct and cut through it like it was cardboard.

"You realize Tom Terror will kill many heroes if he escapes. That doesn't include innumerable innocent victims if he makes it to Earth."

"Why do you care?" I said, feeling more than a little guilty about all this. "You're a servant of the Grim Reaper."

"I...it's complicated."

"Well, so is my life. If I don't bust out of this joint, I'll never see Mandy again," I said. "Besides, I'm lacking in the superpowers department while he's gained all of Ultragod's abilities. Give me one good reason why I should care about this."

I talked a good game, but I shared Cloak's worries. I wanted to escape this place and see Mandy again, but I didn't want hundreds of innocents on my conscience either. I wasn't a sociopath, it seemed, just gleefully immoral. Still, I wasn't budging on this plan until Cloak gave me some answers.

"I was once a hero," Cloak said. *"My foremost duty is to make sure the Reaper's Cloak is used to prevent the rising of the Restless Dead. Everything else, including your supervillainy, is secondary."*

"I'm not you."

"I know. But you need to know why I care. I'm Lancel Warren. The Nightwalker."

Chapter Seventeen

The Great Supervillain Riot

"Yeah, I figured that out awhile back."

"*Wait, what?*"

"Yeah, you're haunting your own Cloak. I get it."

"Excuse me?" Tom Terror said, across the room. "What are you doing?"

"Sorry, I'm talking to my other personality."

"Ah. Carry on."

Given he had Ultra-powers now, I was surprised Tom Terror wasn't able to hear Cloak's voice.

"*Tom Terror always overestimates his creations. I doubt his powers are nearly as refined as Ultragod's.*" Cloak made a snorting noise in my head. "*You should also be grateful I'm desperate to keep zombies from overrunning my city. Do you think it's been easy watching you waste my powers like you do?*"

"I've *not* been wasting *my* powers."

"*And the **stupid** names you give everything! It's never been called the Night Tower or the Night Car. I didn't have 'Night' in front of everything. You sounded **ridiculous** calling it a Night Computer. I tried to be subtle about telling you not to call it that, but you seem oblivious to causal suggestions.*"

"Sunlight called it the Night Computer."

"*Sunlight has a lot of problems. I tried to get him therapy for them, but the Seventies were a strange time. He spent a lot of time with Hunter S. Thompson and was a bad influence on him.*"

"Wait, he was a bad influence on *Hunter S. Thompson?*" I asked, not sure if that was possible.

"You can see why I stopped working with my brother's descendants," Cloak replied. *"They were great gadgetry crime fighters but a little on the strange side."*

Tom's cell door flopped off as a pair of prison guards charged at Tom Terror, firing their laser guns. The blasts bounced against Tom's energy shield before he cut their heads off with his glowing chainsaw.

It was a bloody, gory mess.

"That was unnecessary," I said, looking at the corpses.

"Necessary? No. Fun? Yes." Tom looked at the carnage with a sadistic glee. "Haven't you ever killed someone for the joy of it?"

I hadn't, but he was testing me. "Yes, but that's me."

Tom dissipated the chainsaw and stretched out his hands, shooting bolts of lightning throughout the Archvillains' Wing. It was like being caught in the middle of an electrical storm. Seconds later, all the cell doors opened and alarms started blaring throughout the prison level.

"On a scale of one to ten, just how much of a psycho is Tom?" I asked Cloak.

"Less than Mister Chaos, who is still the most prolific serial killer in American history, but more than anyone else I've ever fought," Cloak said, sounding more like a superhero every second. *"Having second thoughts about your supervillain career?"*

"Not a bit."

For once, I wasn't sure if I was telling the truth or not. Teaming up with Tom Terror was a far cry from anything my brother had ever done. But, really, wasn't that the point?

"You must do what you feel is right, of course."

"Shut up, Obi-Wan."

Tom Terror floated up a foot above the ground and addressed the gathering crowd of supervillains were forming around us. "Members of the Fraternal Order of Supervillains, colleagues, and fellow architects of global chaos...we are free!"

A cheer went up throughout the prison level.

"The Society of Superheroes thought they could keep us prisoner on this barren rock, but they were wrong!" Tom Terror shouted, stretching out his arms as he levitated upward.

"The neo-bourgeoisie capitalist pigs!" Soviet Ape said in Russian, shaking a furry fist.

Thinking at the Cloak, I asked, *"Wait, how do I understand Russian?"*

"I'm translating."

"Should I call you Lancel, Cloak, or what?" I asked, unsure what to say or do. Despite everything, I still trusted Cloak and wanted his advice. After all, he wanted out of this place as much as I did.

"Cloak is fine," Cloak said. *"My old life ceased to matter when I died. Though, I confess, I'm not looking forward to spending eternity with you when you die."*

"We'll have to work on fixing that," I muttered aloud.

Tom continued his speech, not noticing my mumbling. "They are trapped on this planetoid with us! Never has there been a better time to strike down our foes, freeing us from their interference to pursue our superior Nietzschean morality!"

"You know Nietzsche doesn't work that way, right? I knew Fred. He was a pleasant man who would have been horrified at what the Nazis did with his philosophy."

"Shhh. Some of these guys might be able to hear you."

A resounding cheer followed seconds later as the doors to the Minor Supervillains Ward opened, hundreds more supervillains poured in to join us. Their guards there hadn't been able to offer much resistance either.

"Kill them all!" A Ted Bundy-looking fellow said. Hell, he might have been Ted Bundy for all I knew.

Not all the supervillains around me looked comfortable with this train of thought but most did. Enough that I pitied the Society of Superheroes. There were more people than the Society of Superheroes up here, including guards and scientists.

It was going to be a massacre.

"Perhaps not. I'm starting to see the method in Tom's madness."

"Care to fill me in?"

"Not yet. Just do whatever Tom says for the time being, unless it involves killing innocents."

"I liked it better when you called me Master."

"Do whatever Tom says for the time being, unless it involves killing innocents, Master."

Seconds later, Tom floated down and started directing the various other archvillains to take teams to different parts of the moon base. After a few minutes, it was only me and several hand-chosen goons. These chosen goons were not the supervillains I'd imagined becoming like. Down to a man, they were all psychopaths.

"Good," Tom said. "Those imbeciles I just speech-ified should provide us a suitable distraction. If they don't, the other archvillains should at least keep the Society's attention."

"Pardon?" I did a double take.

"Contrary to my stated opinion." Tom paused. "The Society of Superheroes is not composed of idiots. There's no way to shut off the powers of the Metamen here but they disarmed the technology-based criminals and suppressed the power of those who draw their energy from magical forces."

"Such as me."

"Such as you, yes. The Society is going to tear through the majority of those fools like wet tissue paper. A pity superheroes don't kill, a great number of those criminals have no place in my New World Order."

"I know the feeling," I replied, thinking my first act as world dictator would be to execute Tom and most of the psychos here. "So, you freed them to get their butts kicked?"

"Yes, in addition to killing any civilians in the area. Slaying the so-called innocent inflicts mental damage on superheroes that I find superior to physical damage, nine times out of ten. Rule Number One and all."

"Damn, those are actually *rules*?" I asked, stunned. "I thought they were just something Diabloman made up."

"More like guidelines." Tom revealed he'd seen the pirate movies. So much for his 'only intellectual stuff' plans for Earth.

"The actual super-powered inmates, plus those I've picked for their skills or other qualities, will pursue the important part of my plan. Specifically, guaranteeing my escape. If they succeed in this, they will be given a substantial reward for their services. You, Merciless, will have the most important mission of them all. If you accomplish it, you will be given Australia when I take over the world."

"Why Australia?"

"It's about as close to America as you can get without actually having it."

"*I know plenty of Australian Superheroes who'd be insulted by that comparison. Supervillains, too.*"

I rolled my eyes, wondering how Cloak could stay calm. A second later it hit me the Nightwalker had been in thousands of these situations.

"It's your mission to secure the teleporter and bring me the Power Nullifier in Ultragod's quarters. Once I have it, I will possess the power to become every bit as powerful as Ultragod permanently. It's why I allowed myself to be captured," Tom said, his presence darkening the room. I was in the presence of a genuine evil genius.

I was starting to realize why so many people used the 'you're insane' statement to supervillains. "Why me?"

Tom smiled, his teeth looked like those of a shark. "Like I said, you strike me as the kind of person who can be trusted. People who can be trusted have families, friends, and loved ones."

"Uh-huh." I could see where this was going.

"So, it's simple. If you betray me in any way, I'll hunt down your wife or parents or whomever you care about and turn them into chopped liver. Literally. I'll *turn* them into pieces of liver before chopping them up. I haven't used my transmogrifier in *years.*"

I nodded. "Okay."

"*Merciless…Gary…*" Cloak trailed off.

"*Don't worry, Cloak. All he's done is piss me off.* **No one** *threatens my family,*" I said back to him.

"Any questions?" Tom Terror asked.

"Tell me how to get to the teleporter," I replied, smiling. "I'll take care of you. Honest."

"Not quite yet." Tom made a tsk-tsk noise. "While I expect you'll do what I want you to do, I'm going to equip you with some henchmen to carry out this mission. After all, without your powers, you're just a man. I can't leave you *unguarded*."

It was in that moment I decided Tom Terror was worse than Jack the Ripper, Ed Gein, and a dozen other mass murderers put together. Not only was he a multiple murderer, but he was also *smug* about it. "Who are you sending with me?"

Tom gestured over to one of the few remaining supervillains, a man who had somehow managed to get his costume back. It was form-hugging black and white spandex with a big dartboard centered on the man's chest. His entire face was covered but for his mouth and chin, which were plastered with a psychotic smile.

"Howdy! I'm Psychoslinger," the man proclaimed.

"I know who you are." I felt sick just being in the man's presence.

Psychoslinger smiled, pulling on his costume like it was a pair of suspenders. "Gee, thanks, I feel so flattered! An actual archvillain knows who I am."

"Yeah, well what you did to that daycare center was all over the news." I struggled to smile despite my loathing. If I had my powers, I would've burned Psychoslinger to death and scattered the ashes. He was the type of guy you drove a stake through the heart of to make sure they didn't rise from the grave. Of course, given what happened with the Ice Cream Man that may just be practical.

Tom Terror stood between us. "I wanted to pair you with Mister Chaos, but he's already killed two supervillains and fed a guard his own tongue. So, I suspect he's not going to be available for team-ups any time soon. Psychoslinger is the best substitute I could find."

Psychoslinger produced a psychic knife in the air, balancing it on the end of his index finger. "I want you to know, I normally don't kill kids."

"Well, that's a relief," I said, still sickened.

"I prefer to kill women. I've got a mark on my body for every filly I did. I may need to find a new way to keep score, though, because I'm running out of room."

"As a superhero, I wasn't allowed to kill people, but I wanted to kill this one."

"Say no more."

"Y'all ever been to Texas? That's where I operate. Maybe we could have a team-up. I bet we could kill twice as many people as I could alone!" Psychoslinger began juggling his psychic knives.

Chapter Eighteen

Where I Deal with My New Partner

Psychoslinger and I were walking down the now-deserted cell blocks of the prison level. Our directions from Tom Terror were irritatingly precise, highlighting how we could best take advantage of the breakout.

I had no intention of living up to my end of the bargain, of course.

I intended to find the teleporter, figure out how to use it, and get myself off this rock. All I had to do was put up with Psychoslinger's insane commentary until then.

"I've never killed anyone famous before. Sometimes, though, I consider trying to kill the President. The problem is he's guarded by a lot of very scary people. A lot of them have superpowers. Someone tried to kill President Kennedy in Dallas, you know. The Golden Lightning caught the bullet, though, jerk."

"This is hell," I muttered.

"I've been to hell. This isn't even close."

"Have you ever considered what it would be like to kill everyone in the world?" Psychoslinger said. "I have. I'd need superspeed for it, though. That way I could kill everyone individually."

"Alright, it's close."

"I can't say I have."

"Either that or invulnerability. If I had invulnerability I could take my time killing everyone. So, between the two, I'd have to choose invulnerability, but I wish I had both," Psychoslinger said, making a psychic mace as he walked. He turned it into a machete and created a second one, spinning the two blades like he was a human fan. Psychoslinger made his blade work look effortless, making me all the more uncomfortable with his close proximity.

"Okay, I **need** *to kill this guy. I don't care what it takes. Tell me how and I'll do it,"* I said to Cloak.

"In order to defeat Psychoslinger, you need to understand his motivations. Psychopaths are different from sociopaths, however."

"How so?" I thought to him.

"Sociopaths often have some form of ethical code they abide by," Cloak said. *"It's just unique to them, like you and yours."*

"Thanks," I replied, rubbing my temples. *"I think."*

"Psychopaths are, dumbing down the psychology involved, unfettered. Given you can't defeat Psychoslinger without your powers, the best option for defeating him is figuring out what Tom Terror is using to control him. I have a number of suggestions for how we can deduce it."

"Hey, Psychoslinger, what does Tom Terror have on you?"

"I suppose you could do that too."

"Oh, not much. He said he'd help me kill Albuquerque."

I was unsure how to react. "Is that a life-long ambition?"

"Yep!" He said. "How about you?"

"No. I can't say I ever dreamed about killing a major populated area."

"Not even Delaware?"

"No."

"Oh."

I said to Cloak, *"I don't think we're going to get an advantage from psychoanalyzing this guy."*

"Neither do I."

Still thinking at Cloak, I asked, *"Is there any way I can get my powers back? I mean, I seriously want to kill this guy. I don't have an issue with killing people, but this guy is the first guy I've* **wanted** *to murder."*

"No way that I know of. The spells were designed to guard against,

well, villains like you using them."

"Dammit." I grit my teeth.

"Something wrong?" Psychoslinger asked, his voice unsettling due to its cheerfulness.

"Nothing, I'm having an argument with the voices in my head," I replied, getting sick of that excuse.

"I have that problem too!" Psychoslinger slapped me on the back.

Seeing a nearby fire extinguisher, I decided to reach for it and bash in Psychoslinger's brains. Picking it up, I had it knocked out of my hands by a sun-shaped shuriken. The tiny little flying disc released a blinding flash of light that caused me to drop it against the ground.

"What the hell?" I asked, turning around.

"Halt evil doer!" Sunlight lifted another shuriken. "You are under arrest by the authority of senior Society of Superheroes member Sunlight!"

"Man, I hate killing old people," Psychoslinger said, frowning. "They go down so easy. Worse, he's a dude! Dudes are no fun to kill! They do a whole different type of screaming!"

"Wait." Sunlight pointed at me. "You!"

"How the hell did you get here?" I was flat-out *confused* by his presence.

"Teleporter." Sunlight pulled out another of his shurikens. "I recognize your cloak now! You must be the supervillain who killed the Nightwalker!"

I almost shouted. "You fucking sent me the cloak in the first place!"

"You did?" Psychoslinger said. "Awesome!"

"No!"

"Obviously," Cloak said, indignant. *"I died of an aneurysm. Even at a hundred and ten, I was sharp enough not to be taken down by the likes of you."*

I would have made a rebuttal to Cloak if not for the absurdity of the situation.

"Fiend!" Sunlight said, catching his returning weapon. "Prepare to be smote, old school style!"

"Old school is right. Sixty-five-year-old men should not be

wearing tights!" I did not have time for this bullshit.

I wasn't afraid of Sunlight. I was afraid Psychoslinger would kill him and I'd be blamed for it. Could you imagine what that would do to my rep? Killing the Extreme was one thing, people would respect that. Killing Sunlight would label me as a murderer of eccentric elderly superheroes.

"You're all heart."

"I know," I thought back.

Psychoslinger had already conjured two psychic knives to throw into his face by the time I realized I needed to keep the crazed former sidekick alive.

Seeing no alternative, I charged at Sunlight, yelling. "Mercy is for the weak!"

"Is that your battle cry? If so, it needs work," Cloak said.

"Do you ever shut up?" I ducked and dodged Sunlight's shurikens. He was tossing two or three at a time now. Each one caused a blinding flash of light when they hit the wall, which made it hard to dodge the next one.

"I confess, since dying you've been my one source of entertainment. Try not to kill my grandnephew."

Taken aback by my charge, Sunlight failed to dodge. As a result, I smashed him into the wall behind us with all the force I could muster.

"Ooomph!" Sunlight said, grunting. "It'll take more than that to put down—"

I interrupted him with a punch to the face. He somersaulted over me and jump kicked me in the head. Even at sixty-five years old, Sunlight had a bunch of kick. No pun intended. Then again, so did I. Kneeing the man in the stomach, I dropped him long enough to start strangling him with my cape. After he stopped struggling, I threw him against the wall and tried to figure out a way to render him insensible. Spotting Sunlight's utility belt, I pulled some rope from it and started tying him up.

"You won't believe me, but this is for your own good," I whispered in his ear.

"Thank you. I appreciate you doing this. As exasperating as Robert could be, he is still family."

"I'm doing this for Mandy and my reputation, not you," I muttered under my breath. "This guy has about exhausted my non-existent mercy."

"Varlet!" Sunlight howled, showing he was still conscious. He couldn't do anything other than shake a fist in my general direction, though. "I'll get out of these bonds and hunt you to the ends of the Earth."

"Yeah. You do that. A little help here, Cloak?"

"Take the third capsule on the utility belt from the buckle and break it front of his face. That's the Solar Sleeping Gas. Don't use the second capsule. That's the Solar Happiness Gas."

"I don't even want to know."

"I didn't name them!"

Grabbing the third capsule, I cracked it open underneath Sunlight's nose, a purple mist pouring out of the capsule. Sunlight passed out, a good thing since he'd already started slipping out of my crude bonds.

"Hey, no kill-stealing!" Psychoslinger shouted, running up behind us. Seeing Sunlight was alive, the psychopath took his knives and started grinding them against one another. "Ooooo, a tied-up superhero. This should be fun!"

I closed my eyes, trying to figure out how to prevent Psychoslinger from killing him. The problem was that it was a bit like keeping a dog from barking. "Yeah, bound and gagged superheroes are pretty damned fun. Sadly, we can't kill him."

"What, *why?*"

I blathered out the first thing that came to mind, "Because of Rule Number One!"

"Rule Number One?"

"Yes," I said. "It's in the by-laws for the Fraternity of Supervillains."

"Again…why?"

"So, uh, we can get more fights in the long run," I said, trying to think of a reason he'd accept. "Up the pay-per-view rights price."

"Oh!" Psychoslinger said, a figurative light bulb popping on above his head. "I get it. We get more press this way!"

I was stunned this was working. "You catch on quick."

"You're like my supervillain mentor!" Psychoslinger said, extending his hands to embrace me.

"Never say that again." I walked past him on down the hall. "Ever."

"I can't believe that worked."

"Me either."

Psychoslinger trailed up behind me, a big grin on his face. It was a bit like having a murderous puppy adopt you.

"In any case, I think I can keep this guy from killing anyone else," I thought to Cloak. *"All I need to do is make up rules that he has to follow. It's a long shot, but I think I can pull it off. If I work hard, maybe I won't end up with a hundred murders tagged to my record."*

"Hey look!" Psychoslinger said, pointing to two guards coming around the corner. They were wearing suits of scaled-down power armor like the kind worn by the Prismatic Commando. In their hands were a set of electrical-shock prods, the variable settings on them ranging from knocking out a full-sized normal human being to putting down a super-powered elephant. They also had laser-pistols on their chests and energy shields on their backs. I imagined they were Foundation for World Harmony trained and probably capable of kicking my ass every which way from Sunday. I didn't think they would be too happy about my escape and searched for a way to talk my way out of this or fool them.

Before I could react, Psychoslinger hurled two psychic daggers through their helmets, killing them instantly. Their armor should have contained defenses against psionic attacks as well as being composed of reinforced steel. It meant Psychoslinger was packing a lot more punch than I'd initially surmised. It also meant I was now an accessory to murdering two innocent guards.

Great.

"Look at that," Psychoslinger said, laughing. "A pair of hole-y guards!"

"Yeah, that's just fucking hilarious," I said, trying and failing to keep my immense sarcasm out.

Staring down at the guards, their helmets dripping blood and other liquids down on the ground before me, I almost launched myself at Psychoslinger. This was real, and I might have been able to stop Psychoslinger with Sunlight if I'd tried to. At the very least, I'd had an obligation to try.

"*Steady. His time will come.*"

"You don't sound like you approve," Psychoslinger said, a dangerous edge to his voice.

Clenching my fists, I counted to five before uncurling them. Turning to Psychoslinger, I put on the fakest smile imaginable. "I dunno, it was kind of quick, shouldn't you have done their legs first? Make em beg a little?"

"Oh!" Psychoslinger said, slapping his head. "That's why you sound upset. I get it. No, these guys are just mooks. We save that for the real prey."

"So this is just...warming up?" I asked.

"Yeah. It may be against the rules to kill heroes but that doesn't mean we can't torture them."

That was what I was afraid of. "Yeah, I suppose it doesn't."

If I continued to travel with Psychoslinger then I would, undoubtedly, be party to more murders. He was a complete psychopath and, worse, was working for Tom Terror. If I helped Tom Terror escape with both the power-nullifier and his teleporter, then I was potentially unleashing the equivalent of a world-ending disaster.

Tom Terror hadn't managed to conquer the Earth in eighty years but he'd come close on several occasions. He'd even managed to take over an alien planet and rechristen it Terrorworld. The thing was, Tom Terror only had to win once, and the world would enter an age of darkness.

Or, he might fuck it up again and I'd be free. Better still, I'd have a friend on the inside who was smart enough to let me out. The best supervillains never stayed locked up for very long and it was precisely because of these sorts of jailbreaks. It was times like these I had to question just how committed I was to my philosophy of letting nothing hold me back.

Would I really burn the world to be with Mandy again?

Yes, I would.

But it would mean her knowing me as a monster.

And I wasn't sure I could stand to have her look at me that way.

Or Keith, or Gabrielle, or all the people I loved in this world and the next.

Fuck. No wonder so many supervillains were committed loners.

"I can't advise you on this, Gary," Cloak said. *"I have too much blood on my hands to judge a man for his deeds."*

"Then shut up."

I continued to think, following Psychoslinger and hoping we didn't come across any more guards or heroes.

I also knew that hope was in vain.

Chapter Nineteen

Where I Discover that Sci-Fi Horror is Still Horror

A half-hour later, we were lost. Apparently, Tom Terror's precise instructions were a complete load of crap.

"This place is a maze!" Psychoslinger growled, shaking his fist. "Let's find someone to torture some information out of."

I sighed and pulled a map off the side of the wall that was next to an emergency staircase. Consulting it, I pointed down the hall.

"We have to go down there, past the cafeteria, past the armory, under the ecological preserve, through the courtyard, and beyond the civilian housing to reach the Heroes' Wing."

"Armory?" Psychoslinger's head perked up. "Like guns or... bigger guns?"

I continued consulting the map for intelligence about the Society of Superheroes. "More like all the super-technology, alien weapons, magical items, and otherworldly stuff the heroes have confiscated over the years. You know, which isn't in their rooms as trophies."

I paused, realizing what I'd just said.

"We have *got* to go there!" Psychoslinger said, clenching his fists. "I want exploding boxing gloves!"

I debated telling him the obvious flaw with that desire. You know, losing your hands, but realized I didn't care if he did or not. "I don't think it works like a store. Also, all the other supervillains are going to be going for the armory too. Which will mean they're going to be intercepted by all the superheroes who will realize this. Which means it is exactly the opposite of the way we need to go in order to make use of the quote-unquote distraction Tom Terror has provided us."

Psychoslinger stared at me and I worried if I'd pushed him too far. It was a delicate balance dealing with psychopaths like him. I'd used to work with a few at the bank. Push them too far and they would slit your throat. Push them at all and they'd walk all over you.

Psychoslinger conjured a glowing boomerang in hand.

I looked down at the map. "Of course, if you really want, I suppose we have to go there anyway."

Psychoslinger's entire attitude changed. "Ah, you're alright, M! We should be sex brothers!"

I stared at him. "I...am not familiar with that term."

"Well, first we kidnap a hooker..." Psychoslinger continued the conversation but I mercifully, no pun intended, tuned him out from that point on.

I was spared having to devote any of my attention to what was a disgusting story by the sight of something almost as disgusting. On the other end of the hallway was an eight-legged black creature with a long scorpion tail and ant-like body. It had no eyes but a huge phallic head with mandibles on the ends of its mouth. It was standing over the corpses of four prison guards it had torn to shreds despite their armor and extraterrestrial weapons, feasting on their insides.

Oh God, the smell.

I recognized the creature from television and movie adaptations, as well as newspaper reports: a Deathmonger. Deathmongers were the equivalent of chemical weapons in the greater universe, outlawed but still used biological monstrosities. Superheroes could tear through them like wet-tissue paper, but normal human beings? Like I was, presently? They were lunch meat.

I took three steps back. "Game over, man, game over."

"Eh, it's just a big dumb animal," Psychoslinger said, throwing a pair of his psionic boomerangs at the creature's head.

They slammed into its skull.

And caused it to look up from its meal and hiss.

Aw crap.

I proceeded to hit the ground with the speed of a bullet train as the Deathmonger leapt over my head and slammed into Psychoslinger, starting to claw out his insides and tear parts of his body. Oddly, Psychoslinger's body didn't produce blood but seemed to disintegrate into psychic energy as he was torn to shreds. Remember the old joke about the two men being chased by a bear, I gave Psychoslinger a salute and ran away from the Deathmonger. I picked up one of the fallen guards' electros-staffs and high-tailed it down the hall.

"You realize that's just going to excite it, right?"

"No, I'm not an expert in space monsters!"

"Keep running. You're almost to the prison decontamination zone."

A nightmarish roar echoed from behind me.

"Deathmongers belonged in the biological preserve and extraterrestrial zoological research center. If they were released, that could be a million terrible horrors ready to be unleashed on the people here. Every man, woman, and child in Avalon may be threatened."

I tried to imagine a million terrible things like the Deathmonger. My mind blanked after the first three. "Why the hell would they have that here?"

"On the moon? So our research to benefit humanity and other races doesn't endanger Earth!"

"It's a stupid idea to keep that near supervillains!"

"Admittedly, I agree on that, but it was a budget concern. That and keeping all the supervillains' weapons and equipment nearby. It, too, is being researched for the greater benefit of mankind."

I'd been wondering about that. "So how do these things see?"

"Motion sense!"

I saw the Decontamination Area not too far away. About thirty-yards down a straight hallway. Decontamination was a series of joined hallways with separate control stations that worked like a combination of airport security and a medical center. Given the staggering number of oddball methods supervillains might escape, they had methods for guarding against everything from nanites to fungus capable of eating through concrete to sentient viruses. Guinevere had given me the rundown while explaining to me, in vivid terms, how I was never going to be able to get out of here.

Shows what she knew.

That was when I heard the Deathmonger bouncing behind me. Turning around, I saw the creature move around a corner to about fifteen yards away. It was moving slowly, saving the kill. Looking around, I saw the hallway was mostly filled with atmosphere processors and heating fuel that I didn't possess the scientific training to figure out how to turn into a makeshift weapon.

I lifted up the end of the electro-staff and charged it, pushing its power up to the maximum as I backed up. "Nice kitty."

The Deathmonger prepared to pounce.

I was so dead.

"Gary, the piping right up above you! Hit it now!" Cloak shouted.

I didn't hesitate and did so, causing strange gray gas to flood down on the creature which ignited from the charge and burned the Deathmonger—horribly. My hands were terribly burned, and I screamed, only to drop the staff and start running again, clutching my mangled hands. I couldn't feel them anymore and hesitated to look at them. The monster continued to scream as more heating fluid continued to pour down on it, but it gave no sign of dying.

"We need...to...nuke these things...god almighty...from orbit!" I said, in-between painful grunts. "It's the only way to be sure."

I ran through the Decontamination chambers as fast as I could. The monster behind me lumbered at a quarter of its speed, which was still running distance for a regular human. I ran through the last of the contamination chambers, and I saw a big red button on one of the controls. Unable to use my hands, I slammed my elbow on it. Behind me, a transparent steel room closed its doors and locked the monster inside. It was burned heavily and looked very upset, as much as a creature with no eyes or recognizable human features could do so.

That's when a mechanical female voice said, "HOSTILE

ORGANISM DETECTED. BEGIN DECONTAMINATION."

A glowing green energy filled the chamber.

Followed by the Deathmonger exploding.

Its acidic innards and blood started melting the walls of the chamber, only for the green energy to burn them away.

"My mommy always said there were no monsters, no real ones, but there are." I stared at the empty chamber.

I was going to lose my hands, I knew it.

"Will you stop quoting that damned movie," Cloak muttered.

"Make me."

Turning around, I was almost immediately forced to back away as I saw a *second* Deathmonger crouched in front of me.

"Aw, shit."

The creature looked different than its counterpart, being smaller and more agile looking, with less armor. I guessed it was the male of the species since I vaguely recalled the organisms had sexual dimorphism that favored the female. I also suspected it was the mate of the one I'd just killed since, unlike xenomorphs, Deathmongers were a pack-race rather than hive. Which meant, given they were as smart as apes, it was probably intelligent enough to want me to suffer for killing its mate.

Oh well.

Not much I could do about it now.

I closed my eyes.

"See you in a bit, Cloak," I said, mentally. "I hope our next wearer is less of a jerk than me."

"Alakazam!" I heard a voice with a thick New England accent shout.

I blinked, opening my eyes and watching the Deathmonger in mid-pounce start to change. It fell to the ground, twisting and thrashing, growing smaller and smaller. Eventually, much to my surprise, it became a one-foot-long fluffy white rabbit.

Which hissed at me.

"Gah!" I said, bolting away. "Get this knigget away from me!"

"What'd he do? Nibble your bum?" the aforementioned voice said.

"That is a foul-t..." I trailed off, not in the mood for any more movie references. Which meant the situation was truly dire.

I shook my head and looked up, blinking as I saw the Black Witch. It was a testament to how much pain I was in that I didn't immediately start drooling. The Black Witch was, much like Guinevere, one of the candidates for the title 'World's Most Beautiful Woman.' However, while Guinevere was just beauty in general, love and rainbows as much as centerfolds, the Black Witch was very much the latter alone.

Compared to many of the more stripper-esque costumes worn by some supervillains and supervillainesses, usually to their detriment when punches were exchanged, the Black Witch's attire was positively demure. My wife's ex-girlfriend was wearing a skin-tight jumpsuit that accented every curve and proportion with a long black leather trench coat over her shoulders. She had perfect skin, teeth, blue crystal eyes, and long raven-black hair that trailed over her shoulders. If Kate Beckinsale's character from *Underworld* and Eva Green had a child through science, it would probably resemble Selena Darkchilde.

"Hey, Sal," I said, calling her by the name she hated.

Selena narrowed her eyes, clenching her teeth. "Hold your hands out, Gary. I could make this not hurt but I'm not going to."

I did so, getting my first look at the horrific ruined mass of my hands. I couldn't properly feel anything in my hands because the nerves had been burned away. All the pain was from all the nerves connected to them feeling how much damage I'd endured.

"Abracadabra," Selena said, pulling out a cheap toy stage magician's wand and waving it over my hands.

I tried to stifle my scream.

I failed.

I can't describe the kind of pain I felt so I won't even try but it was over in an instant.

My hands smoked, a glowing aura of Olympian magic surrounded them.

They were also healed.

Completely.

Which meant she could do magic.

Interesting.

I stared at them. "Sal, I could kiss you."

"I'll pass," Selena said, putting up her wand. "I will never understand why, of all the men in the world, you're the one who persuaded Mandy over."

"I'm pretty sure she was always into guys as well as girls. You can be both," I said, wiggling my fingers. "I do owe you, though."

"I'm not doing it for you, I'm doing it for *her,*" Selena said, sticking her thumb up over her shoulder.

Looking behind her, I was surprised to see there was a small gathering of supervillains and heroes around the place. There was Bronze Medalist, a late-thirties African American speedster who was the Silver Lightning's former sidekick and partner (in both senses of the word). He was dressed in a red and green jumpsuit that covered everything but his face and had a pair of yellow goggles over his eyes. I remembered him mostly from those ill-conceived anti-drug PSAs from the Eighties and his energy drink commercials.

Beside him was General Venom, dressed in his stars-and-stripes armor with lightsaber-esque power sword and shield, still doing his attempt at ill-conceived redemption it seemed. General Venom had been a superhero in the 1960s called the Star-Spangled Banner before the Vietnam Wars had messed up his brain so much he'd come to believe the United States government was secretly under the control of Tsavong shapeshifters and needed to be overthrown. Not even cleaning them out in the 1980s had stopped his terrorist attacks.

Behind them was the Red Schoolgirl, a wild-eyed and haired Japanese girl in a black sailor fuku holding a Muramasa katana that continually dripped blood. Her hair was in Chinese bunches with ribbons hanging down the side. There were rumors the Red Schoolgirl was insane and no one knew if she was a hero or a villain. Beside her was the Human Tank, a bulky-grey-camouflage-colored metal-armored villain rarely seen out of her suit. The Human Tank was one of my brother's old cronies from New Angeles. She was a dull, serious woman who didn't talk too much from my recollection. It had taken me *years* to realize she was a woman.

"*She transitioned during your childhood.*"

"Oh, now I feel like a jackass," I replied.

There was no sign of the 'she' who Selena might be referring to, though. None of these people knew me from Adam. Hell, Selena was more likely to help me out and we *hated* each other.

Stepping out from behind the others was a figure I recognized all too well. She was short, as short as Mandy, but muscular with long dark hair she kept in a ponytail behind her. The woman was about my age, pretty albeit not like the selection of supermodels that seem to be oh-so-common around here. Frankly, I preferred the muscled look and there was something familiar about her in addition to her being the third most famous superheroine in the world.

Ultragoddess.

Ultragoddess was an olive-skinned Afro-Hispanic woman with a gold and white costume reminiscent of Ultragod's but altered to include a short skirt over bare legs and thigh-high boots. Given Ultragoddess was invulnerable to anything short of a nuclear warhead there wasn't much point in worrying about her legs. At one point, I recalled she'd even tried a midriff-bearing version of it but switched back after the already-prevalent catcalls had switched to outright obscenities.

Ultragoddess was, in many ways, the heroine of my generation. Not only was she the daughter of the world's most powerful superhero and his rejuvenated bride, civil rights attorney Polly Pratchett, but she'd grown up with us. We'd seen her as Ultragirl, Ultrateen, and even the ill-fated Ultranater in the Nineties. The media had tried to turn her into their perfect paragon, like their father, and I'd always gotten the impression it had made her mad as hell. Part of that was Gabrielle's constant stream of chatter to that effect.

Wait...Gabrielle.

I felt my head as it seemed a bunch of memories were trying to come back at once. Forcing them to the surface, I lifted up my fingers and tried to imagine a pair of glasses and a blonde wig on her head. I remember long nights with my Xbox, pizza, and her. I remembered the investigations we'd done into all the local superheroines and crime. I remembered how she insisted on making love in the dark. How she'd been the first girl I'd ever said I love you to. The only one other than Mandy.

Oh God.

My eyes widened.

"Hello, Gary," Ultragoddess said, looking down. "Long time no see."

"Gabby?" I whispered.

Chapter Twenty

America's Sweetheart and I Hash Things Out

All the immense joy, happiness, and (let's be honest) love I felt for her was drowned out by the staggering amount of *anger* I felt. "YOU BRAINWASHED ME INTO FORGETTING YOUR SECRET IDENTITY?"

"*Gary, calm down.*"

"Don't you tell me to calm down!" I shouted at my cloak.

"Who is he talking to?" the Red Schoolgirl asked in Japanese.

"His magical cloak," General Venom said. "They contain the souls of their dead users."

"Cool!" the Red Schoolgirl said. "Like my katana."

"You just *think* it's haunted," General Venom said.

Gabrielle blanched before looking to one side. "I'm sorry, Gary, I truly am. I realized after you were kidnapped that I was putting you in danger by our association. I could stand anything the supervillains of the world could do to me, but I wasn't willing to risk your life. I'd break if anything happened to you. I had to make a choice. I chose to serve the world. I heard you got married in the meantime. I hope you're very happy."

I shook with outrage. "This is not about you! This is about trust! This is about basic decency! How could you?"

The Red Schoolgirl zoomed with an inhuman speed underneath me, holding her blade next to my throat. "Do not speak to *sempai* like that."

That was when a gigantic Ultra-Force hand grabbed the Red

Schoolgirl in a fist then slapped her up against the side of the wall.

Ultragoddess' voice narrowed. "Do. Not. Touch. Him."

The Bronze Medalist snorted. "Girl, one of the first things I learned about relationships was don't you ever try and get in between an argument with lovers. They will chew you up and spit you out."

"I get that," the Red Schoolgirl said in a squeaky voice. "Can't breathe."

Ultragoddes dismissed the giant hand. "I'm sorry, Motoko, but this is none of your business."

I felt the sides of my head, a migraine coming on. "Words cannot express how pissed off I am. I am going to have to invent a new word to explain how angry I am. *Karflagled*. I am so karflagled off at you right now!"

"See, this is why I date men. Less drama," the Bronze Medalist said, pointing at me.

"You don't have a right to complain, Gary," the Black Witch said. "You went off and got married a few months later. Not exactly much room to reconcile."

Gabrielle took a deep breath. "I may have encouraged him to find happiness for himself."

The Black Witch's eyes widened.

"Cloak, tell me that I wasn't brainwashed into finding Mandy," I said, my voice pleading.

"No, you were just desperate and emotionally vulnerable from my examination of your memories. Surprisingly charming, though. I think it helped she was coming off a bad breakup herself."

"Thank God," I muttered.

"SO THIS IS YOUR EX-BOYFRIEND?" The Human Tank said in a robotic synthesized voice.

"Sort of," Gabrielle said, looking up to me. "We were engaged for like a minute. That was sort of a crisis point."

I remembered the ring now. I'd forgotten I'd bought it and wondered where all my savings had gone. She'd kept it, it seemed. I then noticed a tiny ring-shaped bulge hanging from inside her costume around her neck.

I shook my head. "Listen, Gabby, we *will* talk about this, but we have a lot of stuff going on, right now."

"HEY, WATCH IT WITH THE SECRET IDENTITY," the Human Tank said. "SHE'S VERY SENSITIVE ABOUT THAT."

"No kidding!" I snapped.

"We know it, though," General Venom said.

"Who are you people, anyway?" I asked, looking around the three. "I know who you all are, obviously, but I'm surprised to see you working together."

Gabrielle sighed and put her hands on her hips. "We're the Shadow Seven."

I stared at her. "Running a blank here."

"Because it's a *secret* team," General Venom said. "A group of mixed heroes and villains who run missions for the Society of Superheroes off the books against corrupt organizations that can't be legally fought."

I sputtered. "Superheroes can't be anti-establishment!"

"I confess, that is awfully shady," Cloak said, concerned. *"Combined with this Star Chamber-esque court, extraordinary rendition, off-world prison, and so on—I can't help but feel the Society is losing its way."*

"That's not what I mean! You're stealing the whole point of being a supervillain!" I had never been more offended in my life.

"Gary, are you a supervillain?" Gabrielle asked, horrified.

"Uh...kind of?"

"Ha-ha-ha!" the Black Witch laughed, grabbing her face. "Oh, this is *priceless*."

"What did you do?" Bronze Medalist asked.

I felt queasy. "I killed the Extreme. All of them."

There was a shocked silence and the Shadow Seven exchanged glances. Then everyone, except Gabrielle, started clapping.

Tough crowd.

Gabrielle stared at me, not condemning but concerned. "Gary, the Extreme did a lot of black operations for various governments. Horrible but necessary things for a lot of very important people. They're going to find you and throw you in a hole."

"As opposed to the hole your father threw me in," I said, sarcastically.

"The Extreme were monsters," the Black Witch said. "They murdered Sally Arcane and god knows how many others."

"They were—" General Venom started to say.

"You don't get to speak," the Black Witch said.

I paused, realizing something. "Wait a damned minute; I saw about half of you coming in to the prison. You were all locked up."

"Well, not all of us," the Bronze Medalist said. "I get to chill out in N.A. when not saving the world."

"We watch the others in the prison for trouble in-between missions," the Black Witch said. "Obviously, we were doing a piss-poor job."

I was appalled. They were *prison snitches*. How could Gabrielle have fallen so far to employ such?

"Your sense of morality is decidedly warped."

"Hello, I'm a supervillain."

Cloak sighed.

"Also, why are you the Shadow Seven?" I asked. "There're only six of you."

"On our last mission, Exsanguinator was possessed by a demon the Dark Undermaster summoned. It forced him to kill his family and we were forced to kill him. Gabby drove an Ultraforce stake through his heart then made a lamp that conjured real sunlight to destroy him," the Red Schoolgirl said, looking back at her.

"It is a reminder of how dangerous the battle against evil can be," General Venom said. "Those who commit crimes may laugh at the righteous and exchange derisive glances but in the future, it will be the righteous who laugh last."

"I don't think you get to claim righteousness after forty years of domestic terrorism," I said, shaking my head. "Why are you with this guy?"

"To save lives," Gabrielle said, looking at the Decontamination area then back at me. "Do you know the situation?"

"He does," Cloak said, volunteering me. *"He's also happy to help get it under control."*

I grimaced. I wasn't eager to make an enemy of Tom Terror, but I wasn't about to deny them either.

"I can't offer you a pardon for multiple murders," Gabrielle said, staring. "A lot of the Society of Superheroes believe the Extreme were heroes and deserving of our protection, even if I think they undermined everything we stood for. I will, however, help you get away, if you agree to assist us. There're thousands of noncombatants here in Avalon, and the idiots rioting have released things that they can't possibly understand the dangers of."

"Oh, someone understands the danger," I said, looking at her. "Everyone else is expendable."

"Tom Terror," Gabrielle hissed. "He is the only person I would break the first rule of superheroism for."

"Gabrielle, are you sure this is a good idea?" the Black Witch stuck her thumb out at me. "I know this guy as well as you. He couldn't kill time. I can't believe he killed the Extreme."

"Things change," I said, then gritted my teeth. "I'm not exactly operating at my best, though, since my powers are being suppressed."

Gabrielle nodded. "Computer, authorize ambient magical energy field withdrawal for prisoner Gary Karkofsky. Code: Ketra-18."

"Authorization granted," the computer's voice said.

Like someone was removing a blindfold from my eyes, I felt the power of the Reaper's Cloak return to me. My head filled with all manner of mystical information that I didn't even realize had been downloaded into my subconscious. Conjuring a snowball in one hand and a ball of fire in my other, I made them dissipate before nodding to them. "Okay, I promise to help you save this place. Just so we're clear, though, I'm only doing it because you returned my powers to me and not at all because I think a universe without the Society of Superheroes would scarcely be worth thinking about."

"Okay..." Gabrielle trailed off, confused.

"I have to preserve my supervillain credibility," I said, putting my hand over my heart.

"WHO ACTUALLY SELF-IDENTIFIES AS A SUPERVILLAIN?" The Human Tank said. "THAT'S LIKE CLAIMING YOU'RE EVIL." "I *am* evil," I said, smiling. "The wickedest of the wicked. Everyone is the hero of their own story but me, who is most certainly the villain protagonist."

"You do realize the whole Fraternity of Supervillains thing is meant to be ironic, right?" General Venom asked.

"I don't think he does," the Red Schoolgirl said.

"We've wasted enough time," Gabrielle said, gesturing with her head down the hall. "Gary, you take the front with me."

"I do not see what Mandy sees in you," the Black Witch muttered.

"I am a fantastic lover," I said.

The Black Witch looked over at Gabrielle.

Gabrielle stared back daggers.

The Black Witch took position in the rear, deciding it'd be better to get as far away from her as possible.

I decided to ask one of them about the decision, not wanting to talk to Gabrielle just yet. "Bronze Medalist—"

"I actually won two gold medals and one bronze. Yet, for some reason, they call me Bronze Medalist. Can you guess why?"

"Uh—"

"It's because people think of getting the bronze medal as losing. Which is ridiculous. It means two people in the world are faster than I at track and field. Two. I think that's something to be proud of."

"Yes!" I said, grimacing. "I agree!"

"*You realize he's playing with you, right?*" Cloak said.

"Not going to risk it," I whispered. "I don't suppose anyone is going to tell me what is going on?"

Gabrielle led me down a hall to an observation deck that showed the main part of Avalon, the miniature city outside the temple where the majority of the citizenry lived in addition to the heroes. The place was presently under attack by two gigantic creatures that would give H.P. Lovecraft nightmares.

The first was made of countless corpses sewn together and fused into a hideous vaguely humanoid form, the corpses all still animated with the souls of the damned and depraved who were forced to serve as the monster's host body for all time as their punishment.

The second being was a construct composed of monstrous eyes formed into a whip-like tentacle that reflected horrific atrocities from all the world's various wars and genocides, things I felt a brief experience of looking at it before glancing away.

They were flinging out spells and grabbing up citizens to add to their nightmarish frames. It was as if someone had combined a vision of the Inferno with a Godzilla movie.

My response was succinct. "What. The. Hell."

Gabrielle crossed her arms. "Gog and Magog."

"The monsters from the Torah?" I asked.

"Yes," Gabrielle said. "Nephilim born of Azazel and imprisoned in Hell after the Spiritual Flood. They're just some of the many horrors from the Old Testament summoned by the Devil King to vex the Society. These two will not stop until they have killed everyone here and then they will descend upon the Earth, with or without gear to transport them."

I stared at him. "Tom Terror unleashed this as a distraction too."

"Yes," Gabrielle said. "He infiltrated P.H.A.N.T.O.M agents into the staff as well as corrupt ones to get many of his followers their equipment. These things will kill the Earth's people if they can, but Tom will gladly turn the world into ashes if it means he can be king of them."

"What about the other heroes?" I asked.

"They're busy with other threats," Gabrielle said. "Equally bad ones."

I nodded. "Okay. I'll stop these."

"Thank you, Gary."

"For Mandy."

Gabrielle looked down. "I see."

"You know, I always thought the monsters of the Torah would be less...literal," I muttered.

"Live and learn," Gabrielle said, smacking her fist. She then blew out the observation deck windows and flew off.

The Human Tank smashed her fists together and said, "LET'S KILL THESE BITCHES." She then ignited her rocket pack before wings stretched out from her backpack and she took off into the air.

The others followed, each content to fight for the world.

While I had been content to rule it.

Damn, did I feel lousy.

Scared too.

This was way above my pay grade.

"This is why I kept the Solar Devastator around. You never know when you're going to be facing Kaiju."

I took to the air, levitating. "Cloak, shut up."

Chapter Twenty-One

Where I Earn My Maccabean Street Cred

As terrifying as their current skyscraper-sized forms were, and as keenly aware as I was it wouldn't take that much for one of them to puncture a hole in the side of Avalon's dome to kill us all, it helped to remember Gog and Magog weren't newcomers.

Again, I hadn't realized the Nephilim were literally the creatures from my rabbi's lessons I'd learned growing up, but I'd heard of giant monsters going by that name fought by the Society before. It said something about the kind of world we lived in that this was something I only vaguely recalled.

"Gog is the stronger of the two," Cloak said, his voice a low whisper. *"The smarter as well. He will spawn all manner of horrors from himself and make deals with mortals to subjugate the world in the service of Chaos. Magog, by contrast, is nothing more than a mindless force of destruction."*

As I levitated towards the two towering monsters, Magog spit forth a house-sized ball of hellfire toward a crowd of people. Bronze Medalist got all but a pair of them away as it descended, only for me to grab both and turn us insubstantial. Because the fire was magical, I lowered us to the level underneath us and dropped them before ascending.

"Yeah, I'm getting all sorts of warm and fuzzy feelings from the creature spoken of as one of the primordial enemies of Israel."

"He may try to murder you first."

"Seriously?"

"When we say these things are literally the things from the Old Testament, we're not making fun. They follow the rules of the masks they wear."

Shadow Team Seven divided into groups. General Venom used an energy-construct pegasus and his energy sword to fire blasts of light at Magog while encircling him. Bronze Medalist evacuated as many people as he could from the area before starting to use his inertia to send massive chunks of debris at it. Black Witch unleashed pretty much every offensive spell in Dungeons and Dragons, attempting to strike down the massive corpse creature. The Human Tank did what tanks did best, firing at it repeatedly. The Red Schoolgirl assaulted the dozens of corpses falling from its body to form a miniature zombie apocalypse.

Which left Gabrielle to face Gog alone.

She started by conjuring a building-sized Ultraforce claw hammer and then wailing the crap out of it.

Then she got nasty.

I wasn't sure what, exactly, I could bring to bear in this encounter, but I'd made a promise I intended to keep. I might not be winning any Humanitarian of the Year awards, given I was a bank robber and multiple murderer, but I had standards, dammit, and I intended to keep to them. I would probably come to regret that but, fortunately, would likely die before that became an issue.

"You frighten me," Cloak said.

"I try," I said, cheerfully.

In the end, I decided my best strategy was to join the Red Schoolgirl in destroying the various zombie demons that were falling off the side of Magog. Despite being made up of countless corpses fused together, more than the entire population of Avalon put together, Magog was shedding bodies like dandruff. These bodies, rather than rejoice at being freed, started moaning and running at anyone they could attack.

Icing their legs, I proceeded to hurl handfuls of fire at their faces. "I'm not a huge fan of zombie fiction. I make the occasional exception in video games, but I've got to say, the number of knock-offs lately are saturating the market."

My fire seemed to have a surprising effect on the creatures, every single ball of flame I hit them with caused the zombies to catch fire before burning to nothing in seconds. It took me a second to realize why that was before I remembered the Reaper's Cloak was designed to send wayward souls on their way. I may put the psycho in psychopomp, but that didn't mean I couldn't take advantage of that fact.

"*Demons and Nephilim collect the souls to mortals to use as power reserves,*" Cloak added. "*If you remove these bodies and send them off to their true afterlives, it will weaken it enough to perhaps send it on its way.*"

"Is that any different from throwing fireballs at them?"

"*No?*"

"Thanks, that's really helpful."

"I am the promised doom of all nations!" Magog shouted, its voice a hideous choir of a thousand dead. "All beings will know and rue my apocalypse."

"The smell is definitely apocalyptic," I said, blasting yet more zombies as they seemed to come faster and more numerous towards me.

"Why are you quipping in combat?" the Red Schoolgirl said, slicing through one, decapitating another, and then bisecting a third. I'd say she was cutting through them like wet tissue paper but I'm pretty sure that would have given more resistance.

"Don't most heroes and villains?" I asked.

"No!" the Red Schoolgirl said. "Besides, they're zombies! They don't care."

"Well I care!" If you're going to do a fight with a hideous world-ending evil, then the best thing was to do it right.

The Red Schoolgirl shook her head and sliced another through the head down to its groin. "Weirdo."

Magog wasn't a one-trick pony, however, and shot forth a storm of red lightning from its chest in every direction. The Human Tank was struck by one of these bolts and ended up falling from the sky, only for Bronze Medalist to propel himself through the air and grab her before settling safely down. That proved to be a trap, though, as another bolt struck them both in the back and caused them to fall down onto the ground.

I wasn't sure if they were unconscious or dead, but the difference was mostly academic to superheroes. As long as you didn't get your brain or entire body destroyed, the Society of Superheroes could revive you. It said something about the world the Society of Superheroes hadn't been able to get that tech to the common man despite their best efforts to do so.

Unfortunately, I didn't get a chance to deal with that as the numbers of zombies falling from Magog doubled, then doubled again. I had to throw far more fireballs just keep up and was rapidly running out of juice, especially since the moon wasn't exactly a center of necromantic energy. General Venom didn't last long in the air, either, getting struck by a whip-like appendage composed of the living dead. This knocked him from his horse right into one of the Black Witch's spells.

"We're not exactly covering ourselves in glory here!" the Black Witch said, summoning a host of shadow construct ravens that started tearing away corpses from Magog's body and eating them.

"The society took a few hours to beat Magog alone last time," the Red Schoolgirl said, her sword starting to glow as she grew faster and more brutal in her attacks. Her voice started to shake and change to something lower. Almost mannish. "**Kill, maim, destroy!**"

"Is that normal?" I called to Black Witch.

"No," she responded. "That's a bad sign!"

"I never would have guessed."

A frightening berserker's fury came over the Red Schoolgirl as she intensified her attacks a dozen-fold and started screaming in archaic Japanese Cloak couldn't translate. Glowing red kanji appeared all over her body as she threw all caution to the wind. She did much more damage to the zombies, but they started clawing at her, biting her, and weighing her down with their massive ranks. Not even my blasts were doing much to keep them off.

"She's being possessed by her ancestor, Oda Nobunaga!" the Black Witch said. "Get her away from the horde before he gets her killed and absorbs her soul!"

"What kind of outfit are you running?" I said, going closer and throwing most of my remaining reserves at her.

"A mixed superhero/supervillain team, dumbass! I thought we established that!" Black Witch said, conjuring a shielded bubble as Magog transformed into, I kid you not, a gigantic dragon made out of linked together corpses. The thing spread out its wings, pulled its neck back, and breathed out a tidal wave of hellfire down on her. Everything around her was scorched to ashes including the building she was on but her shielded bubble held firm.

"I am way out of my league here," I muttered, running up at Black Witch and dodging my way out of the zombies I'd done my best to keep a safe distance from while pitching flaming death at.

"*Be careful, Ms. Ishikawa's blade is capable of killing Reaper's Cloak wearers even in their intangible form,*" Cloak said. "*I lost friends to the Mad Samurai in World War 2 when he wielded it.*"

"That is such a racist codename."

"*He called himself Divine Warrior of the People, but he killed hundreds of innocents, so my response is—screw that guy.*"

Fair enough. I found myself dodging flying limbs, legs, heads, and worse when I got near the berserk and increasingly battered looking Red Schoolgirl. She had several bad bite marks and I was never more glad the whole 'zombie infection' thing was one of the few myths that was just that. I'd hate to face the Red Schoolgirl when she was dead, cannibalistic, and hungry.

That's when I ducked under one of her wild swings. "I will skin you alive, gaijin, and nail your pelt to my door!"

"Okay, the racism here is just getting really annoying," I said, blasting three zombies out of the way before freezing her sword in her hands. She growled as it suddenly lost its bisecting power. Ironically, she didn't drop it but started using it like a bat to knock away zombies instead.

"Sayonara, Schoolgirl," I said, grabbing her by the shoulders and causing her to turn intangible as we both fell to the level below and landed in a maintenance closet. She promptly clobbered me with her iced over sword but while being hit in the face with an icicle wasn't fun, it was a lot better than being decapitated by it. Besides, if there was one thing I knew how to do right, it was take a punch.

Falling backward into a pile of mops, brooms, and buckets, I iced over the door to the room to prevent her escape, then levitated, insubstantial as a ghost. The Red Schoolgirl screamed numerous obscenities at me in modern Japanese but was unable to catch me as I disappeared. I didn't know anything about her powers, but I figured being unable to kill anything would help her regain control over herself. She could worry about getting all those demon zombie bites disinfected.

Coming back up to the battlefield, I found myself surrounded by many demon zombies. They looked decidedly brassed off at having been denied their prey. Worse, I could see the Black Witch's shields buckle under Magog's zombie dragon form— shooting lightning from its eyes. That was, seriously, sweet to look at, but bad for our tactical situation.

As the zombies around me descended, I prepared what little fire I had left to deal with them, only to see a gigantic Ultra-Force fan blade slice through them like a lawnmower moving around me. I was covered in demon-zombie bits and gore but never felt so relieved. Looking up, I saw an Ultra-force battleship had been conjured in the air beside Magog and was unloading with every one of its two-hundred gun emplacements on the Nephilim.

Gabrielle had defeated Gog and come to reinforce us.

I'd never been so happy to be rescued in my entire life.

"No one takes out my friends, so says Ultragoddess!" Gabrielle shouted, not really being all that good at the mid-battle banter. I wasn't about to call her out on it, though. Even if I couldn't add much more to this battle than cheerleading, I was all for it.

That was when a gigantic Ultraforce, science-fiction cannon the size of a WW2 artillery piece appeared on the top of a nearby building. It had a telescope on the top of it leading to some sort of sniper's scope occupied by a small individual. I, for a second, thought it was Ultragod, before seeing the prominent P.H.A.N.T.O.M skull and lightning bolts emblem on the side.

Tom Terror.

Shit.

"GABRIELLE!" I shouted, waving my hands.

She didn't hear me or just thought I was trying to flag her down. A bolt of Ultraforce energy fired from the canon, undoubtedly enhanced by the complicated circuitry and physics Tom Terror could visualize in his mind. The bolt struck against Gabrielle and caused her energy reserves to blast out of her mouth, arms, and legs. Gabrielle started falling like an angel from Heaven, only for me to throw the last of my energy reserves into levitating and cushioning our fall. Even so, we hit hard against a hover-car hood in front of a Chinese restaurant. In the distance, I saw Tom Terror flying off, not even bothering to see what had happened to Gabrielle. He was utterly confident his sneak attack had worked.

He might have been right.

"Stay with me," I said, holding Gabrielle, ignoring the immense pain I felt from having hit it head-on.

Gabrielle looked alive, a little singed but otherwise fine. The weapon had just drained her of everything she'd had left.

Leaving us both powerless before Magog.

"You will die, little human," Magog grumbled as the dragon moved over me. "The Brotherhood of Infamy will destroy your hometown, murder your family, and bring the Great Beast into this world. I will enjoy the feast that my father will leave for this world. Now, though, you will go to meet your mistress in Hell."

I stared up at Magog, clutching Gabrielle's unconscious form against my chest.

I would give anything to protect her.

I loved her every bit as much as Mandy.

Even now.

Shit.

Why did I have to have these revelations now?

"Anything?" a voice whispered in my head.

It was not Cloak's.

"Yes," I agreed, immediately.

"*Gary!*" Cloak shouted, as if I'd made the stupidest decision of my life.

"Then take my power, champion, and know we will meet

again. Then I will collect upon this favor." The voice sounded like Mandy's and Gabrielle's synthesized together. I knew who it was I'd just made my deal with.

Death.

Samael.

The Reaper's Cloak's mistress.

Magog pulled his head back to breathe down another tidal wave of hellfire as I felt power within my hands like I'd never felt before. I could have broken my deal by not using it, but I'd meant everything I'd said to death. Summoning flames in my hands, I whispered, "Burn, you son of a bitch."

An immense amount of fire poured from my hands, a tornado of flame that struck the monster in the chest and caused the entirety of its massive frame to start burning. Thousands of souls were freed in an instant and thousands more joined in the ensuing ten minutes I kept burning it. A crowd of civilians, heroes, and supervillains gathered around to watch me as I focused my flame with overwhelming hate.

And, eventually, Magog was no more.

Not just in this reality.

But any reality.

I'd killed the Nephilim permanently. Like Sauron after the One Ring had been destroyed or the Kurgen after his head was cut off.

It was a big deal.

Probably.

I couldn't think about it, though, because all that exertion came to hit me in an instant. My eyes rolled back into my head and I fell over—unconscious on top of Gabrielle.

I really hoped I wasn't going back to jail.

Chapter Twenty-Two

The Ghosts of the Past
are the Hardest to Exorcise

I found myself with a monstrous headache, worse than when I'd regained my memories, and woke up.

To mist.

I was surrounded by an endless fog in a dark and foreboding set of surroundings. I couldn't see anything beyond a couple of feet away and I wasn't sure I was standing on the ground either.

"Okay, this is weird," I muttered. "Am I dead?"

"No, just unconscious," Cloak's voice said in the mist. It wasn't coming from my costume anymore. "You're not even gravely injured, just exhausted. If you were close to Death, I expect she'd be trying to speak with you now."

That was when a handsome man in his early forties walked through the mist, wearing an older-style suit with a winning ring on his right hand. He had dark, well-groomed hair, white skin, and a pair of dark foreboding eyes. He was the sort of fellow who, if you were looking for the secret identity of a superhero, you'd look right at this guy.

I offered my hand to him. "Nice to meet you, Lancel." It seemed wrong to call him Cloak here.

Lancel helped me up. "I tried for years to get people to call me Lance. It didn't take."

"Sorry," I said, dusting myself off. "So this is my afterlife? Or yours? I can't say I'm too impressed."

"I don't think its forever," Lancel said, looking around. "I can feel the weight keeping me bound here weakening the more you come into your role. I thought Death would be mad at me forever for stealing the Reaper's Cloaks, but it seems she's more forgiving than her reputation would suggest."

"You stole the Cloaks?" I asked, surprised. "From Samael."

"Persephone, Hel, Thanatos, Baron Samedi, or whatever name you want to call him or her. Death assumes the appropriate mythological form for her audience. She was always a terrifying female specter to me. The supernatural exists, no matter what humans like to label them, and mythology is just their medium for communicating with us." Lancel nodded. "I'm not proud of it but I didn't begin my career as one of the good guys. I was the secret leader of an organization called the Brotherhood of Infamy. It was a cult devoted to the worship of the Great Beasts in hope of destroying the world so it could be remade into something better."

Wow, that was like discovering Santa used to kill children in his spare time. "Wow. Why the hell would you do that?"

Lancel looked over at me. "Not everyone deals with their grief constructively."

I looked at him. "I know something of that, myself."

Lancel gave a half-smile. "In the end, when the time came to destroy the world for our paradise, I couldn't do it. I still had too many friends and my brother to tie me to the world. I think, to really believe in a utopia, you must hate the world. As angry as I was at the world, I wasn't angry enough to take my revenge out on everyone and everything. So I spent the next eighty years trying to make up for my mistake."

"The other six cloaks are still out there."

Lancel nodded. "I'm afraid so. As entertaining as this diversion with Tom Terror is, I can feel whoever possesses them are misusing them. They also all bear the curse Death placed upon them to bring the dead back to life to scourge the living. That has the potential to destroy the world if it's not stopped."

I remembered Gog and Magog and wondered how many other such creatures were out there. "So do a lot of things. You can't just look after your own mess, Lance."

"No, I suppose I can't. Does this mean you've decided to come over to the side of the righteous?" Lancel asked.

I looked down. "I don't know if I can."

"That's surprising, given you almost just sacrificed yourself to save Gabrielle."

"Ever see *Return of the Jedi*?"

"I may have caught it in theaters," Lancel said, chuckling. "Is this going to be one of your extended references?"

"No," I said, shaking my head. "Just a short and sweet one, like me. I always thought the Force was overly forgiving letting Vader into Jedi Heaven. Darth Vader was willing to kill the Emperor for the love of his son and die to save him. Which is great and all but, what about all the other millions of people he helped the Empire kill, like the Alderaanians? It's easy enough to die for the people you love. It's hard to do it for the rest of the world. Gabrielle is, *Mandy* is, but I'm not."

"That is, perhaps, a bit much to ask of anyone. Sometimes we forget that heroes are not meant to be the standard by which we should judge others, but those people who go above and beyond."

"What you said, chief." I'd been mulling over this stuff for the past few days. "My powers feel *really good*. I like using them. I loved the money, the fame, and the respect. I like Cindy and Diabloman, to be honest, and I imagine I'll like plenty of other supervillains who are as far from Psychoslinger as humanly possible. I hate the people like the Extreme and those bastards who employ them. If you're asking me if I'm going to give up a life of crime, probably not."

Lance looked down.

I took in a deep breath. "But maybe there's a spectrum to these sorts of things."

Lance looked up, surprised.

"On one end of the rainbow, you've got guys like Ultragod and Gabrielle. The people willing to sacrifice everything in order to do stuff," I said, trying to force down my anger over the fact my girlfriend had chosen the world over me. "At the other end, there's the Extreme, but maybe there's something similar with supervillains. Heroes and anti-heroes. Yet, if there're these, why not anti-villains?"

"I'm not sure that's a word."

"I'm pretty sure I read it on TV Tropes."

"Again, I have no idea what you're talking about."

I looked at my hands. "Or maybe the line between heroes and villains is just imaginary. A construct of where you're looking and what you support."

"Most people learn that when they're fourteen."

"My life got skewed at that age."

Lancel placed his hand on my shoulder. "There is still Tom Terror's riot going on outside. It's dangerous. You need to wake up and deal with it."

"I will," I said, staring. "Then I'm going to use Ultragod's teleporter and get the hell out of here. I'm also going to help myself to anything that is going to keep me and my friends out of jail."

"That is a dangerous self-defeating road, my friend."

"Only if I lose. Next time, I won't."

Lancel frowned, his voice softening. "It is a long, hard, and dangerous road you've set yourself upon, Gary, but I suppose we both knew that. I can only offer you my support and friendship. Also, my dear hope you never have as much to atone for as I do."

"Right back at you, Lance. Where's the exit?"

Lance took a step aside. "Just go through the mist. A word of caution, though, these mists are made of the same substance all ghosts are made of: memories. You'll have to pass plenty of them to get through. Ones that are better left behind."

"I never left my memories behind. Even before I got the Reaper's Cloak."

Lancel kept his expression even but I could tell he understood. I walked past him into the mists and hoped to God I didn't go crazy.

At first, it wasn't all that unpleasant. The mists weren't all that cold, being somewhat cool at best, but gradually became cooler as I progressed through them. I heard voices in the mist, too, of my brother, parents, and others who'd influenced my life.

"You're a disgrace, Gary," my parents said. "Keith almost ruined us. Did you have to finish the job?"

"You get more like me every day," Shoot-Em-Up said. "Man,

if I'd killed the supervillains you did, I would have gotten twice the money from my book deal."

"If you wanted to honor me, you could have looked after my daughter," Keith said, whispering. "You're going to make her life harder."

"We're dead because of you," a bank teller whispered. "All of us died because you made us a target by being a supervillain."

"You could be redeemed," Mandy said.

"You could be a hero," Gabrielle said.

"You're just going to drag down those you love instead," Cindy said.

I shook my head. "Try harder. I know all this."

The mists took me up on the challenge and I was soon reliving my past. It was five years ago, and I was rocking the Kurt Cobain look. I had on jeans and a white t-shirt underneath a black jacket. I was smoking a cancerless cigarette while sitting on a black Honda Accord hood, parked on a cliff overlooking Falconcrest City. The smog and lights blotted out the stars, but I could see the moon above. Mandy was sitting beside me, wearing a black bra and no shirt with her black blue-jeans barely pulled up. The two of us had just had sex in the back of her car.

"So, History, huh?" Mandy said. "You want to be a teacher?"

"I wanted to pursue my Doctorate in Unusual Criminology and be the sort of asshole who writes books and attends talk shows to explain why supervillains do what they do. That doesn't seem like it's going to happen, though." I'd been rejected from the program, even though I had more than enough credits. The fact I didn't have a Masters in Unusual Criminology shouldn't have prevented me from pursuing a higher education, but things hadn't worked out that way.

"I think they realized you were the guy who arranged for hackers to break into the student loan records and delete everyone's debt. The FBI is still trying to recover those files."

"My hacker is the best," I said, smiling at her. "There's nothing they'll be able to prove."

"So, going to continue the good fight?" Mandy smiled. "Become some masked online vigilante?"

"Sadly, my days of Guy Fawkes masks and activism are

over," I said, shaking my head. "They're onto me now so I'd just wind up getting caught. Better to quit while I'm ahead."

That and my niece was starting her freshman year and I didn't want to ruin her chances of getting a decent life. Despite it taking every cent my parents had, they'd managed to look after Keith's daughter after her mother abandoned her. Tina Karkofsky had been raised by Kerri and had a bright future ahead of her.

I wished her luck.

"Smart," Mandy said, not really sounding all that impressed. "How about you?"

Mandy stared forward. "My schedule is surprisingly clear. If I had plans for doing anything after college, they're over now."

I nodded, deciding now was as good a time as any to make my offer. "Well, we could do it together?"

"Oh?" Mandy asked.

"Yeah," I said, handing her a ring box.

Mandy blinked. "Seriously?"

"Wow, and I thought my parents' story of their marriage proposal was unromantic," I said, staring. That had involved a pregnancy scare and a shotgun if my mother's stories at Thanksgiving were anything to go by.

Mandy smiled. She then took the box and pulled out the ring, putting it on her finger. It was far plainer than the one I'd bought for Gabrielle before she up and vanished on me. It was all I could afford. "Are you sure your parents would be okay with you marrying a bisexual Gentile pagan?"

"I'm sure they'd hate you but you're not marrying them."

Mandy snorted. Wiggling her finger. "Are you sure you want to do this? You don't have anyone else you'd rather be with?"

I looked at her. "Do you?"

Mandy didn't answer at first. The Black Witch was serving twenty-to-life for trying to Death Curse some corrupt priests involved in a sleazy cover-up. I thought they should have given her a medal. Finally, Mandy said, "I want to be your wife."

"Cool."

Not exactly the kind of story you'd want to tell your grandkids. Still, it was one of my few unambiguously happy memories. I was kind of surprised the mists thought it would break me, if that's what they wanted to do. The voices that followed were an eerie collection of voices like Cloak's but different. I took them to be the other six Reaper's Cloak wearers for reasons I could only attribute to intuition.

"Mandy will suffer if you continue on this path."

"Worse, she will change."

"You will never be able to have the family you want with her."

"She does not want the children you desperately crave."

"You will take what is best from her and leave her a monster."

"You will have her body but never her heart."

I shook my head at the lame-ass statements and just carried on, hoping we were almost done. "Mandy loves me, and I love her. The fact she's in love with someone else doesn't change that. You can love more than one person. I love my family, my friends, and other people too. That's just how relationships work."

"Is it?"

I was once more in another memory. This time, it was earlier that year with Gabrielle cursing up a storm at the 'Game Over' screen in front of the Xbox 360. She was playing the story mode of *Corruption: Beware the Supermen*. It was a controversial tie-in game I wasn't sure how the Society of Superheroes' marketing people had let slip through the cracks. You could play as any of the superheroes of the Society as well as several pardoned villains. It's just the game was damned hard with certain characters.

"Ultragoddess f-ing sucks in this game!" Gabrielle said, tossing the remote to one side. She had her hair tied in bunches and was wearing one of my many *Star Wars* t-shirts, with no pants on. She had a pair of glasses on that were bigger and more obvious than any normal pair I'd seen. "It's like playing Ultragod except half the power. Which is B.S. because she's *stronger* than Ultragod."

I walked over, wearing a pair of boxers and a carrying a plate of plain cheese pizza. I personally liked to kill entire forests of woodland creatures for my pizza but then again, I'd never exactly been a strict Kosher Jew. I figured if God could forgive me working on Saturdays, he could forgive me enjoying the delicious taste of unclean animal.

"Public perception is a strong thing," I said, walking back to the refrigerator in our apartment to get myself a Coca-Cola. We'd been sharing it for the better part of the last three months. "When people think of Ultragoddess, they still think of the teenage girl who guest-starred on all the cutesy shows in the Nineties. They don't think of the girl who managed to throw down with Entropicus one-on-one or who was trained by Guinevere and all the other warriors of the Society since damned near-birth."

Gabrielle looked over at me. "What do you think of her?"

I popped my drink top and took a swig. "Well, she saved my life, so I can't be too hard on her. On the other hand, I sometimes wonder about your obsession with her. Sometimes, it seems like you love her and other times it's like you hate her."

Gabrielle looked at the screen. "Gary, what if I told you I was Ultragoddess."

It was another moment where all the little clues came together and her still-light light mesmerism fell away. "Wow. I am a *moron*."

Gabrielle looked down. "Not really. Isis cast some spells on me to make it harder for people to recognize me. I also use a lot of Ultra-mesmerism to make people unable to put the pieces together. It's almost unconscious now. I also do my best to project an Ultra-light illusion of myself in most public appearances to add a foot to my features as well as change subtle details, so people will be less likely to recognize me. Guinevere does something similar to those with evil intent in their hearts, so she can be with her family without fear of reprisal."

"That's...terrifying."

"Is it?" Gabrielle looked at me. She pulled off her glasses. "Gary, do you know how many times my mother was kidnapped?"

I swallowed, wondering where this was going. I was surprisingly cool with her revelation of her identity. I think it was like Luke's revelation to Leia in, again, *Return of the Jedi*. I'd somehow always known, and it wouldn't be until it was taken away I would get angry over it. "I remember it being a joke in the school yard growing up. Whenever a villain wanted to get at Ultragod, they would kidnap Polly Pratchett. So…a lot?"

"A lot," Gabrielle said, staring. "What people don't talk about is those weren't funny situations. In the 1930s, the Hollywood Haunter tied her to a set of train tracks. Which, again, is the most cliché thing a villain can do. But you know what? Being tied to a set of train tracks with a train coming is *fucking terrifying.* My mom bore the scars well, standing up to the worst of the worst, but if not for the fact Ultragod has a lot of friends and alien technology; she would have been killed or disfigured many times."

I nodded. "The precautions superhero families have to take is like the Witness Protection Program I understand. The Society of Superheroes relocates their families and friends under assumed identities when they choose to go public. As much as mobsters hate snitches, they hate superheroes more and itch for payback." That was basic Unusual Criminology 101.

"Mobsters are the least of a superhero's loved one's problems," Gabrielle said. "There're terrorists, supervillains, aliens, and the fact weirdness just seems to follow you wherever you go. Ninety percent of superhero marriages end in either premature death or divorce because of the stress. The remaining ten percent? Most of them are with fellow superheroes."

"You found the ring."

Gabrielle looked on the verge of crying. She pulled out the ring from under her shirt. It was tied to a thin silver chain. "Yeah."

"I'm not afraid," I said, finishing my drink. "Let me get on one knee—"

"No." Gabrielle shook her head. "You're not afraid, but I am."

"Gabby," I took a deep breath, suddenly afraid. Afraid I'd lose her and that was the most terrifying feeling I'd ever have. "Before you, I was angry all the time. I hated the world. I hated myself. I hated everyone else for letting the world become like it is. You know what I did to Shoot-Em-Up. You know what happened to my brother. You know…everything. You don't understand but it was dark before and when I'm with you... when we're together." I struggled for the right words. "It doesn't hurt anymore."

I was crying now.

So was Gabrielle. The tears were running down her cheek. "Gary, *they know.* I've been careless. If a B-Lister like the Cackler can figure it out, then others will, and they'll target you. They'll target your family. They'll target everyone around you. I'm going into space on a peacekeeping mission soon, and I won't be here to protect you. I need people to think we've broken up and you mean nothing to me."

I slammed my fist into the back of the refrigerator. "Then let's fool them. Pretend to break up. I'll change my name, fake my death, or create a new identity. Hell, I'll *become* a superhero. Whatever you need. I don't care how long you're away as long as you come back to me!"

"I won't lose you to violence. I'd rather not have you at all than that." Gabrielle was bawling now. She stared at me. "Look into my eyes."

I did, instinctively.

And then found myself in an empty apartment, cleaned out of her stuff with hours having passed and a vague sense we'd broken up.

I cried until morning.

Then got angry and made a silent vow to hold onto the anger harder and tighter than ever.

It was easy.

That was when I passed out from the mist.

Chapter Twenty-Three

My Awkward, Awkward Conversation with My Ex

I woke up getting mouth-to-mouth from Gabrielle. Which was an awkward and pleasant enough situation from my perspective to qualify as adultery. Gently pushing her away before she started chest compressions, I coughed.

"I'm not dead," I said, taking a deep breath. "Yet. No need for cosmic retcons of the universe, necromancy, turning me into a vampire, or revealing that I'm actually a clone of the original Gary Karkofsky."

Gabrielle looked at me, smiling. She then frowned. "You know, you joke about that, but all of that stuff has actually happened to my friends. None of it was very funny."

I grimaced. "Yeah, sorry I suppose it wouldn't be."

We were on top of a roof in New Avalon, overlooking much of the devastation wrecked by Gog and Magog. None of the other Shadow Seven were present and I was surprised to find myself worried about them.

"How are the others?" I asked, turning back to her.

"Alive," Gabrielle said, looking up at the barely intact dome. Some of the energy projecting heroes were patching up the damage from stray supervillain blasts or attempts to kill everyone by a nihilistic few. "Everyone took a major banging but, aside from General Venom, no one suffered any serious injuries. He suffered a broken spine and would be paralyzed if not for the fact he's cybernetic like the Prismatic Commando."

"A pity, the ex-terrorist could have died a hero."

"He made a lot of mistakes," Gabrielle said, looking into my eyes. "That was before he found religion and became a man of peace. I don't believe anyone is beyond redemption."

"I do," I said, staring at her. "But we're not talking about him, are we?"

"Gary, I know I don't have any right to ask—"

I sighed and sat up "You're right, you don't. You gave up that right when you decided to make up my mind for me."

Gabrielle blinked. "I suppose I deserve that."

"And worse," I said, sighing. "However, I'm not so much of an asshat that I'm going to get anything but hate and self-loathing from being cruel to a person I..." I paused. Using the L-word would open a can of worms, and another for good measure. I wasn't the sort of guy who cheated on his loved ones. Even when I'd been cheated on, mostly by Cindy, I hadn't returned the favor.

I hadn't cared enough to get mad over it, either.

I cared very much how Mandy felt.

"I see," Gabrielle said, probably getting more from my hesitation than I intended to share. "Are you happy?"

"Being a supervillain or being married to Mandy?"

"Yes."

I took a deep breath, considering my answer. "As ill-conceived, stupid life-choices I might choose to blame on an early-onset mid-life crisis go, becoming a supervillain has proven to have its ups and downs. I've been involved in some truly amazing stuff, much more fun than working as a bank teller. It's also nearly gotten me killed a half-dozen times in as many days. I'm not sure I'm going to be able to keep up with the pace, if this is going to be my life from now on. On the other hand, I don't feel like I'm sleepwalking through life anymore. I've seized control of my destiny even if it's a destiny that is trying to beat me in the face with a pair of brass knuckles. So, you could say my feelings are mixed."

I pointedly didn't answer her question about Mandy and me. I knew the answer, I just didn't know how to tell her.

Gabrielle smiled. "Supervillain or hero, you've saved a lot of lives today."

"Don't tell anyone else about that."

"I'll let it be known you were leading the Shadow Seven and we formed a temporary alliance to get rid of Gog and Magog only for you to backstab me at the first opportunity. It'll increase everyone's street cred considerably."

"You'd do that for me?"

"I have some experience dealing with career criminals, Gary. Remember, people may think of me as a Pollyanna, but I lead a covert black ops superhero team that exists for the purposes of doing dirty jobs. I'm not one to make moral judgments."

I looked at her. "There's a difference between your team and the Extreme, Gabrielle. You fought to protect people. They fought to fight."

"My team also fights for a paycheck, perks, and hopes of eventually getting out of jail. Bronze Medalist is only on the team because he likes to fight and wasn't getting enough combat time with the Society's main team. The Silver Lightning's influence, I suspect. The Human Tank will probably earn her freedom only to be pulling off jewelry store robberies in a few months' time. This is her third time being incarcerated."

"Some people never learn, I guess," I said, shaking my head.

"Your brother was on the original incarnation of the team, back when it was in the service of the Foundation for World Harmony. Before my time."

I blinked, looking up. "Really?"

Gabrielle nodded. "The stories about your brother you told me made me think not all supervillains were like Tom Terror and his cronies. With the governments all closing ranks and working on becoming more repressive, I figured I'd revive the program and see if we could use it to do some good. A couple of toppled dictatorships, a wrecked Exterminator droid program, six destroyed P.H.A.N.T.O.M bases, and a freed prison camp or two make me think we're doing a good job."

"It's going to take a while to adjust my mental image of you to include badass commando, Ultragoddess, and my geeky ex-girlfriend. You're like Sarah Connor meets Willow Rosenberg meets a black Michelle Rodriguez who can fly."

"Thanks...I think."

"So, how is the prison escape?" I asked, wondering if we were chatting things up as things continued to go to hell.

"Thwarted, so far," Gabrielle said, frowning. "There're dozens dead. Maybe as many as a hundred, and they were people we knew. Casualties could have been much worse but there's at least one advantage of being in a place filled with superheroes and that's people who look after civilians first. More than a few prisoners are missing, though, including Tom Terror. There's missing equipment, too, though nothing too big. Security systems are down, though."

I cursed, hating the fact Tom had probably gotten away with his plan. At least he hadn't gotten the Power Nullifier he'd sent me to fetch. "I'm sorry that bastard got away."

I regretted ever agreeing to team up with him.

I bet most villains felt the same way after they did.

Why did he have such luck recruiting them again?

"Because you're criminals who never learn from your mistakes," Cloak said.

"Hush you," Gabrielle returned. "It's possible Tom hasn't gotten away, actually."

"Oh?"

"Light manipulation is one of the powers granted by the Ultra-Force, Gary," Gabrielle explained. "Tom Terror could have used it to fly out into space and down to Earth at any time, but that's not who he is. He thinks he could have conquered the Earth and turned it into the capital of a vast interstellar human-o-centric galactic empire by now, if not for my father."

"Mostly because it's true." I pointed out. Tom Terror was fully capable of toppling alien empires and building his own. He was just too stubborn to realize it would be better to operate on another world than keep trying to hash it out on the one planet that had the brainpower and muscle to stop him.

"I think he's probably still around," Gabrielle said, looking around. "Invisible and cloaked from all forms of detection. He won't try to leave until he's taken a shot at trying to kill my father again."

"Or his loved ones," I said. "He almost killed you while you were fighting Magog."

"Almost," Gabrielle said. "Which, with a dollar, will buy him a bag of chips. He's smart enough not to come at me directly. Unlike my dad, I'd send him on a one-way ticket to Hell. Something he richly deserves."

I couldn't disagree with her there. Ironic. "So, what's my situation? Am I to go back to my cell?"

"My father would insist," Gabrielle said. "So would the rest of the Society's Inner Council. Which is why I'm going to authorize you to go anywhere you want to go in New Avalon, including my father's room. There, you'll find a teleporter that will take you straight down to Earth. It's his private one, separate from all the locked down ones which run off the central power grid."

She was sending me to the same one Tom Terror had intended to go to. "Thank you, Gabby. That's not going to stop your father from picking me up tomorrow, though. I'm not sure I know where to hide on Earth that is far enough away from your father."

"Nowhere," Gabrielle said, chuckling. "He's kept an eye on you since we dated. Moses checks in on you once a day. I think he may have had Isis cast a tracking spell on you too."

I narrowed my eyes. "That son of a...no wonder he found me so quickly!"

Cloak laughed in my head.

I really wished I was back in the mists, so I could punch him in the face.

"That's a fair cop."

"I'll talk to the Inner Council about it. You saved a lot of lives here and that's going to count for a lot. There's also the fact half of the city just watched you kill a Nephilim. We may be a group composed of heroes, but no one here is stupid either. Between those who are grateful for what you did and those who think you're out of their league, I doubt many superheroes are going to want to come down to capture you personally. You may still be on the books as a criminal, but I imagine they'll leave it to local law enforcement."

"I can deal with that," I said, nodding.

"Don't underestimate them," Gabrielle said, offering her

hand to me. "As much as I hate to say it, there're superheroes who sympathize with the Extreme, and would call me a hypocrite for believing in lethal force but not their way of unlimited total warfare against supervillains. That's not even covering the government super-soldier and anti-terrorist teams they're building. You need to be careful they don't start raining down black ops against you or your family. Make friends, bribe someone, or learn to lay low."

I took it and the two of us stood up. I was still a bit winded from my exertions fighting Magog, but I'd felt worse even before getting superpowers.

"You're telling me to be paranoid about the government?" I asked, looking at her.

"Gary, I used to think you were the kookiest conspiracy theorist this side of Fox Mulder," Gabrielle said, pointing at my chest. "Now? After five more years of being a fully active S.O.S. operative? I don't think you were paranoid *enough.*"

Okay, that was...terrifying.

"I'll watch for drones and missile strikes," I said, crossing my heart. "Also, giant robots who might smash their hands into my bedroom window at night."

"I hate those things," Gabrielle said, in all seriousness. "If you're genuinely happy about being a supervillain, Gary, I support you as your friend and hope you'll carry it out with the same good heart I know you bring to everything else. I may even have some team-ups for you in the future, if you want."

"Really? You support me that much?"

"Of course, I think this is a blindingly stupid idea and you're throwing your life away," Gabrielle said, crossing her arms. "Seriously, you could do so much more on the other side of the law."

"See? That's more the reaction I expected."

"The sane one?"

I paused. "Perhaps. Still, I'm not quite ready to hang up my Reaper's Cloak just yet." Not that I could if I wanted to.

Gabrielle just shook her head. "Do you want me to give you a lift over to the residential quarters?"

I looked from my position there. There weren't a lot of

civilians or superheroes nearby. "Nah, I think I can make it. Besides, I want to avoid being spotted in a too friendly position with one of the world's most beloved superheroines. They might get the wrong idea."

"And what idea is that?" Gabrielle joked.

I paused. I couldn't let that go. I had to answer her other question.

"You asked me if I was happy with my marriage to Mandy. The answer is yes."

Gabrielle was silent for a moment "I see."

"It's not perfect. We're not perfect. God knows, I'm not perfect. However, we've had a good five-year run. Which is better than most nowadays. She's a hero, too, though she hasn't gone out to get any spandex just yet."

"You realize superheroes don't actually wear spandex, right? We wear alien polymers which provide protection against the elements while also capable of being covered in illusion spells that make it look sexy."

"Really? That's why everyone looks like they've gone to the gym or had plastic surgery?"

"Quite often. No one wants to look unattractive when the eyes of the world's population are upon you," Gabrielle said, looking down at her chest. "There're other methods too. This is mostly a wonder bra."

"I seem to recall..." I bit my tongue. No, Gary. Bad. "The thing is, though. Yeah, I'm happy."

"I'm glad," Gabrielle said.

She was lying.

I understood her feelings.

But they didn't change anything.

"Has there been anyone else for you?" I asked, hoping she'd found some measure of love and affection since our breakup.

"I almost married a space prince of the Thran Empire."

"Oh, really?" I asked, surprised and pleased. A little bit jealous, too, since human emotions are messy complicated things.

"Yeah, it turned out he was actually a robot constructed by Emperor Tyranax to seduce me so I could have my brain removed and replaced with a computer after the wedding."

"Ah," I said, not sure how to react, and really annoyed with the slight bit of pleasure I got from that. "That's terrible."

"Yeah, it was, but the sex was good."

I blinked, then gestured over my shoulder to the residential quarters. "Okay, then. I think I'll just be going then."

Gabrielle stopped me by taking my arm, she turned me around and gave me a short kiss on the lips. She looked at me, then down at the ground. Ashamed of herself. "I'm sorry."

I stared at her, then started walking away much faster. I didn't say any parting words to her and hated myself for it. In the distance, on another rooftop, I saw the Black Witch. She was standing next to a laundromat's neon sign that read, "We Do Capes." The Black Witch was far away but I knew she was watching me and had probably seen everything. Given she was a witch, she'd probably heard everything too. I could only imagine her feelings.

I probably agreed with them all.

"You should tell your wife about this encounter," Cloak said.

"No kidding," I said, levitating away. I was fully charged now and didn't feel in the least bit worried about using my abilities. "I'm sure she'll understand."

"Oh?"

"See? I'm getting better at lying to you all the time."

Chapter Twenty-Four

Oh Come on, There's More?
I Thought the Big Monster was the Climax

The residential quarters were, bluntly, a mess.
You'd think most supervillains in a riot would be interested in getting their freedom and would go about in some manner of orderly fashion of doing so: they'd take hostages, go for
the hangar bay, seize the teleporters, or even arm themselves.
Plenty of them did, don't get me wrong, but a staggering number of them made a beeline right for the rooms of the Society's
heroes.

Given a choice between freedom and the slight chance
they could catch their enemies sleeping so they could murder
them, they chose the latter at least half the time. As such, the
residential area looked like, well, a riot had gone on in it.

There were regular intervals of bodies, mostly janitorial
staff and maintenance personnel. People murdered for no other
reason than most heroes didn't live on New Avalon. It was like a
Fireman's Station, really. People kept their stuff here, but no one
wanted to take up permanent residence.

Plenty of rooms had been forced open and it was interesting
to see the temporary quarters of Earth's finest. A few of them
were easy to recognize at a glance like ones filled with Egyptian-
themed stage magician paraphernalia, medieval weaponry,
baseball trophies, and so on. I won't lie to you, I broke away
from my escape to search through several of them. I stole a mint
condition autographed Babe Ruth trading card, a copy of *Action
Comics* 1#, the copy of the Declaration of Independence given

to the Society at the time of writing, and the Hand of Infinity. Which should have had better security.

"*I can't believe you just risked your life to save this place and now you're taking time to rob the Society,*" Cloak said, genuinely appalled.

"Why does it surprise you?"

"*I'm saddened I have no answer to that.*"

"I'm just glad the cloak has extradimensional pockets. This opens so many interesting new opportunities."

Ultragoddess hadn't been kidding about the fact the security systems were down and I was permitted damned near everywhere. There were a couple of survivors I chanced upon, but I just turned intangible and walked through them. Weirdly, this resulted in the majority confusing me for the Nightwalker and the rest just left confused. Which was fine by me. I didn't want to hurt anybody, and I was well and truly *done* with this place.

"Now, where is Ultragod's room," I muttered, disliking the fact the maps weren't labeled in the residential area.

"*Gary, we should talk about that deal you made with Death.*"

"Where I more or less pledged my body and soul?"

"*Yes, that one.*"

"It's a bit late to worry about that now, isn't it?"

"*All magicians who want to proceed past the earliest levels of magic must have a supernatural patron to provide them with access to greater supernatural resources: angels, demons, gods, Great Beasts, or Elder Ones. To gain the highest levels of sorcery, one must humble oneself tremendously and become less of an instrument of your own will than a tool or avatar of your divinity.*"

"Yeah, it works like clerical magic in *Lances and Labyrinths*. I get that."

I could hear Cloak clench his nonexistent teeth. "Yeah, *okay, let's go with that. That fire you created back there? The magic you unleashed? That is only available to the most powerful servants of Death. The ones who are living avatars of her will.*"

"So, you're saying I'm awesome?"

"*I'm saying* she shouldn't have given you that."

"But she did and I'm grateful."

"*There will be a price. You need to be prepared for it. Death gives nothing away for free and to save one today is to lose everything tomorrow.*"

"I'll give everything of myself. I'm not afraid."

"*You—*"

"Please don't say I should be. That's so damned cliché."

"*Fine.*"

I didn't get a chance to say anything more because I saw a glowing psionic boomerang coming straight at my head.

"Crap!" I said, jumping out of the way, only to have my right arm cut at the shoulder. It wasn't bad, but it hurt like hell.

That was when I saw Psychoslinger step out from one of the nearby rooms. "You left me to die, Merciless. That was very rude!"

I thought he did die! I, immediately, retaliated by unleashing a fireball about a dozen times larger than the tiny ones I usually unleashed. It was closer to using a flamethrower than before, but my sheer hatred for the man gave me a boost.

The flames washed over Psychoslinger with to no effect.

Well, crap.

"Nothing to say? That makes it worse!" Psychoslinger shouted. "I mean, if I wasn't able to reconstitute myself from death due to being a psionic being then I might actually have died for good! Which would have sucked."

He started hurling more boomerangs, not really aiming but trying to make me jump up and down. I turned insubstantial for good measure but when another grazed my leg, I ended up hitting the ground from the injury. It seemed Psychoslinger could penetrate my intangibility too.

Way, way too many bad guys could do that.

"*Tell me about it,*" Cloak muttered. "*It made my power flat-out useless at times.*"

"Not helping!" I shouted.

I switched to ice, this time, freezing Psychoslinger's legs to the ground, then his arms, and then covered his entire body in a gigantic block of the stuff like the Chillingsworths often did. Psychoslinger then disappeared from inside it and appeared outside of the ice block, unharmed. I blinked, wondering if he could teleport or if he could just regenerate himself that fast. Either way, this was getting worse all the time.

"I am getting really-really upset!" Psychoslinger shouted, raising his fingers and pointing like they were hand-guns. "Pew-pew-pew!"

I almost laughed even as psionic bullets shot out of them and exploded against the wall behind me. He wasn't aiming at me this time, otherwise he could have taken me out. Even so, I used my insubstantiality to move underneath the ground and behind him. I should have run away, but hindsight is twenty-twenty.

I prepared to try to put something in his head when Psychoslinger spun around and conjured a psionic bat he clocked me in the head with. It would have killed me if not for the durability the cloak provided, but it still hurt like hell. He then kicked me, struck me in the chest with his bat, and then hit me again across the back for good measure. I hit the ground like a sack of potatoes.

That was when Psychoslinger grabbed me by the hood of my cloak and held a psionic shiv to my throat. I found, much to my surprise, I couldn't turn insubstantial while he held it. However the supervillain had gotten his superpowers, I had to give him credit. He'd won the superpower lottery. He was not only immune to everything I could throw at him but effectively immortal.

"No one is immortal," Cloak whispered. "Remember how you controlled him last time!"

I questioned Cloak's definition of control, but it seemed Psychoslinger was a pathologically impulsive manchild, and that gave me some insight into handling him. "All right, all right. You pass the damned test."

"Test?" Psychoslinger said, snorting.

"To join the Fraternity of Supervillains, obviously," I said, sighing bored. "Tom Terror set up the whole business with the Deathmonger. I was to see how you dealt with it, whether you attempted to finish the mission, and then gauge how you reacted to the perception of betrayal. Congratulations, you passed. Albeit, you took longer than I expected to get here."

"Bullcrap!" Psychoslinger hissed, showing the first sign of genuine anger I'd seen from him.

"Oh, come on, Psychoslinger, did you really think it'd be that easy?" I said, sighing. "You're here, though, which shows you've got some initiative."

It was a ridiculous assertion, except for the fact Tom Terror wasn't exactly known for his fatherly treatment of subordinates. He was a terrible boss, one of the worst, yet people kept flocking back to him. I had the suspicion it was because supervillains were like pack animals and flocked to the biggest source of power they could perceive.

"I don't believe you," Psychoslinger said, sounding conflicted. "I think I'll carve the truth out of you."

"Fine by me," I said, showing no fear.

Psychoslinger hesitated.

I'd ruined his buzz.

I pointed down the hall. "We've got a job to complete, though. Get the Power Nullifier, give it to Tom, kill Ultragod, and get out of here. After that, you could try to kill me but, let's face it, Psychoslinger, would I really be this calm if I didn't have an ace up my sleeve?"

Psychoslinger stared at me.

Then dropped me.

"You *were* in the archvillains wing," Psychoslinger said, muttering. "I've been at this for years and they haven't put me there. They say I'm a serial killer. Which is complete garbage. I am a SPREE KILLER and mass-murderer, dammit."

"The Society gives no respect," I said, getting up and dusting myself off. "Ready to go kill the world's most powerful hero?"

"Hell yes!"

"Gary, where are you going with this?" Cloak asked.

"I have no idea."

Chapter Twenty-Five

Things go from Bad to Worse
(It's a Frequent thing)

Psychoslinger and I continued past the bodies of the dead New Avalon staff he'd created while searching for me, heading up a flight of stairs to a long hallway that ended in a single doorway. It was here our journey would end. According to Cloak, who was willing to help me in hopes of defeating Psychoslinger, this was Ultragod's room. Walking up to the doorway, I saw a large metal box with a set of controls just to the left of the solid steel door.

It was the Society of Superheroes' version of a common door lock, preventing anyone but authorized personnel from entering. I was authorized to move through this place with impunity but, apparently, that didn't extend to Ultragod's quarters. I wonder if he suspected his daughter might try and break her ex-boyfriend out of prison or if he'd just changed the locks recently.

Psychoslinger suggested we kidnap one of the local technicians and force him to open it for us, but I didn't think that was the best option. Psychoslinger would kill any who helped us as soon as their usefulness ended and probably before.

I was tempted to turn myself in, but I hadn't seen anyone yet who Psychoslinger couldn't kill outright. Instead, I'd just let him direct me and done my best to keep us stealthy as I struggled to figure out a way to stop someone immune to my powers.

"*Will you help me here?*" I asked Cloak.

"Follow my lead," Cloak replied. *"Start by unscrewing the panel then..."*

With that, he gave me precise instructions on how to hack the terminal. I worked for half an hour on hacking the terminal, finally bandaging two wires together that caused the door to open with a whoosh.

Psychoslinger stared at me. "That was brilliant! Where did you learn to do that?"

"I'm a mad scientist in addition to being a sorcerer. I have a secret fortress filled with android servants underneath the South Pole."

"I want one of those!" Psychoslinger clapped his hands. It was like he *wasn't* threatening to kill me in order to make me go along with his plans. "Tell me how!"

"Later," I said, giving a dismissive wave before heading into Ultragod's room.

The interior was a wonderland equal to the Night Tower. There were advanced-looking devices, alien artifacts, glass cases, and a number of statues that looked like they should belong in ancient Rome. It was bigger on the inside than on the outside—taking advantage of the "uncertain technological properties" available to the Society of Superheroes. A giant hologram of the galaxy hovered near the ceiling, generated by a number of glowing crystal pyramids at the base of the floor. Ultragod had an interesting sense of style.

"Amazing," I whispered. "I need to take everything here."

"No."

"Oh hush."

"This is boring," Psychoslinger said. "I was hoping we'd get to see Ultragoddess. Killing Ultragod's daughter would make me the most feared supervillain in the world. Well, you know, aside from you and Tom." Great, now he was attempting to butter me up. The fact he was threatening to kill Gabrielle should have made me angry, but I imagined Psychoslinger trying and it made me laugh. It amused me to think of the myriad ways Gabrielle would tear him apart. Unfortunately, she wasn't here, and I was left alone with the psychopath who outclassed me in every possible way.

"Rule Number One."

"*You could try killing him with your intangibility powers,*" Cloak said.

"*Let's call that Plan B,*" I said back to him.

"*What's Plan A?*" Cloak asked.

"*I'll tell you when I think of it,*" I replied.

Psychoslinger threw up his hands in frustration. "Man, who knew being a supervillain could be such a drag. You know, I think I'm going to abandon them when I get back down to the Earth. I'm going to kill a bunch of superheroes, their families, and their dogs too."

"Really? Their dogs?" I asked, disgusted.

"Okay, that may be going too far, but anything non-canine," Psychoslinger surprised me by saying. Then again, psychopaths could often bond with animals more easily than with people, I'd read somewhere. It was the one quality that hinted they might be more than complete monsters.

Other psychos tortured animals just fine, too.

So maybe I was reaching.

"Let's find the teleporter as it's our chief priority," I said. "After that, we can get the Power Nullifier."

"*Smooth. He'll never see through that plan. I've underestimated your skill as a criminal mastermind.*" I could *feel* the sarcasm.

"Sure!" Psychoslinger said.

I tried not to smile. Instead, I thought smug smart-alecky remarks at my cloak. "*You were saying?*"

"*I'm beginning to think I've overestimated the intelligence of the average supervillain.*"

"Supervillains are a cowardly and... something," I said. "*I forget the rest.*"

"Be wary," the Nightwalker said. "*Psychoslinger is likely to turn on you at any moment.*"

"No kidding." I headed over to a device which looked like a set from the original Sixties *Star Trek.* "I think this is the teleporter. Either that or Ultragod is a friend of Gene Roddenberry."

"You're right," a booming voice said above me. "On both counts."

I looked up at Ultragod, hovering a foot above my head, his cape trailing behind him.

"Well, crap." I said, staring up at Ultragod. "Cloak, I'm about to get my butt kicked, aren't I?"

"*Indeed.*"

Ultragod punched me through a set of glass display cases before I could react. Ultragod was upon me a second later, this time punching me through a set of purple alien pots. By the time I landed on the floor, my back was filled with shards of glass and pottery. I'd been beaten before, sometimes to the point of unconsciousness, during my angry youth.

It was nowhere near this bad.

"I had hopes for you." Ultragod floated towards me. He conjured a gigantic fist made of energy that picked me up between its fingers. "I thought you were different. Yet, here you are, working with monsters like Psychoslinger and Tom Terror. The choices we make define us. I'm sorry to say yours have revealed your true character. I was hoping better, given what Gabrielle said about you."

"Pfft." I spit blood from my mouth. "This is not what it looks like."

Oh God. Did I actually say that?

"Ninety-seven New Avalon citizens are dead. Several superheroes are critically injured, a few may not make it. That's not counting the prisoners killed in the resulting battles or by their fellows. Do you have anything to say before I pound you and Psychoslinger into next month?"

"How about...goodbye?" Psychoslinger lifted a strange multi-barrel gun with dozens of blinking lights. A blast of white energy shot forth from it and struck Ultragod in the back.

The glowing fist holding me up dissipated as the superhero crumbled to the ground, clutching his chest as if his heart was exploding.

"What the...hell?" I struggled to get up and fell to the ground. I was still hurting from Ultragod's attack.

"I found the Power Nullifier in one of the display cases. Just look at him, he's crawling on the ground like a baby. This is so awesome." Psychoslinger laughed, shaking the weapon like a toy.

I struggled to get up, falling to the ground a second after I got to my feet. "Yeah, awesome."

Well, that was unexpected.

And *really bad*.

Ultragod looked terrible. After being blasted with the Power Nullifier, he looked like he'd come down with a severe case of the flu. Worse, he looked like he was dying. In an instant, the tide had shifted and now the world's greatest superhero was at our nonexistent mercy. Which is exactly what I *didn't* want.

"Gary, you have to help him. Tom Terror built the Power Nullifier as a weapon to **kill** *Ultragod, not disable him. Without his powers, Ultragod will be killed by his inherent radiation within minutes."* I seemed to recall Tom Terror having tried something similar on Gabrielle way-back-when, only for it not to work because the Ultraforce was inherent to her.

I wanted to help, I did, but I wasn't sure how. God almighty. Why was reality doing this to me? You know, aside from all the horrible stuff I'd done in the past few days. Psychoslinger placed the Power Nullifier beside Ultragod, taunting the Lord of Light with the reverse setting being *just* out of reach. The weapon looked like an oversized children's toy, yet it had reduced the strongest man in the world to a shivering wreck. Psychoslinger kicked the legendary superhero across the jaw, conjuring a psychic dagger before driving it into his left hand and doing the same to his right. The wounds weren't lethal, but they were enough to cause Ultragod to cry out.

"You want to join in, Merciless?" Psychoslinger said, giggling. "I figure there are all sorts of things we can do to him without killing him."

Somehow, between here and when he'd ambushed me in the hall, we'd become friends again. Or he was going to kill me soon so there was no point in not playing with me first.

"I'll pass. I've got a teleporter to catch. You, however, knock yourself out." I needed to find a weapon to get rid of this bastard. My back tooth came loose as I ran my tongue over it and spit it out along with a mouth full of blood. Ultragod had cleaned my clock but good.

"Thanks!" Psychoslinger gave me two thumbs up. "You're all right."

"Your approval fills me with shame, but I've got better things to do than stand in your way." My eyes searched the trophy room around me for something that might help. There were alien flowers, weapons that I didn't know how to access through their casings, and holograms of Gabrielle with various boyfriends. About half of them were of her and me.

Awkward.

Psychoslinger picked up Ultragod by his tights, hoisting him up to eye-level. Looking into the superhero's eyes, he said, "I wonder what it would do for my rep if I cut the face off the world's greatest superhero? How beloved will you be if your face scares small children?"

I decided I had no idea what half of this crap was, and I'd just have to improvise. "Psychoslinger?"

"Yeah?" my psychotic companion said.

"I'm actually on his side," I said, deciding to distract him. Maybe Ultragod could think of something. Maybe Psychoslinger would kill us both.

Either way.

I was a supervillain.

Which meant I did what I *wanted*.

Not what was smart.

Psychoslinger seemed to understand what was happening because he dropped Ultragod and threw a pair of psychic daggers at me. I was already turning intangible by that point and slipped into the floor before levitating up behind him. Grabbing a humanitarian of the year award from the wall, I attempted to put it inside his chest as I done with the Extreme.

"Fun times over, Psychoslinger," I said, before noticing there was nothing inside Psychoslinger's chest. It was like he was made of electricity. "Crap."

"I'm *made* of psychic energy, you fool! There's nothing you can do to stop me!"

"The one time I try to do something nice..." I trailed off, wincing.

"Albeit for the selfish reason of not wanting Gabrielle to hate you

any more than Mandy would for letting the world's greatest hero die."

"Not the time, Cloak!"

Spinning around, Psychoslinger tried to take my head off with a psychic scimitar. I ducked, just barely avoiding having my chest bisected.

"Bitch!" Psychoslinger hissed. "Stand still!"

"I'll pass," I replied, deciding discretion was the better part of valor. Using my intangibility to pass through objects around me, I dodged attack after attack. One of the hurled blades managed to nick the back of my leg, knocking my feet out from under me. I noticed I was once more at the teleporter, directly under the control system in fact.

"You had me fooled, didn't you? You had me thinking you were one of us, but you were really one of them! Naughty-naughty!" Psychoslinger walked at me, smiling as he conjured a series of six-inch claws on the ends of his fingers. It made him look like one of the Tomorrow Society's villains.

"Tell me," I whispered to Cloak, coughing, "how do I work this thing?"

"Push the green button and turn the dials up to maximum. Then hit the outline where Psychoslinger is in relation to the room."

"Gotcha." I smiled.

Desperation made my hands move unnaturally fast, allowing me to finish the operation within a fraction of what time it would normally have taken. If I had moved any slower, though, I'm sure Psychoslinger would have taken my head off.

Speaking of which, Psychoslinger stared as a glowing particle effect appeared around him, followed by a weird static noise. For a second, he looked confused, and then terrified. Seconds later, he was gone.

I wanted to say something witty, but I was too tired to. "Okay, what the hell, did I just do to him?"

"You teleported him without any destination, so I suspect his atoms are scattered across Earth's atmosphere."

"Good." I coughed. "Couldn't have happened to a nicer guy."

"I always tried to save life, even that of supervillains. This is the first life I've taken since defecting from the Brotherhood."

"Are you okay?"

"*Somewhat.*"

"That's all we can ask for."

I limped my way over to Ultragod. The world's greatest superhero was bleeding on the ground, looking half-dead. Picking up the Power Nullifier, I pulled the only lever on it to the opposite of its original position before firing another blast into Ultragod's chest. The superhero started looking better almost immediately, getting up off the ground within moments.

"You saved my life." Ultragod sounded surprised. "Thank you."

"You are now my hostage." I aimed the gun at his chest.

"What?" Ultragod stared.

"*What?*" Cloak joined him.

"With this positronic Merciless Gun, I am holding the world's greatest superhero hostage! Unless the sum of one *million* dollars is delivered to my favorite charity, namely me, I will use it to obliterate you!"

"Lancel, is he out of his mind?" Ultragod asked, looking at my cape.

"*That would explain a great deal.*"

"Okay, I want you to set the teleporter so it takes me back to Falconcrest City." Poking him in the chest with it, I gestured for him to go to the device.

"You realize the battery contained just enough energy for two shots, right?" Ultragod pointed at the futuristic 'gun' in my hands.

"Obey the Merciless Gun!" I shook the useless weapon. "Or you'll be obliterated!"

Seconds later, Tom Terror zoomed in through the door. "Ah, you survived. I must admit, I'm surprised."

Perfect timing.

Now I had to deal with him too.

The guy who was more terrifying to me than Magog and Psychoslinger put together.

"*He's just a man,*" Cloak said.

"*So were you,*" I replied.

"Don't worry," I said, hoisting the gun. "He's already taken a blast. He's doomed. You, of course, should be the one to finish him off."

Ultragod fell to one knee, faking weakness. I was glad he'd finally copped to my plan.

Tom Terror looked at me. "I'm surprised. I thought you'd betray us to his daughter at the first opportunity. That was why I selected you, after all. I recognized you from my research. You were my Judas Goat to lure her to her death."

"Sorry that didn't work out," I said.

"Are you?" Tom Terror said, reevaluating me. "Hmm, I suppose the only emotion strong enough to replace love is hate. You will be able to relish your lover's tears as you play a vital role in the death of her father."

Wow, Tom was a nutcase. "It's all I ever wanted."

"What happened to Psychoslinger?" Tom asked.

"Psychoslinger decided I was a threat, either that or he got bored. I've got him covered, though. This gun is so powerful even Ultragod would be destroyed should I fire it."

"*Gary, what are you doing?*"

"Evil!" I snapped, waving around my useless gun. "Work with me, Cloak."

Tom seemed uninterested in my random mutterings. "Well, no one will miss Psychoslinger anyway. Still, his loss affects my plans somewhat. I'm afraid you'll have to settle for New Zealand," Tom said, landing nearby Ultragod. He looked pleased with himself, not even bothering to check whether Ultragod was really down for the count.

"Yeah." I smiled. "Sure."

Ultragod smashed Tom Terror in the face with an energy construct boxing glove. It came so fast, Tom didn't have time to react. A second later, a gigantic hand smashed Tom flat, creating a little cartoon-like impression of his body in the floor. Taking a look inside the foot-deep hole, I saw Tom was still alive, albeit barely. I was tempted to finish him off. Instead, I decided to let the heroes deal with it. I didn't want a zombie Tom Terror coming after me like the Ice Cream Man did.

"Poor Tom, he was never as strong with that elixir as he thought." Ultragod turned to me. "What is this all about? I worked with Nightwalker for eighty years and I understood all of his plans better than what just happened."

"Is he going to be all right?" I asked, staring down at Tom's unconscious body.

"My Ultrahearing says he's still breathing. He's broken about every bone in his body but he's alive," Ultragod said, poking him with his foot. "I'll have a medical team stabilize him, but he'll be incapacitated for the next... oh... year or so."

"*He* calls it Ultrahearing," I said to Cloak. "I don't know why you're ashamed of affixing the word 'night' to stuff."

"*Gary...*"

Turning back to Ultragod, I asked, "He can't hear us, though? I want to be sure."

"No," Ultragod said. "He'll be out for days."

I sighed. "Tom threatened my family. I figured this was the best way to convince him not to. Tom won't blame me for escaping in the confusion the way he would if I helped you."

"*You would have helped anyway, Gary. I think, Moses, you should let this one go.*"

"All right." Ultragod looked at his bleeding hands. "You're surprisingly cunning, Merciless, I misjudged you."

"No, you didn't.

"*You really didn't. He is a fascinating mixture of good and evil. Which means someone really needs to smack him until the evil is gone.*"

"Hey!" I snapped.

"*It's true. All that stuff about not judging you? I take it back. I think you need a lot of judgment.*"

I rolled my eyes. I was happy Ultragod was alive, either way. "Cloak is right. In the end, I would have saved you anyway. It wouldn't have been selfless, though."

"Excuse me?"

"I don't need you on my tail for the rest of my life. So, the best way to stop you from doing just that is to trick you into feeling indebted to me."

"Indebted to you." Ultragod crossed his arm. "How amusing. Are we still keeping up this supervillain charade?"

"Absolutely. You see, I've got no problem with you opposing

the real psychos. You can come work for me after I've conquered the world."

"You're still after that, huh?" Ultragod sounded disappointed.

"Yes," I replied, proud of how all this had worked out. "World domination is all the rage and I need the world to be intact for it to be worth anything. So pass it along to your Society of Superheroes brethren I won't be killing any of them in the near future. However, I will take them all in as servants to my grandiose Merciless Star Empire." I was pretty sure I was rambling nonsensically.

Then again, I just fought a giant corpse dragon and helped defeat the most dangerous supervillain in history.

I had reason to feel high.

"Lancel, what *is* he talking about?" Ultragod asked, raising an eyebrow.

"*I honestly have no idea. However, we do need to get back to Falconcrest City.*"

"Obey the Merciless Gun!" I shouted, waving the useless Power Nullifier at Ultragod. "I'm totally not rambling because you beat the crap out of me. This is serious stuff here!"

Ultragod went over to a nearby device and healed his hands under a purple ray. "All right, Merciless, we'll play it your way. What are your demands? Try not to ask for a billion dollars, most of our budget comes from the U.N grants and they're not rolling in cash these days."

"Safe transport to Falconcrest City, a full pardon, and…a million dollars," I said. "Even with inflation, a million is asking for a bit much, but you're right. Anything less and I'd be selling myself short."

"Fair enough," he replied.

"Really?" I said. I hadn't actually expected him to give in on that.

"Really." Ultragod sighed. I think he expected better of me. "I'll have it transferred to your account from petty cash. It's also less than a hundredth of the bounty for capturing Tom Terror."

"Well, send it to my family. They need it for putting up with me and my brother." I waved around my gun again. "As for the rest? Inform all the other superheroes to fear the wrath of Merciless: The Supervillain Without Mercy! I may not be killing or harming them, but I shall wreak a *terrible vengeance* on any who seek to strike at me."

"*Not killing or harming them is the definition of mercy.*"

"Shut up."

"You don't have to be a supervillain, Gary," Ultragod said, his voice lowering. "You could use your powers for good. In time, you could become as famous as Nightwalker."

"*I doubt it.*"

I rolled my eyes. "This whole speech would be a hell of a lot more impressive if it didn't come within minutes of you beating the crap out of me."

"Ah, yes, that."

"Yeah." I stepped onto the teleporter pad. "I'm a supervillain. That's all I've ever wanted to be and that's what I am. If you doubt that, use your Ultrahearing to listen to my heartbeat and see if I'm lying. *I want this.* I still do after all that's happened. Warts and all."

Ultragod's gaze was piercing and I felt ashamed for my words. "I'm sorry to hear that, Gary. So will—"

"Don't mention her name," I cut him off. "Also, refer to me as Merciless."

"Merciless." Ultragod frowned. "I suppose you've earned that."

"Yes, I have." I wanted to go back to my wife and forget this entire trip. Some things were just too painful to deal with.

I couldn't, though.

This would be with me for the rest of my life.

The price of doing business.

Ultragod walked over to the teleporter controls and started working them, the machines started to whirl and blink. "You know, if our positions were reversed, you wouldn't hesitate to remove someone who threatened to take over the world. I could teleport you right back to jail or into a bunch of rocks."

"You could, but you're Ultragod."

"I am indeed," Ultragod said, right before he engaged the controls. He didn't mention his daughter in our final conversation. I was grateful for that.

Everything went white.

And I went home.

Epilogue

Where I Find Out What's Been Going On

I emerged in the middle of the suburbs. A second later, I vomited across the ground.

"I should have warned you about that. Teleportation is horrible, it's why Ultragod flies and I used the Nightshu...ahem, I used a shuttle."

"Do you enjoy tormenting me?"

"I admit, a little. This whole supervillain fantasy of yours is ripe for parody."

"Well, at least you're honest." I felt the inside of my mouth with my tongue, realizing it was free from blood. In fact, my entire body had been healed. "What the hell?"

"Molecular reconstitution is part of the features we got when we purchased teleportation technology from the Interstellar Trade Guild," Cloak said. *"I should warn you, side-effects are possible."*

"Like what?"

"An uncontrollable need to rant and make witticisms no one else finds too funny. Given you do that already, you should be fine."

"Cloak, did you just make a joke?"

"Maybe."

"Good. Maybe there's hope for you, yet," I said, smiling. Taking a second to look upwards, I appreciated the sun shining down upon me. Never had its rays felt so good. "Prison...it changes you. I'm not the same man I was before going on the inside. I can't go back, I won't."

"You were in prison less than twenty-minutes."

"Details."

Spitting up a bit more of the foul taste in my mouth, I walked onto a nearby lawn and looked at my surroundings. We were in Falconcrest City, all right. In fact, only a few blocks away from my house. Picturesque square houses surrounded me as far as the eye could see.

There was a conspicuous absence of something, though. People.

Usually, around mid-afternoon, you'd see someone mowing their lawn or watering their gardens. The neighborhood looked like everyone had packed up and headed out, a few cars were abandoned in the middle of the street.

"This is ominous," I said aloud. "I half expect Rod Serling to show up."

"Maybe it's a nuclear drill."

"This isn't the Fifties." I frowned. "We know now nuclear weapons will kill everything on Earth but the Ultra Family, Ymir, and the Behemoth." Not that it had prevented, literally, dozens of supervillains from trying to instigate one over the years.

I was still woozy from my teleportation and I hoped this was all just a coincidence and everyone was watching a popular reality TV show or something to that effect. I'd already gone through the wringer and wasn't eager to go through any more adventures. As much as I loved supervillainy, I was ready to take a couple of months off from it to get my head back together. If I had to use the Reaper's Cloak to prevent the dead from rising, then I could easily restrict myself to target practice every day.

Yeah, training sounded like a good idea.

I was getting a lot of on-the-job training, but that wasn't going to help much against the big baddies. I had turned to Diabloman to give me insight into becoming a criminal mastermind, but that wasn't enough. I needed to get some martial arts lessons from him or Mandy, or whoever. I also needed to ramp up my firepower.

I'd made a deal of some kind with Death, and would probably pay the price for it, if I wasn't already, but I didn't know what sort of benefits I was reaping from it. Hehe, reaping. I hadn't intended that pun. It just went to show how exhausted, mentally and physically, I was.

Even so, the question remained, did I have my powers permanently boosted or had it been a one-time thing in order to deal with Magog? I'd been able to throw a lot of fire at Psychoslinger but that just might be residual power leftover from the initial boost against the Nephilim. It had also proven to be worse than useless.

"Cloak, do you know?" I asked.

"*I'm afraid not,*" Cloak replied. "*Death never showed half as much interest in me as she does in you, it seems. I do, however, feel changed. I believe she has increased your reserves substantially. The curse is still present, though, which makes me think she intends to leave that on until she is certain you're a worthy bearer or not. She judged me unfit for my entire life.*"

"What qualifies as a fit bearer?" I said, looking around.

Nobody.

"*I don't know,*" Cloak said. "*Gary, what do you intend to tell your wife?*"

"Take the money and run."

"*Not what I meant.*"

"I made my choice," I said, not at all regretting it. Much. "Gabrielle may still be in love with me and I may still love her, but I love Mandy and she loves me. We may not have been each other's first loves but we're married and that means something."

"*I approve,*" Cloak said. "*In that one respect, I believe you are a mature, responsible adult.*"

"You shut your damned mouth."

I decided to walk to my house quickly and get in touch with Mandy as soon as possible. I was serious about taking the money and running for a vacation. I wasn't ready to tell my parents I was a supervillain but all the stress in the past week was enough I needed the comfort of my family.

They'd probably object to Cindy and Diabloman coming along but I'd use the money we'd collected, as well as whatever we could sell of the Nightwalker's stuff that wasn't needed for Mandy's training, to make it worth their while. I'd like to sell the stuff I looted from the Society of Heroes, but will probably donate it to charity, either that or return it. They were okay guys, and I didn't feel too happy about robbing them. I was keeping the copy of Action Comics 1#, though. Mandy would probably want to use our time in New Angeles to train as well, and in a few months, we'd be able to tackle this whole superhero and supervillain thing better. It had been amateur hour before.

I hated amateurs.

Deciding to get off the roller-coaster ride while I still could, I focused solely on getting back to my wife. Climbing over the side of a neighbor's backyard fence rather than turning insubstantial or levitating over it, I enjoyed the physical exertion and walked across another empty street. This was starting to freak me out.

That was when a newspaper carried by the wind rolled on by. Leaning down to pick it up, I read the headline: *Zombie Outbreak Affects City*. My eyes popped when I saw the date on the paper.

"I've been gone a *month*?"

Mandy was going to kill me.

That was when a desiccated corpse came up from behind and wrapped its arms around my shoulders. Another zombie, this one more like the Ice Cream Man than Magog's horrors. It was less articulate, though, and bit into my shoulder. It hurt like hell but didn't break my enhanced skin. I screamed in rage and incinerated the monster. More came out of the woodwork. It seemed dozens had been hiding all around the neighborhood, perhaps setting up an ambush for unlucky passers-by. I incinerated them too.

It seemed the roller coaster ride was just beginning.

To be continued in:

THE GAMES OF SUPERVILLAINY

Book Two of The Supervillainy Saga

About the Author

C.T. Phipps is a lifelong student of horror, science fiction, and fantasy. An avid tabletop gamer, he discovered this passion led him to write and turned him into a lifelong geek. He is a regular blogger and also a reviewer for The Bookie Monster.

Bibliography

The Rules of Supervillainy (Supervillainy Saga #1)
The Games of Supervillainy (Supervillainy Saga #2)
The Secrets of Supervillainy (Supervillainy Saga #3)
The Kingdom of Supervillany (Supervillainy Saga #4)

I Was a Teenage Weredeer (The Bright Falls Mysteries, Book 1)
An American Weredeer in Michigan (The Bright Falls Mysteries, Book 2)

Esoterrorism (Red Room, Vol. 1)
Eldritch Ops (Red Room, Vol. 2)

Agent G: Infiltrator (Agent G, Vol. 1)
Agent G: Saboteur (Agent G, Vol. 2)
Agent G: Assassin (Agent G, Vol. 3)

Cthulhu Armageddon (Cthulhu Armageddon, Vol. 1)
The Tower of Zhaal (Cthulhu Armageddon, Vol. 2)

Lucifer's Star (Lucifer's Star, Vol. 1)
Lucifer's Nebula (Lucifer's Star, Vol. 2)

Straight Outta Fangton (Straight Outta Fangton, Vol. 1)
100 Miles and Vampin' (Straight Outta Fangton, Vol. 2)

Wraith Knight (Wraith Knight, Vol. 1)
Wraith Lord (Wraith Knight, Vol. 2)

Curious about other Crossroad Press books?
Stop by our site:
http://www.crossroadpress.com
We offer quality writing
in digital, audio, and print formats.

Made in the USA
Middletown, DE
05 August 2021